Her Texas Cowboy

by

Casey Dawes

Mountain Vines Publishing

Book cover design by GetCovers
Edited by Amy Ewing

Published by Mountain Vines Publishing
Missoula, MT

Her Texas Cowboy

Chapter One

"The Alamo is smaller than I thought it would be," I told my sisters, Diane and Liz.

"That's because you're thinking about Fess Parker, Kathleen," Diane said. "He was tall. Over six feet. Davy Crockett was a lot shorter."

"How do you know?" I challenged her.

"She looked it up on the internet," Liz said.

"She needs a divorce from that computer," I said.

"Then we'd never get anywhere," Diane retorted. "I need it to plan out our stops."

My sisters and I had been on a RV road trip for over six months. Diane was in charge of logistics, and I was grateful for that. Before this trip, I'd never been out of the state of Montana.

"So, are we going in or what?" I asked.

"We need a selfie before we do," Diane said.

After we'd left Yellowstone in June, my sister decided to pick up a selfie stick so we could have a record of ourselves in front of amazing places. While both Liz and I kidded her about it, I liked having the memories.

"We may as well get this over with," I said with a mock groan.

"Sure you don't want to get a coonskin cap first?" Liz joshed.

I gave her the stink-eye. Raising two children had perfected the expression.

Instead of cowering, my sister laughed.

I obviously had more work to do.

We arranged ourselves in a spot that would allow Diane to capture us and the small, bullet-ridden building behind us. I'd always wanted to see the Alamo, imagining it out by itself in a dusty field, just like it had been portrayed in movies with John Wayne and Fess Parker.

Instead it was part of a courtyard surrounded by modern buildings reflecting the sun on this bright Texas mid-January day.

"Smile!" Diane said.

I dutifully arranged my mouth in the appropriate fashion.

After she'd taken several pictures—"to make sure one of them comes out"—Diane collapsed her stick and stowed it and her phone in her large purse.

We showed our tickets and were allowed entrance into the church. Going from the bright sun to the dimness inside the adobe walls made it impossible to see for a few moments, but I could immediately feel the weight of history as soon as I stepped over the threshold.

People had died here. Even though it was close to two hundred years ago, I could still sense their presence. I said a brief prayer for their souls.

We stepped softly through the exhibit, reading the details of the story. It was amazing that a battle that lasted only two hours became a rallying cry for both the Texas War of Independence and the Mexican-American War.

I'd always loved history, but as we'd traveled through the battlefields of the Revolutionary and Civil Wars, I'd begun to feel that too much of it was dominated by bloodshed instead of reason.

I wish I had a skill like either of my sisters—painting or photography—that could express feelings without having to resort to speaking. Even now, Diane had contorted herself into a strange position and was pointing her camera at a wall.

We eventually left the church, all of us quieter than we'd been before we entered. After walking around the grounds for a while, we perked up a little, and by the time we made it to the gift shop, I was almost back to normal.

"You have to put this on!" Diane said, handing me a coonskin cap.

"That's for a kid," I said.

"But you were such a big fan of Daniel Boone!" she said.

"He wasn't at the Alamo," I pointed out.

"But it was still Fess Parker, and he still had a coonskin cap!" She grinned. "Just for a picture. Please?"

"No," I said.

But Liz snatched the cap from Diane's hand and popped it on my head. Before I could pull it off, Diane had gotten her picture.

"You two ..."

"Remember when we used to dress her up like a doll?" Diane asked.

"She was compliant as a baby," Liz agreed. "Wonder what happened?"

"I realized what bullies my older sisters could be," I said, tossing the cap back into a bin full of the things.

I left the two of them reminiscing and went to the bookshelf. After thumbing through a number of them, I picked up *Forget the Alamo*.

"Why that one?" Liz asked as we stood in the checkout line.

"Because I know the general facts, and I saw all the movies glorifying the people who died here, and I wonder if they got it right. Strike that. I know they didn't get it right. I want to see what someone else has to say."

"I never knew you were that much of a reader," Diane said.

"I never had time before," I shot back.

I'd been running the ranch that belonged to all of us, first with my husband Michael's help, and then by myself after he got ill. I barely had time to get supper on the table, not to mention anything else.

"Did you see the Bowie knives?" Diane asked. "Didn't Grandpa O'Sullivan have one of those?"

"I barely remember the old guy," Liz said. "But, yes, I think he had one."

"Wonder what happened to it?" Diane asked. "I remember seeing it in Dad's office right before I left for college. Any idea where it went?" She turned to me.

"I have no idea," I lied. "I haven't seen it in ages."

The clerk motioned me forward, and I was grateful. I remembered seeing it in the ranch office for a long time, and then it had disappeared. I had a good idea what had happened to that knife, and it wasn't a subject I wanted to discuss.

~ ~ ~

From the Alamo, we headed to the San Antonio's River Walk. It was as beautiful as we'd heard it was, even in winter. The eponymous river wended its way through town, from the mission area by the Alamo to the 1700s Villa de Bejar outpost which ultimately became the city that surrounded us.

Our feet and legs had grown accustomed to walking long distances since we'd begun the trip. We tried to go on some kind of hike every week to keep in shape. While I'd never be svelte like Liz who'd hogged all the skinny genes in our family, a body I vaguely remembered having before the birth of my children was coming into focus.

It felt good and healthy, without having to resort to that most evil word in any American woman's vocabulary: diet.

We decided to eat at one of the many Mexican restaurants on the walk, choosing one that seemed to go well beyond the standard fare of tacos and enchiladas.

My sisters had forgotten about the knife, and I was grateful.

"Diane," Liz said. "You outdid yourself on this RV park. That swimming pool is amazing. It's big enough for everyone, and it feels so yummy when you get in because it's just the right temperature."

"The spaces are big enough, too," I added. "We're not all crammed next to each other."

Diane beamed. For as much as I ribbed her about her computer skills, she was handy to have around.

"I figured if we were going to be here for over two months," she said. "I should pick a good place. Besides, they were offering pickleball lessons. I've wanted to learn for a while now."

"I'll come cheer you on," Liz said. "You should come too," she said to me. "You might meet someone."

"True," Diane said. "We only have six months more to find her a man."

"Don't want one," I said. "Besides, my official year of mourning for Michael isn't up yet."

"A year of mourning went out with the Victorians," she replied.

"But you never know when love will come along," Liz said. "You have to be open to possibilities."

"I was open to possibilities in high school," I shot back. "And I spent forty years living in reality. I'm not biting twice." I took a big sip of my lemonade.

"Where are you going to live when you get back to Montana? Didn't Patrick, Sydney, and the kids move into the ranch house?"

"Yep." I didn't want to confess that I hadn't quite figured all of it out. Patrick had told me I was more than welcome to stay in Liz's childhood bedroom, and their kids could double up. But I really wanted my own place. In all of my sixty plus years of life, I'd never had a room of my own. It was probably about time.

"I was thinking of getting one of those tiny homes," I said. I hadn't really been thinking it. I just wanted to make my sisters believe I had my act together when I knew I was a long way from that.

"You could move into my house," Liz said quietly.

I looked at her.

Liz had moved into one of the old ranch hand's homes when she came back to live full time in Montana. As time went on, she'd remodeled. Unknown to us until recently, her artwork had made her a very wealthy woman. Her home had some really nice amenities, including a large bathtub with jets that I was very envious of.

"I can't take your house," I told her.

"Why not? I'll be moving to the new one in the Hudson Valley once this trip is over. No one needs two houses, for god's sake."

I glared at her for her swear.

She glared right back. My sister went so far beyond being a lapsed Catholic that it was like she was on hiatus from all religions.

"Well, they don't," Liz said again, sounding snippy.

"I can't take your house," I repeated, feeling stubbornness take a firm grip on my personality.

"Then don't. It belongs to the ranch, just like yours does. If you don't want it, it will sit there empty."

I hadn't thought of that. It would be stupid to let that nice house just be empty.

"Thank you," I said, as graciously as I could. "That would be very nice."

Her shoulders relaxed, and she patted my hand. "You do a lot for us. You need to be treated like the queen you are."

I didn't have anything to say to that.

The waiter dropped off our dishes, and we spent the next few moments digging in. The chicken I had was done to perfection, and the mole sauce one of the best I'd ever tasted. We'd definitely picked a good spot to winter.

When the conversation picked up again, it steered away from me. Liz talked about the studio she'd found to rent for the duration of our stay in Texas, and Diane had a trip she wanted us to take to see some of the other missions in the area.

I relaxed and let my sisters' chatter drift around me.

It was going to be a good winter.

Chapter Two

Shit.

Literally.

The duct tape I'd used to patch the holes in the dump hose weren't holding. I hated spending money for new stuff when I ought to be able to fix it. But it didn't appear there was any other choice.

"What's the matter?" Diane asked, as she arrived back from her morning walk.

"Remember when we were at that stop in Louisiana, and there were all those ravens with too much interest in the dumping hose?" I asked.

She wrinkled her forehead. "Kinda?"

"They kept pecking at the hose," I prodded.

"Oh, yeah. It was weird. I don't know what they were expecting to find."

"They made a bunch of holes. I patched them with duct tape. Thought it was going to hold, but it's not."

Diane looked down. "Crap."

"Uh-huh." I sighed and stretched out my back. "Guess I'm off to the RV store. We've got enough money, right?" Diane was in charge of finances as well as logistics. She was the one with the accounting degree, so it made sense.

"We're good. This leg of the journey—except for gas—has been a lot cheaper than the time we spent up in New York."

"Yeah, things were expensive there. Good thing Liz makes a boatload of money if she's going to move there. Who'd have figured our sister was a big deal in the art world?"

"Not me. Honestly, I can't say I thought too much about it," Diane said, a note of sadness to her voice. "I was living my own life, not really aware of what you two were doing. I'm sorry about that. I missed a lot."

"We all missed a lot," I said. "Thank you for suggesting this trip. We needed it." I gave her a hug, my eyes a little misty. She squeezed back, and we stood like that for several heartfelt moments before we released each other. I gazed into her eyes, knowing we were lucky to have found our way back to each other. Many siblings never did.

Then we looked down at the hose.

"I'd best be off," I said. "Anyone have dibs on the car today?"

"I can't remember the schedule."

"Best go look," I said.

We towed Liz's Jeep behind us as we traveled the country so we'd have the ability to go shopping, sightseeing, and run other errands. What we hadn't planned on was our divergent interests and needs—especially to get away from each other once in a while. Diane had bought a scooter that hung on the back of the RV when we traveled which gave her another option. But for the car, we kept a schedule as to who wanted it when.

I looked at the paper stuck on bulletin board we'd put up.

Liz was scheduled for the car.

I walked over to where she was sitting on the couch, drinking her coffee and thumbing through an art magazine.

"Hey, I need to run an errand this morning," I said. "It's kind of an emergency. One of the hoses needs replacing. Can you delay your trip a little?"

"As long as you're the one dealing with the hose, I can delay anything." She beamed up at me.

Liz was fine in an art studio or kitchen. She'd learned to help me out with the dairy cows on our mutually owned ranch, and like everyone else, helped move the beef cattle when it was needed, but beyond that, she didn't like to get her hands dirty.

"I should be back by noon, if not earlier," I said.

"No problem." Liz stretched. "I'm feeling lazy today anyway."

I nodded and collected my things and the car keys.

Soon I was on my way down a two-lane road to Texas RV Supply on another bright southern day. This was nice countryside, rolling hills with lots of trees. They weren't very big trees, not by Montana standards, but at least there was space between them. The dense forests of the East Coast hadn't appealed to me.

Here and there I began to see small herds of cattle, and it made me long for home. This trip was good, but I was ready to get back to my real life. Ranching was hard work, especially since my dad had thought it a good idea to have some dairy cattle along with the traditional steers. Beef cattle could be neglected now and then; dairy cattle needed milking twice a day.

Diane had suggested a new-fangled automated milking set up, but it would take a decent financial investment. Maybe we should simply sell off the herd.

I pulled into the parking lot and headed into the store.

It didn't take long to find what I was looking for, but I wasn't sure if I should get the same length of hose we had or go for a slightly longer one. Sometimes RV parks set their sewage connection a good distance from where the rig had to park.

"You picking up a hose for your husband?" a clerk asked.

Why was it that there was always someone who assumed I had one of those things?

"For my RV," I said.

"But your husband will install it." The clerk couldn't take a hint. "He's right to pick this brand. They're the best."

I turned and faced him.

He took a step back.

"They work just fine until a bunch of ravens decide to poke holes in them. And *I* will be installing the hose like the capable woman I am. Don't have or need a husband." I made a little waving motion with my hand. "Now go away and take care of someone who actually needs you. I don't."

He scurried off, and I heard laughter behind me.

I turned again.

A small, but tough looking woman with a broad grin stood there.

"I do get tired of them," she said. "I travel alone—it's best that way. They never think we can do it." She shook her head. "They think we belong in the kitchen."

"I hate kitchens," I said.

"Ditto."

We chatted for a few more moments, then I picked up the box containing the longer hose, checked out, and left the store.

I decided to take a different, somewhat longer route back to the RV park. I needed more time in this open space where I was feeling at home for the first time in a long while. The red cliffs of Utah had created powerful images, and the long prairies, towns, and cornfields— did this country really need that much corn?—across the middle had introduced me to a different side of America. The East Coast had been overcrowded with people, and the Deep South left me feeling at sea. It was so very different from the way I'd grown up.

But here, in Texas Hill Country, life felt familiar.

The road twisted through gentle slopes, until signs of civilization started cropping up: the inevitable dollar store, some housing developments that had been planted like a crop in an open field, and a Tractor Supply store.

Then I saw it: Jupe Mills of Texas. It was one of those sprawling ranch supply stores like Murdochs in Montana.

Of its own volition—I'd swear it on my deathbed—the Jeep pulled into the parking lot.

I didn't need anything. I should pull out and head back to the park. Liz was waiting.

I hauled my body out of the seat and locked the door behind me.

As soon as I got beyond the cash register section, I took a deep breath.

Yep. There was nothing that smelled like a ranch store except a ranch store.

Women's clothing, hats, and boots were in the first section. My jeans were hanging looser on my body. Maybe I needed a new pair?

I wandered through the section, stopping to try out a hat. The hat was great, but the face in the mirror looked as old as it had for a while. Except the eyes. There was a spark that hadn't been there for decades.

I must have been more miserable in my marriage than I'd ever imagined.

"It looks good on you," a male voice said.

I whipped around, almost losing the hat in the process.

He was only a few inches taller than me, salt and pepper hair with a thick white mustache set above a friendly smile.

"Um. Thank you." I took off the hat and put it back on the stack.

"You look pretty without it too," he said.

Pretty? Was the man blind? Even as a teen no one used the word "pretty" in the same sentence as my name.

Or he could be a serial killer trying to lure me back to his secret hiding place, have his way with me, and then torture me to death.

If so, he was a really hard up serial killer.

He pulled at the brim of his own hat. "Have a good day," he said, then walked away.

It took a moment for the air to close around the gap that his departure had left.

Then the bright lights and sounds of people's voices took over. In front of me, a pair of blondes—perhaps mother and daughter— examined purses. Behind me, the melodic strains of Spanish played in my hearing.

I shook off the strange feeling and walked away from the clothing section, trying to think of what else I might need stranded in ranch land with no spread of my own within five hundred miles. I wandered up and down the aisles, and finally bought myself a new pair of work gloves. I didn't really need them for everyday chores, but every once in a while they came in handy for repairs.

Throughout the whole time I was in the store, I had a feeling that my life was about to change. I didn't really believe in the second sight my mother had sometimes mentioned. Mom claimed her mother had been able to tell when a couple was suited for each other, and her grandmother had been the village matchmaker.

As I walked to the car, I tried to shake off the feeling, telling myself it was only the result of being on the road for so long.

~ ~ ~

Before she left for the studio she'd rented, Liz had put something in the crockpot to slowly cook for hours. Rich smells permeated the small space. Diane had taken her camera and ridden off on her scooter to take pictures shortly after.

Once I replaced the hose, there was little else for me to tend to.

With the RV to myself, I felt the desire to pick up my weaving again, something I hadn't done for several months. Between the holidays and the travel, it had been too overwhelming. Here, however, it felt a little bit like home.

I dug out the loom from where it had become buried in one of the closets. It was a ridge heddle loom, the right size for the table runner I was trying to make. I'd been weaving on and off for years, but this was the most intricate pattern I'd tried: a series of dark gray Celtic knots on an off-white background.

My late husband, Michael, had given lip-service to my craft, but always found something else for me to do when I pulled it out of storage.

I pushed the memory from my mind, took my loom out into the glorious day, and set about weaving. There was magic as my hands moved back and forth, each thin line creating a pattern, like how each decision we make creates a life. My choice to marry Michael after high school dictated the following decades. Now my determination to stay single would build the path for the rest of my life.

Chapter Three

Sunday morning I was looking forward to attending mass. It had been a long while since I'd attended the same church for a stretch of time. Neither of my sisters were churchgoers, although that may change if Diane's new boyfriend had his way. My own attendance hadn't been consistent, and I missed the weekly time that I treasured to reflect and connect with God in the way I'd been raised.

Once again I drove the winding hill country, but this time in a different direction, the route taking me closer to the city of San Antonio. There was a Catholic church in a small town on the northwest edge of the city that had a number of masses. I'd settled on an English one at 9:30. It was the service most likely to have some sort of coffee hour. I was ready to talk to people other than my sisters.

Some local ranchers could be there. I was hungry for some solid discussions about beef prices and the cost of feed.

I pulled into the parking lot of the modern-looking church. They could build things here in the warmer climate that would never handle the cold of Montana.

A number of people walked the path to the front entrance of the church. There were couples, a few old people depending on rolling walkers or a cane to navigate from one place to another, and a number of families with children. Some of those peeled off before reaching the entrance, no doubt to deposit the cherubs in someone else's care so they could have a moment of peace to themselves.

I had always been grateful to wave goodbye to my two before having that precious half hour to myself before the kids came scrambling back in to find us and finish the service.

A Latina woman about my age looked over and smiled, making me feel welcome … a stranger in a strange church.

I politely chatted with the greeter, then entered the large, airy space. The pews were in a semi-circle surrounding the altar, their polished red wood matching the beams in the open space above us. With white walls and plenty of windows, it was almost like being out in the open air.

It was lovely.

The only thing lacking was a bit of padding for my rear end.

I settled into a middle row and looked around me, indulging in people watching. Two women were deep in a discussion that no doubt involved some upcoming event. They had the look of those who ran church functions. A solid group of she-who-must-be-obeyeds. A circle of men who looked comfortable in their sports jackets were no doubt boasting about their golf scores. A few others, less comfortable in their coats and flaunting dressy boots, were the ranchers. The women who walked next to them had taken the opportunity to look their best.

I understood. Getting gussied up for a cow was a no-win situation.

"This seat taken?" a voice I'd heard before asked.

It was the man from the ranch store.

Eerie.

"No. Not at all," I said.

My expression must have shown my concern because as soon as he sat down, he said, "I'm not following you, really. It's a small town."

"I see." Coincidences had abounded on our RV trip so far. I was almost getting used to them.

He was of the cowboy boot and ill-fitting sports coat set, which meant I didn't have to pretend to know golf.

I took a chance.

"Are you a rancher?"

He chuckled, his mustache moving with his mirth. "Did you decide this because I was in a ranch store or because of my boots?"

Heat rose in my cheeks. "Both." I picked up a missal, not sure of what to do next. Small talk with a rancher should be easy. I did it all the time. Why was I having problems talking with this particular one?

"You should have bought the hat," he whispered as we all stood for the processional. "It suited you."

I nodded and focused on the book I held, even though I didn't need it. I could perform the mass as well as any priest … except for the minor technicality that women weren't allowed to take on the role.

Would that ever change? In some ways, the world seemed to be going backward in terms of things women were allowed to do, not forward.

As the ritual continued, I drifted into its familiarity. It was almost meditative, except I was hyper-aware of the man next to me.

About midway through the service, the entryway door opened. Without turning around, I knew the children were here, their energy filling in all the emotional spaces that the adults had left for them.

One girl, about four or five, came running down the aisle next to us, her dark curls flying behind her as she ran in her pretty white dress and shiny black shoes toward the altar. "Papá!" she yelled. "Papá!"

I glanced to the front where the priest stood.

Had there been a major shift in church doctrine when I wasn't looking?

The man next to me chuckled. "Watch."

Right at the end of the aisle, the child veered to the right, to one of the altar servers.

The man hurriedly passed the cruets he was holding to the person next to him and turned back, right as the child launched herself into his arms.

The congregation laughed as the man grinned and held his child. He said something in Spanish to her, and she shook her head. He took on a stern expression and said it again.

This time she slid down, ran back toward the door, coming to an abrupt stop and sliding into a pew a few rows from the front.

"It happens every week," the man next to me said.

"Oh."

The congregation settled back down and mass continued.

Less than a half hour later, it was over. As we stood, the man next to me said, "My name is Rodrigo Ramirez. I am indeed a rancher."

"So am I," I said, waiting for him to ask where my husband was. Like driving an RV, some men were unable to fathom that a woman could run a ranch.

"Did you recently buy one here? I thought I knew everyone in the area."

We started to move toward the door.

"My ranch is in Montana," I told him. "My name is Kathleen O'Sullivan."

"It's nice to meet you." He held out his hand.

I shook it, the familiar callouses of a hard-working rancher rough in my palm. His handshake was solid without trying to prove a point.

His attention was caught by another couple, and we drifted apart.

That was fine by me. While I hadn't noticed a wedding ring— why had I looked?—that didn't mean he wasn't married. Although if he was, where was his wife?

I made it through the gauntlet of priest and attendees and automatically walked toward the parking lot. I didn't have the energy to face a bunch of strangers over coffee.

"Kathleen!"

I turned. Rodrigo came toward me.

"Excuse me," he said. "I was curious as to what you are doing here if your ranch is in Montana."

"My sisters and I are taking a road trip for a year. We're halfway through. We decided to stay here for a few months until the snow leaves the mountain passes."

"Will I see you again?" There was too much eagerness in his question.

"Probably." I'd need to find another mass to attend. In spite of my sisters' fondest wishes, I had no desire to fall into the same trap they had. After forty years of marriage, the last thing I needed was another man. Especially a Latino rancher from Texas. While we had lots in common, we had ranches to run that were over fifteen hundred miles apart.

A woman with a mass of bottle-blond hair and a slim build that was obviously enhanced in the right places came toward us. I had to keep myself from staring. It was a stereotype come to life; a stereotype that I'd thought had gone out of existence in the last century.

"Hi, Rodrigo," she purred as she put a possessive hand on his arm.

"Hey there, Trixie Lynn. I'd like you to meet Kathleen O'Sullivan from Montana."

"Oh, hi." Her Texas drawl was charming, and her slim hand small in mine as we shook.

I tried not to feel intimidated, but high school memories of the clutch of cheerleaders lording it above us mere mortals flooded my brain.

"Are you here long?" she asked. "I hear Montana's a beautiful place. You must miss it."

"I do," I answered honestly. "There's no other place like it."

"Kathleen's taking a road trip with her sisters. Doesn't that sound fun?" Rodrigo asked.

"If you knew my sisters better," she said, "you'd know that sounds like a nightmare." She laughed, a noise that was as staged as everything else about her.

Except her eyes. There was a warning in her eyes.

Rodrigo many not have a wedding ring now, but she intended to put one on him.

I kept it light. I had no interest in her man.

"I know what you mean," I said. "I was totally against the idea in the beginning, but they convinced me. It's turned out okay. We're closer than ever. There's only three of us."

"Who's running your ranch?" Rodrigo asked.

"My son and the ranch manager we hired."

"We? You're married?" Rodrigo sounded disappointed.

"Widowed," I answered. "My sisters and I own the ranch collectively. I … well, my late husband and I … managed it for all of us. He died last year."

"I'm so sorry for your loss," Trixie Lynn said. And then she added, "Bless your heart."

It was one of those Southern expressions I was never going to get used to.

"Yes," Rodrigo said, "Condolences."

"Thank you." I looked toward the parking lot.

"We need to be going," Trixie Lynn said to Rodrigo. "Remember you're having that barbecue this afternoon to celebrate your son's birthday. I've made up a big batch of coleslaw and some berry pies."

"I haven't forgotten. We have plenty of time. Alejandro has been smoking the ribs since early this morning. It will be an amazing feast." He turned to me. "My son is turning thirty today. He's going to be taking on increased responsibility for the ranch that will someday be his. You have a son. You understand." He looked directly into my eyes, and there was an odd moment of intense connection I hadn't expected.

I nodded.

Then he smiled.

"You should come! You and your sisters! We'll introduce you to Texas properly."

"I'm not sure that's a good idea," Trixie Lynn said. "It's a family event. And I'm not sure we've planned enough food for three more guests."

"The neighbors will be there," Rodrigo said. "So not entirely family. And there is always enough food for strangers. Isn't that what tradition and our teachings tell us?" He gestured to the church.

"I'm not—" I began.

"I am. It's settled. You'll come?" He looked at me.

There were dozens of reasons why we shouldn't. One was looking at me with ice chips in her tiger-green eyes.

"I'll discuss it with my sisters," I said. "If we come, we'll bring something," I gave Trixie Lynn one of the looks I usually reserved for men who were being jerks.

"If you want … no need," he said. "There will be more than enough. I promise."

"We will. It's part of *our* tradition," I said.

He gave me the address, and we bid goodbye.

After I got into my car, I debated. While attending a barbecue at a Texas ranch might be interesting, this particular event might be uncomfortable. None of us spoke much Spanish, and I was the only one who had any real interest in ranching.

Then there was Trixie Lynn. She'd already decided I was the enemy, even though I had absolutely no interest in Rodrigo in a romantic sense.

I had no interest in any man. The one I'd loved, the man I'd given my heart to, had turned out to be domineering and secretive, almost destroying my entire family.

Chapter Four

"We need to go, Liz," Diane said when I told my sisters about the invitation. "It's only polite."

"Screw politeness," Liz said. "It will be fun! I've never been to a Texas barbecue, never mind to an event with the kind of people I don't usually hang out with. I wonder what kind of artwork they'll have. Mexican pottery is so vibrant."

"You're really developing a potty mouth," Diane said.

"I've had one for years," Liz said. "You're just getting exposed to it."

"It's been worse since we left New York," I said. "What would Walter say?"

"Walter encourages me," Liz said. "He likes me when I'm earthy." Her voice lowered on the last word. She blinked her eyes and licked her lips.

"Ew!" I said. "Keep it to yourself!"

"I can kind of relate," Diane said. "It's been a long stretch."

I put my hands over my ears. "You two are over-sexed."

Liz pulled my hands down. "So is he good-looking?" She turned to Diane. "He must be good-looking. Otherwise she'd have no problem going."

"He's an older Latino man with a mustache," I said. "If you define that as good-looking, then there you go."

"We obviously have to attend this," Liz said. "I can tell nothing from that description … except my sister is obviously asleep where men are concerned."

"I like it that way," I protested and turned away to fill a glass with water.

Even before he got ill, Michael and I had stopped being intimate. I'd figured that's the way it was, although memories of Mom and Dad kissing passionately when they thought no one was looking occasionally resurfaced.

With Michael, the change was partly due to our growing distance in our day-to-day living. I had my things to do around the ranch; he had his. As long as the kids got to where they were supposed to be and did okay in school, he was happy with them. As for me, he didn't fuss as long as dinner was on the table at the correct moment, and everything else ran smoothly around the house.

"C'mon, Kathleen." Diane interrupted my thoughts. "We're going to be in this area for a long time, let's meet some people."

"You could go to church and meet people," I pointed out.

The pair of them gave me their best "that's not happening" expressions, fists on hips and all.

I sighed. I should never have mentioned the barbecue. That would have been the only way to get out of this.

"What are we going to bring?" I asked.

~ ~ ~

We were running late by the time we left the RV. Liz had nixed my original outfit, and Diane fussed with my hair and insisted on make-up.

I felt like a prize cow going to the state fair, hopefully to win a blue ribbon before being sold to the highest bidder.

Liz had pulled together fruit and potato salads, so we wouldn't arrive empty-handed, a forbidden situation.

Liz was driving, taking the curving road like she was on a racetrack. My job was to make sure the salads got to the barbecue in one piece.

"Wow," Diane said as we reached the address.

The long driveway began with the traditional arch made of huge logs of gleaming wood. Massive longhorns graced the top part of the square arch. Below it, a sign announced, "Ramirez Ranch." The sides ended in two stone pillars connecting to an iron fence. A beautiful iron gate was open, welcoming us to the long, paved drive.

It was extraordinarily different from the three peeled logs our grandfather had used to mark the beginning of the often-rutted dirt road that led to our ranch house.

In the green field to the right, a few cows grazed, while a lone, longhorn steer claimed the field to the left.

"We're not in Kansas anymore," Diane said quietly.

"Nope," Liz agreed and put the car back in gear to head down the long drive.

It stretched for nearly a mile before curving around a small hill to a valley where a cluster of well-kept buildings nestled. There were a number of cars around the main house, more than one of them a high-end vehicle.

"These aren't our people," I said. "Let's go home."

"Nonsense!" Liz said. "Where's your spirit of adventure?"

"She doesn't have any," Diane said.

"Just go," I muttered. "We don't belong here."

"Too late," Liz said and nosed into a space along the fence.

Rodrigo had spotted us, and was walking toward us with a smile on his face.

"Is that him?" Diane asked.

"Uh-huh."

"Oh," Liz said. "Definitely good-looking. Definitely."

"Good thing you're already taken," I said.

"But you aren't," she shot back.

"Shut it," I warned. I pushed my car door open and stepped out, plastering a smile on my face as I did so.

"You came!" Rodrigo beamed, his moustache gracefully arching above his mouth.

"I did," I stated. "And I brought my sisters."

By that time, Liz and Diane had gotten out of the car.

"Ah, yes. I can see immediately that you are sisters. Your father must be a lucky man to have such beautiful women as daughters. Your mother must be stunning as well."

Good grief. A flatterer. This party couldn't end soon enough.

I stood there, unsure what to do next.

"Unfortunately," Liz said, holding her hand out in greeting, "our parents have passed. I'm Liz, the middle sister." She nodded at Diane. "Diane is the oldest, and Kathleen is the baby."

"I'm not a baby. I'm sixty-three years old for god's sake."

It took all I could do not to clap my hand over my mouth for taking the Lord's name in vain.

Rodrigo didn't seem to notice.

"Welcome, welcome," he said.

I turned to the car to retrieve the salads, handing one to Diane and the other to Liz.

"Thank you for your thoughtfulness," he said, gesturing to the bowls. "Now, come and I'll introduce you to the others and get you something to drink."

He led us down a path through a garden lush with foliage of different hues of green.

"This is lovely," Liz said.

"My wife planted it. She did all the landscaping around the house." He paused and looked around. "She was a very talented woman when it came to domestic arts. I'll show you our home later so you can see for yourself."

"She's gone?" Diane asked gently.

"About five years ago," he said. "Cancer."

"I'm so sorry for your loss," she said while Liz and I murmured our agreement.

"It was a while ago. We had a good marriage," he added with a finality that put an end to the discussion.

As we made our way to the patio where the guests were gathered, I turned his phrase over in my mind. What did a "good marriage" mean to him?

Heck, what did it mean to any of us? I would have sworn Michael and I had a good marriage, but that had turned out to be a false assumption.

We reached a large patio area with a massive barbecue and stone fireplace in one corner. Another corner held a beautiful hand-constructed fountain, incorporating bright Mexican pottery from which water spouted.

More of the late wife's handiwork?

A gaily decorated piñata hung from one of the vine-covered overhead beams, ready for the small children who darted here and there among the adults like small lizards.

Rodrigo made the round of introductions, but few of the names stuck in my head. They were beautiful, lyrical names that were the antithesis of the meat and potato names of my relatives. Instead, I sorted them by identity: neighbor, relative, or friend.

The one name that stuck was Juan, Rodrigo's oldest son. He was a gracious copy of his father, although a little less garrulous. His chatterbox wife made up for it, although her conversation was frequently interrupted by rapid commands in Spanish to her two children.

We finally got settled next to a pair of kindly neighbors who were happy to learn about our travels.

That's when Trixie Lynn made her entrance.

She'd changed her clothes since this morning. This version still showed off her trim figure, but gave a nod to the wide skirt and wide belts several of the younger women at the barbecue wore. Her cleavage was accented by a beautiful squash blossom necklace.

As she carried a tray containing bowls of salsa and chips to one of the scattered picnic tables, she nodded like a queen greeting her subjects.

When she reached the table, people helped her unload the tray. Bowls were whisked away as she walked to Rodrigo and put a possessive hand on his arm before looking at me with a fake smile.

"Ouch!" Liz said. "What did you do to her?"

"Nothing."

One of the neighbors we'd been chatting with returned with few bowls of chips and salsa for us. We'd all picked up bottles of water on our introduction rounds, deciding to save our alcoholic indulgences for home.

Rodrigo said something to Trixie Lynn that made her frown, but she released his arm. He turned and came over to us.

"I promised to show you my house. It's best to do it now before we start to eat."

I rose with a smile, an expression I made sure Trixie Lynn saw. Her eyes narrowed.

Triumphant, I walked with Rodrigo into the house, my sisters following behind.

The entryway from the patio led to a large hallway next to the kitchen. A high bar, currently covered with an array of side dishes, separated the two before ending in an arched doorway.

"Oh! That's amazing," Liz said, staring at the gleaming appliances and bright tilework.

"It's how my wife wanted it," Rodrigo said with a smile. "I merely paid for it."

This guy was traditional through and through. Not surprising, but it bothered me more than I thought it would.

Opposite the kitchen was a family room, complete with a large-screen television. Next to the kitchen was a laundry-utility room. One of the two wings off the center contained a formal living room, dining room, and office. The other contained four bedrooms.

There were three full bathrooms in the house, all of them spacious, lush, and sparkling clean. I almost swooned.

"Your place is lovely," Diane said as we returned to the patio.

"Gracias," Rodrigo said. "Later I can show you the outbuildings." His pride in his ranch shone through the few words.

"That will be Kathleen's thing," Liz said with a smile that bordered on a smirk.

Diane nodded.

"Would you like to do that?" Rodrigo asked.

"Sure," I said.

My sisters were going to get it when we got home.

"I look forward to it," Rodrigo said. "I'm especially proud of my horses."

"How long have you owned this ranch?" Liz asked.

Rodrigo settled in a nearby chair and took a sip from a bottle of Tecate beer. "This ranch has been in my family for multiple generations," he said. "My ancestors emigrated from Mexico in the late 1700s. It was a time of conflict with the Native Americans who were here then." He shook his head. "We were a new brand of conquistador, seeking to dominate with a rifle rather than a cross. It was a tragic time."

"And your family has had this ranch since that time?" Liz asked.

"Yes. Through all the different governments and governors. We are still here. We have enlarged the size of the ranch and made it prosper."

He took another sip of his beer.

"My ancestors stuck to it," Rodrigo continued, pride lurking around the edges of his voice. "Even during the difficult years, when Texas was a republic. Mexican law had been more equal, I think. It was forbidden to enslave people. And women?" He smiled at us. "There was a community property law so all land was held jointly between a husband and wife. Women had other rights as well; things they no longer had when the Americans took over in the name of independence."

Trixie Lynn settled into the chair next to him, once again possessively touching him on the arm. The gaze she turned on us wasn't a glare, but it came close.

"Are you boring these nice ladies with your stories?" she asked. With a tinkling laugh she added, "Rodrigo loves history. He forgets not everyone is as interested."

"I like history," I said. What Rodrigo had told us, combined with our visit to the Alamo, intrigued me.

Trixie Lynn's expression crossed the line to glaring.

"There are more guests asking to see you," she said. "And Marcos keeps asking when they can smash the piñata."

The smile lines in Rodrigo's face deepened.

"Marcos is my grandson. He's going to be a great horseman. You should see him ride. A natural!"

Trixie Lynn rose. "It's important you talk to the county commissioner. Remember, he said he could only stay a short while. You told me to remind you." She gave us a fake smile. "I'm sure you'll excuse us."

"Ah, yes." Rodrigo stood as well. "I don't like how he's spending my money. I need to remind him who elected him." He focused on me and smiled. "I'll talk to you later."

What was that strange sensation in my chest?

If I ignored it, I was sure it would go away.

"That woman does *not* like you," Diane said.

"Nope," I replied. "I don't know why. It's not like I did anything to her."

Liz laughed. "It's what she's afraid you're going to do to her plans that's the problem," she said.

"Huh?"

"Rodrigo likes you."

"No, he doesn't. He's a nice man to everyone. They all adore him at church."

"We did leave you in Montana too long," Liz said. "He's a nice, *rich*, single man. Trixie Lynn has her sights set on being Mrs. Ramirez number two. And you're a potential threat."

Now it was my turn to laugh. "She's wrong in so many ways. I'm looking forward to being on my own in Montana. No more love and no more men for me."

"We'll see about that," Diane said. "The more you resist, the harder you'll fall."

"I'm getting a margarita," I said, standing up. Enough of this nonsense. If we weren't in polite company, I'd give my sisters the finger, but as it was, all I could do was turn my back on them and head to the table where the blender whirred.

~ ~ ~

The barbecued meat, served on toasted buns, was perfection. I couldn't remember when I'd tasted better barbecue, and I told the man who'd been at the smoker.

"Gracias, gracias," was his only reply.

"He doesn't speak much English yet," a young man said to me. "He just got here from Guatemala. My papá was his sponsor."

"That was nice of him," I said. "You must be Rodrigo's son."

"I'm Juan." He held out his hand, and I shook it. "Papá says you are from Montana, but you're taking a road trip in an RV. I've always wanted to see Montana. I understand it's beautiful."

"We think so," I told him. "If you ever do get up there, please stop by our ranch. I'll make sure your father has our contact information."

"That's very nice of you."

A small boy, about four or five, ran up to Juan and jumped up and down. "Piñata! Piñata!" he yelled.

This must be Marcos, the young one so ready to smash the paper donkey and reap its rewards.

I felt a sudden longing for my own grandchildren. Although I didn't see them very often because they were busy with their own lives, my children were an important part of my life. They were one of the good things I'd gotten from Michael.

"Your son?" I asked, even though I knew the answer.

"Yes, the little monster himself." He ruffled his son's hair. "Let's go ask Abuelo when the piñata will be ready to smash, okay?"

"Okay!" Marcos looked up at me and smiled. "Who's she?"

I crouched down to his eye level. "I'm Kathleen. I'm visiting."

Large brown eyes studied me, and then he nodded. "Okay!" He grabbed his father's hand and started pulling. "Piñata!"

"Got to go," Juan said with a smile that was an echo of his father's.

Once they'd departed, I stood up and headed back to my sisters.

Trixie Lynn stopped me on my way back.

"It was so nice you were able to join us. We don't get many new people at these gatherings. Usually they're only for family and *close* friends." Her smile was as fake as the eyelashes she'd plastered on.

"It was very gracious of *Rodrigo* to invite us." I started walking again. It was difficult to avoid being snarky with a woman like Trixie Lynn.

"So when do you head back to Montana?" she asked.

"Not for a *long* time," I said. "Well, I'm sure you have things to do, being a busy hostess and all. So I'll just leave you to it."

I gave her a smirk and a little wave of my hand.

By the time I got back to Liz and Diane, there was a cluster of small children jumping up and down under the piñata, vying to be first to swing the stick at the poor paper donkey.

Rodrigo chose a girl to be first, much to the dismay of Marcos. The boy started to protest, but a stern look from his grandfather settled him down.

The girl, obviously skilled at this game, gave a mighty thwack to the underbelly. Marcos was next, and he swung wildly, the blow glancing off the donkey's rear. The rest of the children took their turns, some missing altogether, some with accurate and deadly aim. Slowly the paper became torn and dented. When it was the first girl's turn again, she took careful aim and hit it with all her might.

The paper tore open and candy rained down.

Small children scrambled after the morsels that rolled everywhere. When Marcos realized one of the younger boys hadn't gotten much of the candy, he gave some of his own to the kid.

Juan was raising his son well. Had he learned it from his mother or father?

~ ~ ~

When the sweets had all been scooped up, Rodrigo asked me to come with him to see the rest of the buildings and the horses.

We stepped out into the warm air, and I looked around me. "It's beautiful countryside," I said.

"Yes," he said. "I'm glad you appreciate it."

"I'm a rancher," I said. "We always notice the land."

"It's true," he said. "You'll have to tell me about your place in Montana, but later. Now I want to show off mine."

The corrals and buildings showed no signs of needing repair or painting. This was a ranch that was doing well, with extra cash that allowed for regular maintenance. It was a contrast to my own experience, where things only got fixed if they had to be, and I'd become an expert at getting one more month's life from the aging machinery.

As we walked, he explained his operation and the delicate act of balancing his costs against the prices the small monopoly of beef buyers would pay.

"I'm not a big fan of regulation," he said. "It can often cause more harm than good. But it would be good if there was a way to break these monopolies and stop what looks like price fixing to me. It's harder to be a small rancher when the conglomerate consistently squeezes prices."

"I know what you mean," I said. We discussed the problem as we walked toward a fenced-in field on the far side of the barn.

When we got to the fence, he opened a gate and we walked into the field.

He gave a sharp whistle.

A cluster of four horses that had been at the end of the enclosure lifted their heads.

He whistled again.

The horses immediately trotted in our direction, their distinctive heads held high, manes and tails gracefully drifting behind them. One in particular stood out to me, a chestnut brown with a white star on her forehead.

As they came closer, I realized their body configuration was different from the broad-chested quarter horses I owned. Mine were work animals, bred for the rough weather of the mountain west.

These were beautiful, an indulgence I'd never be able to afford.

The chestnut singled me out. Dropping to a walk, she approached cautiously, sniffing to determine if I was friend or foe. Her breath was warm on the hand I held out, palm up, to introduce myself. As soon as she was done nuzzling, snorting, and inspecting, I reached my hand up to caress her soft jawline.

"She likes you," Rodrigo said. "Unusual. She doesn't like most people."

"What's her name?"

He pointed to her forehead. "Star of Arabia."

"So she's Arabian."

Rodrigo nodded and rubbed the horse closest to him. "They're my pride and joy. Such beautiful animals and so easy to ride. You'll need to come riding with me someday, and you'll see for yourself."

Star decided it was her turn and rubbed her nose against my hair. Deciding she liked the texture, she took a nibble.

"What are you doing?" I stepped backward, stumbling over a small hillock in the field.

I almost went down, but Rodrigo steadied me.

"I forgot to warn you that she likes to do that," he said, his hand still on my shoulder.

Normally, I don't like men touching me, especially those I don't know very well. But this felt natural.

I stepped away and shook my finger at the horse. "No more of that!"

Star looked at me, stepped closer, and settled her head on my shoulder with a nicker.

"Definitely likes you," he said with a warm smile.

Star might not be the only one who liked me.

Chapter Five

It took me a long time to get to sleep Sunday night. For some reason my brain was hung up on Rodrigo. I played over scenes in my mind: him with his grandchildren, his laughter, the moment with the horses that seemed more meaningful to me than it probably was.

Interspersed with those scenes were Trixie Lynn's glares. She clearly had her intentions set on being Rodrigo's next wife. She acted like the lady of the manor, making sure all the guests—except us—were comfortable, and chatting with everyone, a large smile on her face.

The hostess with the mostest.

But it wasn't clear to me how Rodrigo felt about her. Was he playing along with her game because he was clueless? Or was he using her?

I didn't like what it said about his character if the latter were true.

When I finally fell asleep, other scenes filled my dreams.

I had a vision of myself, covered with veils and jewels and little else, riding Star across the desert, trying to outrun a dust storm like Viggo Mortensen had done in *Hidalgo*.

I *loved* Viggo Mortensen. He could share my bed any day.

As long as he didn't become too real. Fantasy men were just fine. Reality was a different story.

The image of the ride repeated itself several times during the night. One of the things I liked best about it was that somehow my body had transformed into something that looked more like Sophia Loren and less like Kathy Bates.

Then the bathroom dreams began. At first they were the bathroom nightmares I'd lived with on a daily basis after I had kids. All four of us had shared one bathroom. My daughter, Megan, had gotten worse as she'd gotten older—make-up, long hair, and hair clips scattered everywhere, along with the occasional intimate apparel that freaked out her brother if he saw it.

Patrick had been the neatest of the lot, but he still left the toothpaste uncapped.

And my husband? It was up to me to put the toilet seat down as far as he was concerned. That's what he'd married me for—to make sure the house was clean and dinner on the table at the appropriate time.

There'd been a few moments of dreamless sleep before the nightmare morphed into nicer visions.

Rodrigo had three good-sized bathrooms, *and* a housekeeper.

Two of the bathrooms had big tubs, one with jets. Plenty of room, heated floors, and gleaming porcelain fixtures.

If I got the man, I got the bathrooms, my subconscious informed me.

But I couldn't hang out with someone just because he had beautiful bathrooms.

Or horses.

By the time I awoke the next morning, I knew all those fantasies were going to stay exactly that. Once this trip was done, I was moving into Liz's house—which had a very nice bathroom—and living all by myself.

It was just what I needed.

~ ~ ~

"I'm off to do some painting," Liz announced the next morning.

"Are you going to be gone all day?" I asked.

"As far as I know," she said. "I've scheduled the car for today. I'll stop and get groceries on the way back. I'll make something simple tonight. We ate a lot yesterday."

"But it was *so* good," Diane said.

"I've never had barbecue that wonderful," I said.

"Well, marry the rancher and you'll have all you want of it to eat," Liz said.

"And the waistline that goes with it," Diane said.

"I'll put a hex on both of you," I warned.

"That only worked when we were kids," Liz said.

I'd teased both her and Diane when we were younger, telling them I had the evil eye inherited from one of our Irish ancestors. I'd "hex" them and tell them bad things were going to happen.

Then I'd engineer a few events to make them believe. The problem was, sometimes bad things happened that I hadn't created. Those events frightened me enough to make me stop.

"There's no need for hexes," Diane said, her voice a little nervous. "I'm sure Trixie Lynn won't let you anywhere near her chosen man."

We laughed.

"Just remember," I said. "Unlike you two and your new romances, I have no intention of getting involved with anyone ever again. Michael's barely in his grave. I don't understand why you think I need *any*one."

"Because you were so unhappy with Michael," Liz said, all teasing dropping from her voice.

"Michael and I were fine." It was over. There was no reason to talk to my sisters about anything that had gone on between me and my late husband.

Liz shook her head. "No. You were miserable. Part of it was because he needed to be in charge, for his own ego. He never acknowledged how smart and resourceful you are."

"We were fine," I repeated. I didn't need my marriage analyzed. It was over. As dead as Michael in his grave.

"No you weren't," Diane said. "Even I could see that in the short time I was there."

I started to sputter, and she raised her hand.

"You don't have to say anything. But I think …" She glanced at Liz. "I think we'd both like you to be open. Something … or someone … else could come along that would give you more happiness than you've ever allowed yourself to have."

I had to look away. I didn't want to think too deeply about what Diane had said. I was the one who held it together when things were unraveling. I never showed anyone how I felt. It was too dangerous. Life could be navigated with a little sarcasm, a good dose of prayer to the right saint, and a lot of duct tape.

"I'm fine," I repeated. I took a deep breath and looked at Diane. "What are your plans for the day?"

"I've got work. Then I'm going to take the scooter and take some pictures."

Good. That put the two of them out of the way so I wouldn't have to deal with questions about my marriage or speculation on what could occur with Rodrigo.

Because nothing could occur with Rodrigo, no matter how many clean bathrooms he had.

~ ~ ~

By the time Diane left it was after lunch, and I'd run out of things to do. I tried to read, but even that had failed to hold my interest for long. I was used to being active, having chores and errands to do. With this trip, we'd rarely stayed in one place long. The exceptions had been the month in Yellowstone and another in upstate New York.

During those stays my sisters had hooked up with men from their pasts.

Good thing it couldn't happen to me. My past was literally dead.

Restlessness put me in mind of Star. It would be nice to spend some time riding her to see if she was as beautiful a horse as she looked.

Riding the range with Rodrigo wouldn't be bad either. I was eager to learn more about his operation. We'd barely scratched the surface of our ranching discussion.

But that meant being in closer contact with him. Making small talk at church would be fine. Anything more was running into dangerous territory.

As I refilled my water glass for the fifth time, I realized I needed to do *something*.

Pulling my loom out from its storage place, I went outside, hoping the constant movement of the shuttle from one side to the other would soothe my nerves

The next gray Celtic knot began to emerge as I steadily worked. There were only two colors, but the setup had taken hours, and I needed to take care to ensure the threads were parted accurately. The pattern was unforgiving. A mistake would show.

"That's beautiful," a woman said.

I looked up, startled. I'd been so engrossed in the detail I hadn't heard her arrive.

"Thank you," I said.

"Have you been weaving long?"

"Several years. I took it up once my children left home."

"I've never had the courage for weaving. It seems too exact. I knit and spin. They're more forgiving." She held out her hand. "I'm Genna."

"Kathleen." I shook it. "You spin? That's always seemed a mystery to me. All that fluff becoming a strand that is strong enough to make clothing."

"It is pretty miraculous. But so is that. All those threads becoming that beautiful pattern."

"I suppose it is."

"Well, I'll see you." Genna took a few steps toward the road before turning back. "You're the only one I've seen doing fiber arts.

Would you mind … um … could I get my spinning wheel and come back? I don't talk much, but it would be nice to work with someone. Back home—in Colorado—we have a fiber arts guild. We spend an afternoon a week working together. I miss it."

I was tempted to say no. I'd met enough people at the barbecue to last me a bit. But then I saw the longing in her eyes. "Sure. Why not?"

Her face bloomed with joy.

"Great! I'll be right back."

Soon she was set up next to me, a strangely-shaped spinning wheel in front of her. I watched for a bit as her hands and fingers took a hunk of chestnut colored fiber and held it just so to create an even thin thread of yarn.

It was indeed magic.

I went back to my loom.

True to her word, Genna didn't say much, and I began to relax.

Soon the rhythm of what we were doing threaded together. Unwritten music surrounded us, as did the ghosts of all the people who'd participated in the past and present of fiber arts. Mongolian men wove camel hair on spindle looms. Women in lonely farmhouses worked on large looms to produce clothing for their family.

It was an art as old as the human desire for warmth and personal decoration.

When we parted a few hours later, I'd made a new friend.

I'd just put the loom away when I received a call.

"Hello?" It was Rodrigo's voice.

"Hello," I said.

"Oh, good," he said. "I'm glad to get you. I realized we didn't make a plan to go riding."

"No, we didn't," I said, not offering anything more.

"What are you doing this week? Are there any free days?"

I walked to the car schedule we kept. "I'm not sure," I lied.

"You must be a busy lady," he said. "Perhaps some other day soon? I'd like to talk to you more about how you ranch in Montana. Maybe I could learn something."

"I doubt it," I said. He seemed to be doing just fine.

"You can always learn something," he said. "Surely there must be some day you have free."

"Can I get back to you on that? My sisters aren't here at the moment. I'm not sure what they have planned. We only have one car, and we need to schedule its use."

"Of course."

We chatted a few more moments, then hung up with my promise to get back in touch.

It sounded lovely. It would be something to do.

We could be friends, couldn't we? I'd put up good boundaries, enjoy the ride, then walk away when we were done.

Just to make sure, I'd say a little prayer. It was too insignificant a matter for Mary or any of the members of the Trinity, so I sent up a quick prayer to the first saint I thought of: St. Jude. Head bowed, I asked for the support I needed to make sure Rodrigo and I remained just friends.

It never occurred to me I was praying to the wrong saint.

Chapter Six

I sat outside the park's laundry room and read the book I'd picked up on the Alamo. Like the Lewis and Clark expedition, familiar to every child who was educated in the Montana school system, myths abounded about the Texas fight for independence from Mexico.

Heat and the various aromas of laundry detergent continually drifted from the open door. I would have preferred to go back to the RV, but ever since the incident in Indiana, we'd agreed to stay with the laundry.

It had been Diane's turn to do the laundry, and competition for the few machines had been high. She'd put a load into the dryer and dashed back to the RV to get some lunch. By the time she got back, she was astounded to see that a woman had removed our intimate clothes—fortunately dry—from the dryer so she could use it for her clothes.

But worse, she was folding *our* undies and socks.

I was glad it had been Diane. Liz would have thrown up.

Diane pointed out the sign that said not to touch other people's clothes, and rescued our garments.

The woman got all huffy, insulted that her *good deed* hadn't been appreciated.

People. I never could quite get the hang of how some of their minds worked.

Today I waited right where I was, armed with water, a book, and snacks.

It was our weekly cleaning and stocking up day. We rotated the chores. By now, both Liz and Diane were competent enough to dump the gray and black water tanks of the RV into the park's sewer system. Diane did most of the straightening. Liz thought chaos was the normal way to live.

Shopping was a chore Liz had reluctantly shared with Diane, but still didn't trust me with. I shopped for cost, not quality. For years, I'd been buying cheap cuts of meat, canned vegetables, sacks of potatoes, large jars of store-brand peanut butter, and white bread that was perfect for rolling into balls.

It made Liz shudder.

I was also a bit of a failure at helping with dinner. Both my sisters claimed I had no imagination when it came to food.

Which is why even trying to be friends with Rodrigo made no sense. What did I know about the culinary traditions of Mexico or southern Texas? These women had been raised from childhood knowing the right amount of spices to add to make basic food taste amazing.

Growing up, I'd believed that salt and pepper were the only two spices available to use.

Rodrigo had a housekeeper-slash-cook, as well as someone who could prepare the most amazing barbecue on the planet. Did the housekeeper come before or after his wife's death? He struck me as a traditional man through and through so it made sense he'd expect the woman to cook and clean. I already had that merit badge and didn't need another. Marrying someone like Trixie Lynn, who was working to appear like a throwback to the 1950s, made a lot more sense for Rodrigo.

I should abandon any idea of friendship, however brief, with the man. I'd get my sisters to go hiking. That would take care of the wanderlust I felt. Or find a trail ride. Maybe I could learn dressage while we were here.

I laughed out loud. Dressage was a rich person's game. Everything had to be just so, including the strange garments people wore when they rode.

In my life, boots, jeans, and a flannel shirt were the preferred riding wear, with a heavy Carhartt jacket in the winter and a slicker tied to the saddle in case it rained.

And what was with helmets? A cowboy hat was a good investment for keeping the sun from a rider's eyes. A few times of being thrown from a horse—either through the horse's or one's own stupidity—taught a person to land someplace other than their head.

Nope. No charming, rich rancher for me. I'd go it alone.

The timer on my phone dinged, and I got up to rescue the laundry before someone else snatched it up.

~ ~ ~

With food in the fridge, a clean rig, and enough room in the tanks to spend quality time in the bathroom, it was time for cocktail hour. I mixed up a healthy batch of G&Ts, while Diane got her beloved fire pit going. Liz poured us bowls of salsa, with one more for the table so anyone stopping by could have a snack.

It was a custom we'd started right at the beginning of the journey. We loved our downtime, a chance to talk to each other in ways we'd never been able to as adults. Sometimes disagreements arose, but the more we were together, the easier it was to navigate them.

We always waved at people walking by, shouting hello to those we'd met, inviting them to come back with their own chairs and drinks—an impromptu party.

It was still early days at this park, so I was glad when I saw Genna, her husband, and their medium-sized dog walking by.

I waved her over, and introductions were made. The dog was a love, just like her owner. Genna's husband seemed to be a nice man, although he appeared to lean toward the geek clan with awkward movements and little conversation.

Soon we had a small gathering, Diane and Liz chatting about places we'd been and listening to the travels of others.

Genna and I chatted about her fiber guild.

"I never knew such a thing existed," I told her.

"I think they've always been around," she replied. "People did a lot of knitting and weaving in the 1960s and early '70s."

"Granny squares," I said with a laugh. "I remember doing lots and lots of granny squares as a kid. I think I even made a blanket."

"We all did," Genna said. "It was part of the back to the land movement."

"I was already on the land," I said with a grin.

"It must have been fun to grow up on a ranch."

"It was a lot of work," I told her.

"Things aren't always as glamorous as they appear on television."

"Ain't that the truth," I replied.

"But all that effort seemed to have skipped a generation. My kids never understood my passion for knitting or spinning," she said.

"I tried teaching Megan—that's my daughter—but she gave up when it was time to purl. Never could get the hang of it."

"I don't know whether it was the slow food movement or what, but the fiber arts seem to be back in fashion," Genna said. "Maybe it's a reaction to parents buying cartloads of cheap clothing for their kids in big box stores."

"I never got that," I said. "Although as a kid, I would have been jealous. I'm the youngest."

Genna groaned. "With two older sisters. Hand-me-downs."

"Totally."

We chatted a few more moments, then she and her husband left.

Someone else mentioned they were having line dancing lessons tonight at the community center. Liz clapped her hands and said it was a great idea.

Great for her. She didn't have two left feet. The last time I'd been on a dance floor was when Michael and I had done the obligatory one at our wedding reception.

~ ~ ~

But a few hours later, I found myself back on a dance floor. There was no arguing with Liz once she made up her mind.

The teacher radiated youth and enthusiasm while gyrating her body. The five men who were there focused with laser sharpness on her hips and ass as she did so, a fact that annoyed me no end. Some men were only tired of sex when they got in bed with their wives.

I'd placed myself at the back of the crowd, Diane beside me. Liz was in the front row, as close to the instructor as she could get.

I tried. I really did. But my left foot and right foot have never made good partners. It was only a matter of time before disaster struck.

I stepped on Diane's toe twice before she moved away from me. Somewhere during the bends for the electric slide, I managed to slap the ass of the woman in front of me.

She wasn't amused.

But true calamity didn't strike until the Macarena. I'd gotten the dance moves down perfectly … well, as perfect as they were going to get for me.

Then the instructor got fancy. At the end of every set of movements, we were supposed to jump a quarter turn to our left.

My sense of left and right have the same sense of compatibility as my feet do. In other words … none.

It was when I jumped right, immediately realizing it was the wrong way, then tried to correct, that I fell.

Hard.

With a loud thump.

No grace at all.

The air was knocked out of me, and I lay on the floor like a turtle on its back, arms and legs flailing above me. I sent up a thank you prayer that I had had the good sense to wear pants.

"Are you okay?" Liz asked as she and Diane rushed to me.

"Do I look okay?" I asked.

"Anything broken? Sprained?" Diane, ever practical, asked.

I tested my limbs and shook my head.

"Well, then let's get you off the floor."

I looked around at the circle of eyes staring down at me and groaned.

"Make them go away," I whispered to Liz. "They don't want to see this."

She nodded and stood.

"She's fine," Liz said. "She just needs a little rest. Why don't you all go back to the dance?" She stared at the instructor, who got the message.

"Let's go from the top!" the instructor yelled brightly.

One by one, the pairs of eyes went away.

Once they'd enthusiastically gone back to waving their arms and jumping in the right direction, I heaved myself to all fours and made it to standing.

"I think I'll sit the rest of this out," I said.

"Let's just call it a night," Diane said.

"I'm okay with that." Liz smiled. "I know you don't hurt now, but some aspirin and water wouldn't hurt."

I nodded and the three of us returned to the trailer where they insisted I lie down on the couch. Picking up my phone, I noticed I'd missed a call from Rodrigo.

I listened to his voicemail.

"Who's that?" Diane asked as she handed me a glass of water and two ibuprofen.

"Rodrigo. He wants me to go riding."

"You should go," Liz said. "You love to ride."

"You told us how beautiful his horses are," Diane added.

"There are too many reasons not to go," I said, gulping down the pills with some water.

"There's only one reason you're not going," Liz said.

"In your opinion."

She shrugged. "You're scared. You're a fraidy-cat."

"We're not ten," I said.

"Doesn't mean you're not afraid. I dare you to go."

I waved away the dare, but it got my dander up just the same. I wanted to leap off the couch and prove her wrong then and there.

I glanced at Diane.

"I double-dare you," Diane said.

I groaned and flung my arm over my eyes. They knew how to get to me.

I'd never been able to resist a double dare.

Unless I found a really good excuse, I was going riding.

Chapter Seven

Wednesday dawned as the next day inevitably does.

For some reason that reality of passing time hit me hard this morning. We had eight weeks here and one of those was already gone. That meant I only had seven more weeks to dodge Rodrigo's offer of a horseback ride.

But it was also seven weeks of my life. It was time to do something I wanted to do.

All I had to do was figure out what that was.

I took possession of the shower before the other two got up. Years of having to get up early to milk the small dairy herd we'd kept were finally paying off.

I took my clothes into the small closet that served as the shower, then stood underneath a strong spray. They had good water pressure in Texas.

Traveling around the country made me notice things like that. There'd been one, somewhat rundown, place in Georgia that could barely produce a trickle, in spite of all the lakes and ponds the area sprouted.

Hair washed, body cleaned and clad, I emerged from the shower. The aroma of coffee from the kitchen enticed me in that direction, so I tossed my night clothes on my bed in the back and headed to the kitchen. Diane was already up, a steaming mug in one hand, a steamy novel in the other.

"How can you read that trash?" I asked.

Diane shrugged and kept reading.

Must be a good one. Every once in a while I thought about picking up a romance novel, but I didn't want to read about something I'd never have again.

No, I'd rather read about something that happened a long time ago.

The irony wasn't lost on me.

I looked at the car schedule. Today was blank. I quickly scribbled my name, even though I had no idea where I would go. Anyplace out of here would be good.

I poured myself a cup of coffee.

Diane was in the shower, and Liz was doing yoga on a mat outside the RV when Rodrigo called.

"Good morning," he said.

"Hello."

"I was wondering if I could entice you with coffee sometime today. There's a lovely place not far from your RV park. Not only do they have good espresso, but their sweet rolls are the best in the county."

"I'm not sure. We may have things planned."

The blank calendar taunted me.

"I'm sorry to hear that," Rodrigo said. "I was thinking if we had coffee first, then it would be easier for you to come to the ranch and go riding."

He had it backwards. Sitting on a horse and talking about the ranch around us would be so much easier than staring across a table at him trying to think of something to say.

"No, that's not it at all," I said. "I've been really busy."

"I understand. There must be a lot of work to do around an RV."

Was there a little bit of sarcasm in his voice?

"It's amazing how many little things break," I told him. "Driving on highways that need repair—all that bouncing—it tends to wear connections and cheap fittings down."

"Yes, of course."

No mistaking it. He thought I was putting him on.

Even I knew I wasn't being entirely truthful.

It was time to pull up my big girl panties and go riding. I'd made the petition to St. Jude; everything should be just fine. No danger of falling into this man's arms or developing a sudden urge to read bodice rippers.

"How about Friday for the ride?" I asked, checking the car schedule before I answered. Liz was already scheduled in the afternoon, but she could paint in the park. I needed to get this ride done and dusted.

"That would work for me," he said. "I can't wait to get you up on Star of Arabia. You'll be amazed at the feeling."

"I'm sure." I thought of all the aching muscles I was going to have once I got off the horse. It had been over six months since I'd climbed on one of the beasts. Thinking about it made me realize how much I'd been missing it.

"Thank you for agreeing," Rodrigo said. "I've been looking forward to you saying yes."

I decided not to ask why.

We made arrangements and ended the call.

"Who was that?" Diane asked as she emerged from the back looking ready to start her day.

"No one important," I said, not ready to discuss my upcoming ride until I had to.

She wasn't happy with the answer, but must have decided to let it go, because she remained silent.

Liz came in the door and walked straight to the car schedule.

"Where are you going?" she asked me.

"I'm not sure yet."

"Then let me have the car. I have a wonderful idea for a painting."

I shook my head. "Not happening. And I also need it on Friday."

"I'm already on the schedule for Friday." Liz had her mat rolled up under one arm, and both fists pressed into her hips.

There was no way around it. I was going to have to tell them why I needed the car.

"It's your fault. You're the ones who dared me."

"You're going riding?" Diane asked.

"Really?" Liz added.

I nodded. "I need the car to get there."

"He could come get you," Diane said.

I almost threw up at the thought of being in a car with that man. It would be almost as bad as the coffee shop, except I could look at the scenery while trying to come up with something to say.

"No. That's not happening," I said.

"I could take you on the scooter," she said.

"The way they drive here? In those big honkin' trucks? Are you out of your mind?"

Liz started laughing.

"What!" I glared at her.

"If you could see yourself right now. The expression on your face is exactly like Mom's when she was whipping up a good mad at one of us."

"As long as everyone understands that I'm taking the car on Friday, and it's *your* fault," I said, pointing a finger at my yoga-practicing sister, "I don't give a rat's ass what I look like."

Diane started laughing too.

I eyed both of them.

Then I couldn't help myself.

I flopped back on the couch and lost it.

By the time we all recovered, whatever tension there'd been had evaporated, like the air clearing after a full-blown thunderstorm on the plains.

"Do I get the car?" I asked.

"Yes," they said simultaneously.

"Good." I picked up my purse and phone, and beat it out of the RV before they changed their minds.

~ ~ ~

I treated myself at a bookstore, picking up a magazine devoted to weaving which I read while indulging in a second, solitary cup of coffee. Scrolling through my phone, I found a local fiber store that promised more than the typical skeins of colorful yarn and a few packages of roving for spinning.

It had been a long time since I'd found a store that had a good supply of yarns for weaving, as well as a knowledgeable staff. While the loom I'd brought with me was on the small side, it was perfect for my relative beginner status. It would also be the right size if I ever found a fiber arts group like Genna had suggested.

In my heart of hearts, though, I wanted to graduate to a floor loom. It didn't have to be huge, just big enough to weave a sizeable cloth piece. I'd seen a video about a woman who'd created her own wedding dress from the wool of a particular sheep, including preparing, spinning, weaving, and sewing her creation.

I didn't have that kind of ambition, but the loom and weaving gave me peace I didn't find anywhere else.

Punching the directions into the phone's GPS, I drove to the store.

The place turned out to be everything I love in a fiber store. Not only was there yarn of every possible color and weight, but there were large spools of roving for spinners, beautifully crafted equipment for all types of fiber arts, and a colorful array of yarn designed for weaving.

I was in the earthly version of my particular heaven.

There were even several types of looms, including a small floor model.

"Can I help you with something?" asked a slim woman with her gray hair cut short in a practical style. Her voice was softly Southern without being sugary enough to bring on diabetes just by listening to her.

"I'm only looking," I said.

"That's fine," she said. "Many of us look for a long time before we find the loom that will be the right companion for the hours we want to spend with it. With the price tag on some of these, it's harder than choosing a husband."

Her dry sense of humor took me aback for a second, then I grinned.

"Do you have questions on any of them?" she asked with her own smile. "I wouldn't want you winding up with the wrong man."

"Already have that merit badge," I said.

"I'm sorry, but I understand. I have one of those too."

Bonding complete, I began to ask questions about some of the models that seemed slightly advanced from the one I had now. The woman, who introduced herself as Donna, answered every question I had with infinite patience.

At the end, I couldn't help myself. I touched the floor model, trying to avoid looking at the price tag.

"Everyone dreams of that," Donna said. "But it's not practical for most people. It takes up a chunk of space."

I nodded. If I were going back to the ranch house, I'd be able to take over one of the old bedrooms.

But Patrick was there now with his family, and it was my fondest wish that he take over running the family ranch. Megan was invested in her husband's sugar beet farm, and Liz's son, Stephan, was an East Coast artist.

No, it was up to my family, as it always had been. Much as I griped about Michael, he'd been a steadfast rancher. We'd kept it going and made a good profit until the end.

"How long are you going to be around?" Donna asked.

I'd told her we were on a year-long road trip.

"Roughly six more weeks," I said.

"I'll give you a list of classes. We'd love to have you join us. It's a good group."

I took the paper she handed me and scanned it. One class jumped out: weaving lace.

"Is this very difficult?" I asked.

"It can be a little tricky to set up, but once you have the pattern in your head, it gets to be like everything else: meditative. But you need to pay attention at some level."

"I'll have to think about it. I'd love to be able to make lace." Somewhere—if Michael hadn't gotten his hands on it—was a stash of old Irish lace that had made its way across the Atlantic and the bulk of the country intact.

I needed to find it and get it to Megan.

Come to think of it, I should make a proper job of it. Clean out that old house so Patrick could really make it his.

Then, I could step off onto the rest of my solitary adventure with a lighter load.

Chapter Eight

For the first ten minutes I fought a feeling of terror.

I'd never had a massage before, but here I was letting a stranger—someone I didn't know!—touch my nearly naked body. I'd balked at stripping down altogether, but was left with my well-used bra and saggy granny panties.

I'd never been one to spend a fortune on lingerie, but when we were younger, before life took over, Michael used to buy me intimate nothings at Christmas and insist I model them for him. They never stayed on my body for a long time.

Even back then I'd been shy about showing off my body. I'd seen enough models on magazine covers to know I looked nothing like them.

This had been Liz's harebrained idea. I'd finally become accustomed to the three of us getting our nails done every once in a while. For the first time in my life, my cuticles weren't ragged, and my nails no longer looked like someone attacked them with a chainsaw.

And it was heaven not having to cut my own toenails.

"Ow!" I yelped as the masseuse pressed deeply into my shoulder.

"Too much pressure?" she asked.

Ya think?

"A little."

"You're very tense in there." She eased up a little, but still managed to get her fingers deep enough that my muscle twanged. Then all of a sudden the ache was smoothed away.

"Ahh."

"That's a better sound," the masseuse said.

Maybe there was something to this after all. Liz had promised I'd feel like a new woman.

The feeling was only going to last a short while. As I drifted into a fluffy white mental space, almost asleep, a thundercloud hovered in the distance, but I couldn't quite make out what it was.

Forty minutes later, I was instructed to "take my time," but to get off the table and get some clothes on.

That wasn't the way she said it, but I got the message. Play time was over.

I pulled on my blouse, capris I'd taken to wearing once we got to warmer weather, and the flip-flops I'd purchased when we started getting our nails done. A brief glance in a mirror showed a face I wasn't used to seeing. My eyes were bright, my skin glowing, and my mouth had an almost seductive smile. Surrounded by a halo of wild Irish hair, I looked like a totally different woman.

Huh.

There must be something to this massage stuff.

I made my way to the nail parlor where my sisters were already seated, engaged in conversation that made them smile. My heart warmed to see them so relaxed and comfortable with each other. It had taken a while, but we were a family again, more than we'd ever been.

A pleasant young woman saw me standing and asked if I needed help.

I shook my head, but she made sure I chose my color and got settled in my chair anyway before listing the types of water I could have. I chose cucumber-infused, having discovered how quickly it quenched my thirst. The masseuse had indicated I should hydrate to wash away the toxins. I wasn't sure about the science, but a glass of liquid sounded good.

"So," Liz said with a tease in her voice. "Did you like it?"

"It was okay," I said to torment her.

"Okay?" Diane practically shrieked. "It was wonderful!"

"All right," I said. "It was a little better than okay."

"Anyone ever tell you you're a pain in the ass?" Diane asked.

"You and Liz have frequently mentioned that," I said with a grin.

They chuckled as our nail techs settled in and began to work.

Until Liz had introduced me to this experience, I'd had no idea how blissful a pedicure could be. I tried not to think about the poor person having to deal with my thick, yellowing toenails, but sent as much gratitude as I could her way. And I made sure to leave a generous tip.

I flicked the controls that started the back massage—one could never have too many massages—and leaned back to sip my water. As we'd grown accustomed to doing, my sisters also retreated into a quiet state. We only came back to life when the nail tech attacked our nails with silver equipment and determination.

"How are the paintings coming along?" I asked Liz.

"I feel like I'm getting closer to the approach I want." Liz's original style had been a series of paint and ink drawings that had made her famous … and rich. She and her agent had been smart enough to make the images available for reproduction on mass market items like prints, T-shirts, and even a shower curtain.

But that had been a substitute for the painting she really wanted to create. After a breakthrough a few months ago, she'd tried charcoal, but it hadn't given her the satisfaction she'd hoped to get. She continued to work at it and remained optimistic.

"That's wonderful," Diane told Liz. "Have you heard from Walter?"

"Yes," Liz answered, a soft smile appearing on her face. "His lease is up at the end of March. He's already moving some new things into the house and talking to architects about remodeling one of the sheds into a studio." She looked at us. "I'll miss you guys, but I'm looking forward to being with Walter and my son."

"We get it," Diane said.

"As long as you all arrive for a big family reunion in the summer," I said. "We need to teach the next generation how to rope and ride."

"Absolutely," Liz said. "Speaking of roping and riding, how are you feeling about your ride tomorrow?"

"At least it will be over," I said.

"It could be the 'beginning of a beautiful friendship.'" Liz attempted a Humphrey Bogart accent as she quoted one of the famous lines from *Casablanca*.

I gave her the stink-eye.

"She's right, you know," Diane said. "I mean, how would you feel if this was a female rancher, and she invited you riding?"

It took a minute to adjust my thinking.

"I'd be fine," I admitted.

"Well, then, forget he's a guy."

"Hard to do with that mustache," Liz said.

"Hey, if I didn't attack my upper lip with a hair pulling gizmo, I'm sure I could give him a run for his money," Diane said.

"Ouch!" Liz and I said in unison, covering our upper lips, although I knew exactly what Diane was talking about. I had one of those gizmos too.

Liz, blessed with all the good genes, probably had a hairless face in spite of menopause.

"But enough of that," Diane said. "All I'm saying is it doesn't have to be a big deal unless you make it a big deal. Just pretend he's a friend ... or acquaintance. Friendship is the best foundation for a relationship anyway. Not that I'm saying you have to have a relationship," she added hastily.

"You talk to male ranchers all the time at home," Liz said. "You never treat them like they're anything special."

"I don't go riding with them either," I pointed out. "And too many of them need to be taken down a peg."

"Rodrigo doesn't seem that way," Liz said.

He didn't. And that idea scared me.

But if I scratched under the surface, I'd bet I'd find out he was like all the others.

So no big deal going riding with him. He had a good act of being a nice guy. We'd just be pals. Cisco and Pancho. Butch and Sundance. Calamity Jane and Wild Bill Hickok.

I sputtered with laughter, almost spitting out my water.

"What?" Diane asked.

I waved my hand. "Nothing," I managed to squawk out.

"Right," Liz said, and picked up a magazine from the shelf next to her.

I closed my eyes to indicate I, too, was done with the discussion as the nail tech slipped toe spreaders between my toes so she could do the polish.

Ten minutes later, we padded over to manicurists' tables where our toes were placed in heated boxes to harden the polish.

The woman examined my hands and shook her head, but at least she didn't "tsk" at me like so many had done. I endured her silent ministrations, and insisted on clear polish in spite of her urging me to at least consider something light pink.

I pulled out a foot and pointed to my green toe nails. "I'm not a pink kind of gal," I said.

The horses wouldn't care, and I'd be damned if I were going to get gussied up for a rancher.

Eventually, we were done, and even though I was relaxed, I was more exhausted than if I'd spent the entire day rounding up cattle. My sisters must have felt the same way because we picked up some take-out barbecue and drove home.

After dinner I called Patrick, homesick for ranch news. He assured me the majority of cows had dropped their calves on schedule, and the calves were checked and tagged. Things were going well, and he and his wife were enjoying it more than they'd expected to.

We talked about selling off the dairy herd come summer, and he agreed it was probably a good idea.

"It doesn't make sense, Mom. They take up more work than

anything, and we don't produce enough dairy to make it worthwhile. I think we need to talk about another animal, though. Something that isn't beef. Between the conglomerates and the climate impact of raising cattle, diversification to something like chickens, turkeys, or even planting some type of beans would be a good thing to look into."

"I'm not sure about that," I told him. "Seems like extra work again."

"It is, but not as much as the cows."

"Better not make them pets, though," I warned. "I doubt your kids are going to want to eat Bert the Turkey for Thanksgiving."

Patrick laughed. "Good point."

"We'll talk about it when I get home."

"Good. When is that exactly?"

We talked about my return, his kids, and the depths of winter in Montana. After a long stretch in Fort Hood, Texas, he'd forgotten how long snow season lasted.

When I hung up, I felt the ranch was in good hands. The fact that the young family was settling in was a plus. It was time for the younger ones to take over so I could retire.

Retire and do what?

While weaving, even on a big loom, was appealing, I didn't see myself doing that day in and day out. I was too much of an outdoor girl for that. It was one of the things that had surprised me about this trip. The ability to be outside most of the time, not trapped indoors by freezing temperatures and howling wind, made me miss Montana less than I'd thought I would.

Maybe change was okay. If I didn't make a big deal out of something, but looked for the silver lining instead, could I be happier than I'd been my whole life? I could continue to blame my late husband for the misery that had been in my life, but I knew that wasn't all true. I could walk around with my own dark cloud at times, for no reason other than there weren't enough daylight hours.

For the most part, my life had been a satisfactory one. I'd loved raising my kids and tending to the ranch. Now it was time to move on from the past and see what the future could bring.

I could simply go on the ride tomorrow and enjoy myself. My sisters were right. I didn't need to make it a big deal. All I needed to do was have some fun.

With that thought firmly planted in my brain, I rolled over and went to sleep.

Chapter Nine

I woke at six, as eager as a schoolgirl Christmas morning. When I remembered what I was so excited about, I buried my head under my pillow with a groan.

In spite of all my self-talk about it simply being a ride with a new friend, I was more upbeat than I should be. I needed to squash those feelings.

Maybe if I visualized Rodrigo as a woman?

I contorted my brain to create the image and the result wasn't even close to pretty. In fact, I had to stifle my laugh or risk waking Liz in the next bed.

For the next half hour, I tossed and turned, trying to think of anything other than the upcoming ride. At six-thirty, I gave it up and carefully got out of the bed, so I didn't wake my sister. It probably didn't matter. Liz slept more soundly than either Diane or I.

Slipping into the shower, I took time—and a good chunk of the hot water—to thoroughly clean myself and wash my hair. I even made the effort to shave, not that there was as much bodily hair as there used to be.

Clean as a whistle, I wrapped a towel around me and exited the shower room. The aroma of fresh coffee filled the RV and I could hear someone stumbling around the front room. Diane must be up.

Returning to the back room, I could see that Liz had managed to turn herself to the wall, but her chest still rose and fell in steady rhythms. I hoped Walter was a late riser. Nothing worse than a night owl and morning lark living together.

After dressing quickly, I returned to the front. Diane had put her bed back together and was enjoying her coffee and morning scroll through the news on her phone. About a third of the way through the trip, I'd offered to swap places with Diane so she didn't have to put her bed back together every morning, but she said it was preferable to bunking with Liz.

Neither of us wanted Liz, with all her attendant clutter, to take over the front room.

"Morning," I said, reaching for a mug.

"You're up early," she commented.

"Couldn't sleep," I said.

"Just have a good time. You like riding. You always have."

"I'll probably do something dumb like fall off the horse," I said, actually considering it a possibility.

"You'll be fine. It's going to be a beautiful morning. I'm almost jealous."

"But not quite. What's on your agenda?" I asked.

"Not much. I'm feeling lazy this morning. I'll call Joe later. I miss him."

"I thought he was going to try to get down here in February?"

Diane shook his head. "His agent wants his second book done by the beginning of March. He's having trouble with the ending."

"That's too bad," I said. I enjoyed watching Diane and Joe together. They were sweet, experiencing the chance at love they'd missed in high school.

Walter and Liz were another matter. They were two high-strung people who somehow fit together in a way I'd never understand.

"I think we're on our own for breakfast," I said. "Liz is dead to the world."

"She didn't get home from the studio until late last night," Diane said. "You'd already gone to bed. She didn't wake you?"

"No," I said. I'd vaguely heard her come in, but had feigned sleep. "I had a really good night's rest." At least I'd have a small sin to add to confession.

I cracked a couple of eggs into a frying pan and started some toast. Riding took more energy than it looked like, and I wanted to be prepared.

Or at least as much as I could be.

~ ~ ~

I pulled into Rodrigo's place right at nine when I said I'd be there. He wanted to get an early start, saying morning and evening were the best times for a ride in hill country.

He came out to greet me as soon as I turned off the car. He was dressed in worn jeans, a soft flannel shirt, and a light jacket with a pair of well-used cowboy boots on his feet.

As soon as he reached me, he opened the door and extended a hand to help me out. I took it to be polite and was a bit dismayed to find I enjoyed placing my hand in his.

"You look very nice," he said, examining the clean blouse, too-snug jeans, and boots I had on—boots that were much more worn than the pair he sported. The jacket I had over my arm, one of my old Carhartt models, also bore the signs of hard use.

I squared my shoulders. The hell with it. I wasn't a rich cattle rancher, no use pretending to be one.

"Got everything?" he asked.

"Yep," I said.

He closed the car door behind me.

"The horses are in the corral by the barn," he said. "You said you wanted to saddle your own horse, but I had the wrangler lay out the tack."

"Thanks."

Rodrigo handed me a rope lead. "I may have to get her for you."

"Let me try first."

"Of course."

I entered the corral, and instantly both horses were alert, their ears pricking forward as they stared at me. Rodrigo was a known entity, so they didn't pay him much attention.

Stepping carefully and keeping eye contact with Star, I started murmuring to her, to reassure her I wasn't a threat. With the lead coiled in my right hand, I held out the apple slices I'd brought with me in my left.

She shifted her weight and Rodrigo's horse took a step closer to him.

"That's a pretty girl," I said rhythmically. "I'm no threat. We'll be good. That's a good girl. Apples, girl. You like apples. That's a good girl."

I was a few feet away when Star gave a snort and shuffled sideways. After pausing a few moments, I continued to walk toward her.

Her eyes widened, but she didn't move.

I stopped and held my flat hand out a little farther.

Then I waited.

Star let out a heavy breath. She shifted from one side to the other, then stretched out her neck to catch the aroma of whatever I held in my hand.

Finally, she took a tentative step forward, then another.

Her breath was warm on my skin as she investigated, then I was rewarded by the soft touch of her nose as she retrieved the apple.

I quietly snapped on the lead.

"There's a good girl," I told her, rubbing my hand on her neck and withers.

She arched her neck around and pushed against my shoulder.

"Yes, Star. You and I are going to get along just fine."

I smiled over at Rodrigo.

He was beaming.

The lead already on his horse, he strode to the barn.

I followed, clucking to Star all the way. Every few feet she nuzzled my shoulder as if to say, "I'm here, you ninny."

"Nice set-up," I said when we reached the saddling area. Everything was clean, well-organized and within reach. The thought of the disarray in my own barn made me shudder.

"They shouldn't need a whole lot of brushing," Rodrigo said. "My wrangler saw to them this morning."

"Got it," I said, as I walked around Star, rubbing my hand on her sides, rear, and legs. I was letting her know she was safe with me and where I was at all times. The movement of her ears indicated she was following my progress.

"Good girl," I said when I was done. I grabbed a curry and made sure the area where the saddle would sit was free of any debris that would irritate her, then followed up with a brush.

"You're a careful horsewoman," Rodrigo said. "I like that."

"I can't imagine being any other way, especially with an animal this beautiful. But they all deserve good treatment. I can't abide someone who mistreats animals."

"Me either."

I looked over, and we smiled at each other, a moment of connection between friends.

~ ~ ~

Not long after, we were saddled up and on our way. Rodrigo said he'd laid out a path that would take us to almost the full extent of the ranch, about a two-hour ride.

"Unless anything unexpected happens," he said. "Or I find a bad fence." He pointed to his saddlebag. "I always carry tools with me."

"Good planning," I said. "Don't know what it is about fences, but they need mending more than they should."

"Yes. I think there must be a chaneque who delights in watching humans fix things over and over again," he said.

"A chaneque?"

"Kind of like an imp."

I chuckled. "It's as good a reason as any."

"Yes," he said.

We rode in silence for a while. I concentrated on Star, determining how she liked to be guided. Her gait and motion under the saddle were as smooth as Rodrigo had indicated.

"When we get over that rise, we can let them go. Then you'll really see her in action. Arabians are like the wind," he said.

"Why Arabians?" I asked.

"My father was in World War II. He enlisted as soon as he could which was toward the end of the war, wanting to fight for his country. When the army found out he knew horses inside and out, they sent him to Oran, Algeria, to serve with the 28th Cavalry Regiment, the last cavalry regiment we ever had. While he was there, he got to see Arabians being ridden across the desert by tribes of nomads. He thought they were the most majestic animals he'd ever seen. He never stopped talking about them."

"That must have been amazing. Terrible that he was in the war, but wonderful that he'd had that experience."

"Our family has always served," he said. "It's a tradition to enlist right out of high school. I did my tour in the aftermath of Vietnam." His moustache drooped along with his expression. "It was a bad time to be in the army. The disarray after the evacuation of Saigon reverberated for years."

"Has your son served as well?"

Rodrigo nodded. "He won't talk about it much. He went to the Middle East."

"We have that in common," I said. "My son, Patrick, served there as well. He thought he was going to be career army, but the life became too much for his wife, especially when their second child came along."

"Our children had a hard war."

"Yes."

We rode the rest of the way to the ridge in silence. Once there, he looked over at me. "Ready?"

"As I'll ever be."

"Good. I'll race you to the oak tree there. I'll even give you a head start."

"I don't need a head start," I taunted him. "I'll win anyway."

"We'll see about that," he said. "Ha!" He leaned forward and waved the end of the reins by the horse's head.

At almost the same instant, I squeezed with my knees and yelled,

"Go, girl! We're not letting any man beat us!"

Rodrigo had a slight lead, but my girl had heart. With me crouched low on her back, we slowly drew even, then edged ahead.

As soon as we reached the oak, I circled her around it, my arm in the air.

I almost didn't see the branch coming, but I ducked just in time. Unfortunately, the sharp movement unbalanced me, loosening my foot from one of the stirrups.

Down I went, kicking my boot free of the second stirrup as I went down.

"Oof!" The wind was knocked out of me as I landed on the hard ground. As I stared up at the blue sky, I wondered why the O'Sullivan sisters always took a literal tumble when they were around men.

As long as all I did was hit the ground, I'd be safe.

A fall of any other kind could upend my life.

"You okay?" Rodrigo asked, leaping off his horse and rushing over to me.

"I will be," I said, mentally checking for any injuries besides my pride. "I'm tougher than I look." I grinned up at him.

Star moseyed over and nudged my ribs with her nose, blowing air in and out and checking me over with her whiskers, her brown eyes concerned.

I was going to seriously fall in love with this horse.

"You sure you're okay?" Rodrigo asked.

The man was another story.

"I'm pretty sure." I struggled to sit up, and he put his hand on my back to help.

"Nice and easy," he said. "At our age, a bump can do a lot of damage."

Even though I was trying to tough it out, I could feel some aches making themselves known. Plus the ground wasn't as warm as the sun-tempered air around us.

Rodrigo helped me to my feet.

I couldn't stifle the groan.

"Should we head back?" he asked.

"No!" I cried. "Absolutely not!"

"I was hoping you'd say that. But do you want to rest?"

I dredged up my most scornful expression. "Do you think I'm old or something?" I asked.

He stared at me, his expression unsure.

"Or something?" he asked.

"You better believe it," I said, letting a grin burst forth. This was a test. Would he get my sense of humor? It was a key quality I needed in my friends.

Very few people got my ironic point of view.

But Rodrigo grinned.

"Yep," he said. "You are something. I'm going to have to get to know you better to find out just what that something is."

"Well, you're going to need to speed it up, because we aren't here very long."

"I'll do my damnedest."

His smile was genuine, the kind that went all the way to his eyes which crinkled under his thick eyebrows. It was a good face, worn with time, but the lines etched were ones of joy and integrity. I instinctively knew he was someone I could trust.

I led Star over to a branch of the tree that lay on the ground. After testing it to see if it could bear weight, I stood on it and clambered back on the horse.

Star looked around as I adjusted myself and made sure my feet were firmly in the stirrups.

"Good girl," I murmured and patted her neck.

Thank goodness the RV park came with a hot tub. I was going to need it tonight.

Rodrigo came up beside me, and we headed down the fence line.

"How long has the ranch been in your family?" I asked him as we rode.

"Many generations," he said. "Of course it has changed a lot since the mid-1750s when the first Spanish ranches began. The size of our holdings grew and shrank then grew again, depending on who we had to share the land with. The Comanches were tough warriors who didn't like the idea that we were settling here."

"Probably can't blame them."

"No, but it is often the way of humans. We're a migratory animal. Tribes pushed each other out of places all the time. Where did they even come from? There are so many theories, even beyond their own origin tales."

I knew what he was saying was true, even if it didn't make me entirely comfortable.

"We're going through another great migration period for the same reasons people have always moved. Africa is being devastated by climate change. People can no longer grow enough food for themselves. And harsh regimes as well as the opposite—lawlessness—

force people to leave to seek a better life." He shrugged. "Or sometimes we move because the grass looks greener on the other side." He looked over at me. "We humans can be a dissatisfied lot." Then he frowned. "I hope I didn't upset you. You seem like a woman I can be truthful with, and not pick my words."

I considered that. I wanted the freedom to talk without censorship. It was a pleasure I rarely allowed myself these days, the exchange of thoughts with others, even those who didn't agree with me. Too often, though, I held back, unsure if my comments would start a conversation or a diatribe.

I nodded. "I think I'm okay with that."

"Bueno. It will be a refreshing change."

"Of course," I said. "You may not always like what I have to say."

"I'm strong enough to deal with it." He chuckled. "In fact, I'm very interested in your thoughts. It's been a long time since I met a woman—or anyone—who wasn't afraid of her own opinions."

I had to look away. On the surface, it seemed like nothing. But underneath it felt like a strikingly intimate conversation.

Fortunately, I noted a distraction.

"You've got some loose wires over there." I pointed to a portion of the barbed wire that was sagging.

"Good spotting," he said as he dismounted. I did the same, pulling my new work gloves from my jacket.

"You brought gloves?" he asked.

"Never go anywhere without them."

He nodded. "True rancher."

I helped him tighten up the wire. He looked at the fencepost, deciding it was solid, and it was simply the wires that had sagged.

Shortly after we left the spot, we rode up on a knoll. The view from the top was breathtaking: rolling hills that went on for miles. Live oaks stood sentinel on some, but some were as bare as a baby's bottom.

"You should be here the end of March, beginning of April," he said. "Bluebonnets as far as you can see. I always take a day and come up here for an afternoon, just taking in God's miracle."

"Sounds lovely," I said. I wanted to ask him if he came up here on his own or with a woman, but I didn't. "In Montana, we have moments like that, but it comes later. It depends on when the snow decides to leave. You can go up to some of the higher elevations at just the right moment, and the meadows are carpeted with wildflowers, yellows and indigo blues. There are patches of tall bear grass on the lower elevations in May that climb higher in altitude as the spring moves into summer."

He nodded, but didn't say anything, as we both sat comfortably with our memories for a while.

"I like being with you, Kathleen O'Sullivan," he said suddenly.

Surprise kept my mouth shut.

He shuffled a little, then patted me on the arm. "You don't have to say anything. I just felt like I needed to say it. Shall we go on?"

I nodded.

We went down a narrow trail with Rodrigo leading. I was just as glad.

It had been a simple statement. Nothing to it, right? It wasn't even that he likes *me*.

He probably likes being around his dog too.

But my senses, as dulled as they were after a forty-year marriage, knew that wasn't the case. Without even trying, I'd stepped over a line I hadn't intended to cross.

Trixie Lynn wasn't going to be happy.

"What do you think, Star? Am I making Montana mountains out of Texas hills?"

Star snorted and shook her head.

"You're not reassuring me, horse," I said.

Star stayed silent.

There was another problem.

In spite of the little time we'd spent together, I enjoyed his company more than any man in my life, including Michael.

Especially Michael.

Definitely Michael at the end of our marriage.

I'd been outraged when I found out what he'd been doing. Some instinct had kept me from ever giving him access to my trust fund, keeping that safe for the kids' education and our eventual old age. But for him to play sleight-of-hand with the ranch funds had been unforgiveable.

I would have rather he'd spent the last decade with a woman on the side.

Star sensed my unease, and her skin quivered under the saddle.

"It's okay, girl. I'm just mad at things that are in the past. Dumb, huh?"

I got another nicker. Star and I were definitely on the same wavelength.

The path broadened out. With a gentle press of my knees, I brought Star up next to Rodrigo's horse.

"Tell me about your ranch," Rodrigo said. "I'm curious about how our outfits differ."

My laugh came out more like a snort.

"We ranch on a much smaller scale. We can only graze one cow and calf unit per acre. It's just not as lush as it is here," I said.

"We can get about twice that," he admitted.

"And our house and outbuildings?" I shook my head. "I can't remember the last time they had a good makeover. We can only afford to do the bare minimum."

"Then why do you continue?"

I took a moment to figure out how to answer that.

"What do you know about the British and the Irish conflict?" I asked.

"Not much."

"Fair enough," I said. "I couldn't tell you word one about Spanish or Mexican history. We were brought up with Irish stories, wild St. Patrick's Days in Butte, and green beer. The Irish were always wonderful good Catholics, and the British nasty land-grabbing Protestants."

Rodrigo laughed. "History created by public relations giants on both sides of the question, no doubt. It's been the same with the US and Mexico."

"I realized that at the Alamo. But true or false, Ireland was the mother country, and land was our birthright that had been stolen." I shrugged. "By the time we got to Montana, other Europeans had made a good start on taking the land from the Native Americans, and whenever they were ready to sell it to us, we were ready to take it, no matter how hardscrabble it was. It wasn't any worse than potato land on the Emerald Isle, and it belonged to us."

"So you can't leave," Rodrigo said.

"Not can't. Won't. I won't give up my family's land. Not for anyone." I surprised myself by how vehement I was.

He nodded. "I understand. I feel the same way."

Another strand of connection threaded between us.

For the rest of the way back to the ranch, our topics became less serious. He pointed out some of the improvements he was making and the remains of the original homestead, but we also talked about music, favorite holidays, and pets we'd loved.

I told him how much I was enjoying Star, and how envious I was that he had her.

And I made sure I stayed on for the rest of the ride.

~ ~ ~

After we'd taken care of the horses, he invited me for lunch. I tried to protest, but I didn't put a lot of effort into it, especially after he told me Antonia, his housekeeper/cook, had made chicken enchiladas and mixed a salad.

I couldn't refuse to eat after another woman had spent her time cooking. Although Liz's cooking lessons had never taken, I still understood how much work it took.

"Thank you so much … gracias," I told Antonia as I took my place at the table.

"It's not a problem. I love to cook for señor's guests …" She gave Rodrigo a look. "Most of them."

He shook his head and spoke rapid Spanish.

She waved him off and returned moments later with two plates mounded with enchiladas. The salad was already on the table, along with a pitcher of ice cold water.

"Unless you'd like something stronger," he said.

"No. Water's perfect."

He nodded and they dug in.

"This is amazing," I said after a few bites. It was a perfect meld of sweet, savory, and spicy.

"It's one of her best dishes," he said. "I'm glad you like it. Be sure to tell her. She takes great pride in her cooking."

"I certainly will."

"Will you come golfing with me?"

"Golfing?" My fork clattered to the table. "You golf?"

"Si. It is a great sport."

"I don't golf." I'd never had any desire to do so.

"Even better," he said. "That will give me an excuse to teach you."

I thrust my fork into a piece of enchilada. How was I going to get out of this in a way that didn't offend him?

Chapter Ten

Should I go to a different mass? Skip it and confess next week? It wouldn't be the first time I'd skipped mass and confessed. I lay in bed and debated.

Sunday mornings were usually done by rote. I'd been doing the same thing every Sunday for the last sixty-some-odd years. Get up, shower, dress, and grab some coffee and enough sustenance to last me through the mass without my stomach grumbling.

Follow the mass, sometimes with more attention than others. The beauty of rituals done all one's life is the ability to do them without thinking. That leaves the brain free for other important things, like how to fix the tractor without money for new parts.

But the last thing I wanted this morning was time to think. It was all I had been doing since I left Rodrigo's yesterday. We'd spent the time during lunch getting to know each other better. It had been easy. He'd even laughed at my attempted jokes.

He'd talked easily about his late wife, leaving me with the sense that they'd had a good marriage. I was amazed to find a twinge of jealousy for their happiness.

Several times during the lunch, I'd wondered what I was doing. Getting to know and enjoy spending time with a man I was never going to see again made no sense. Especially since I wasn't interested in a man—any man—at all.

I pushed the covers away and got up. May as well face the music. If I didn't go, I was sure Trixie Lynn would have something to say. I was quite sure she was the guest Antonia had referenced. The woman made delivering barbs with a smile into an art form.

All my dawdling made me late for church. The parking lot was fairly full since this was the most popular service. I walked as quickly as possible, took the program the usher passed me, and found a seat toward the back.

The first thing I did was scan the congregation for Rodrigo. I tried to do it as subtly as possible, but needed to crank my head about to see every corner.

What was it with Texas women and big hair? I'd thought we were all done with that after the '80s.

I'd just spotted him when the woman seated next to me gave me the stink eye.

It took all the restraint I had not to stick my tongue out at her.

Content to know he was there, I was a dignified old lady throughout the rest of the service, concentrating on the rituals and trying not to think about why I was content.

After the service, the church emptied in its usual process. Ready for more coffee and torn between wanting to see Rodrigo and hoping to avoid him, I hustled over to the meeting room where the socializing occurred.

As soon as I entered, I spotted him. He smiled and walked toward me, two steaming cups of coffee in his hands.

"I didn't think you were going to make it this morning," he said and held out one of the cups to me. "It's the way you like it. Milk only."

"Thank you," I said.

We stood next to each other in silence for a few moments, drinking our coffee and scanning the crowd. He smiled at people he knew, while I nodded at acquaintances.

It was like being in my own church at home, a familiarity and comfort of community.

Trixie Lynn spotted us and started making her way over.

I stifled my sigh.

"Would Tuesday be a good day for golf?" Rodrigo asked.

"You're serious about this, aren't you?"

"Deadly. But I'm going to start you with miniature golf."

I had a vague idea of windmills and small children running amok with metal sticks.

"I have to check the car schedule, but I think I could do that."

"I can pick you up," he said. "That way you won't get lost."

"I've been driving all over this country," I said. "I haven't gotten lost yet." Maybe misplaced a few times, but I wasn't going to let him know that."

"I'm sure you are capable," he said. "I'd like to pick you up, though."

I hesitated. Picking me up sounded too much like a date. And we were not dating.

"I'll get back to you on that."

"Hello, Rodrigo," Trixie Lynn said with a gush of over-friendliness. "I feel like I haven't seen you all week. I've missed you." She gave me a dismissive glance. "I see you're still here, um ..."

I stayed silent, daring her to refuse to remember my name.

"Ah, yes. Kathleen. You and your sisters look so much alike, it's hard to keep you straight."

We looked nothing alike, but I wasn't going to bite. We'd be gone in a little over a month, and she could have the rancher all to herself. "How was your week?" Rodrigo asked. His smile was gentle.

He suffered fools and angry women far better than I did.

Then I remembered him telling me he had three sisters.

Good training.

"My week has been so busy," Trixie Lynn said. "I'm in charge of the white elephant sale. It's coming up in a few weeks. There have been *so* many donations this year. It's almost as bad as the pandemic years when people had nothing to do at home but clean out their stuff."

"I remember that time," I said, trying to emulate Rodrigo's kindness. "It was difficult to get anywhere near Goodwill to drop off things."

"I'm desperate for help," Trixie Lynn said, ignoring me as she put her hand on Rodrigo's arm. "Do you think you could spare some time … or perhaps Antonia could help?"

His face got as pale as naturally dark skin could get.

I couldn't help my smile.

"Uh …" he stammered. "Not really … I'm busy, and I'm sure Antonia is too. She's got some big cleaning project … spring you know."

"It's only January," Trixie Lynn pointed out.

"She's getting started early," he said.

"I could help," I said, then smacked my lips together.

They turned to me, astonished looks on their faces.

"I mean … well … if it's in a few weeks. I'll be here for a while yet."

"I need people to clean things and get them ready for sale," Trixie Lynn said. "It's dirty work."

"I'm a rancher," I said, squaring my shoulders. "It's all dirty work."

She looked torn between wanting to tell me to get lost and hug me for solving her problem.

"Thank you," she said, opting for politeness. "Let me have your phone number, and I'll text you the details."

"Don't forget to write it on the schedule," Rodrigo reminded me.

"What?" Trixie Lynn asked.

"They share a car and keep a calendar to show who needs it when. Clever, isn't it?"

"I suppose. Be easier if everyone had a car."

"Difficult enough to tow one car behind a forty-three foot rig. Three would be impossible."

"Do you have a driver? That must be like steering a semi."

"You're looking at her," I told Trixie Lynn.

"You drive it?"

"Yes, ma'am."

"Oh." Trixie smoothed her blond hair, then did the same to her skirt before looking at Rodrigo. "I can't even imagine steering such a big vehicle," she said. "I've always thought that would be a man's job."

Oh, puh-leeze.

"Kathleen is a very capable woman," he said. "I admire her for that." He smiled at me, igniting Trixie Lynn's ire.

"She needs to be, I suppose," she said. "I'm glad I've had a man around most of my life to handle the heavy lifting. That's why it's so hard now, since my husband died." She actually batted her eyelashes at him.

"I'm sure you'll find someone," Rodrigo said.

"There aren't many eligible men my age." She stepped a few inches closer.

"You could always learn to do things yourself," I said. "Most of it's not hard."

"Well …" She turned her hard eyes and fake smile my way. "Some of us don't have the upper body strength that others do. We use our body for other, more feminine, things." She arranged herself in a way that was clearly suggestive of what her own body was capable of doing.

Good thing my father finally convinced me that physical fighting wasn't the way to solve problems.

"They're not mutually exclusive," I said. I didn't try to move. If I had tried to put my legs in those positions, I'm sure I would have broken something.

Rodrigo cleared his throat and ran his finger under his collar.

I pulled out my phone. "Give me your number, and I'll text you to find out when you need my help," I said. "I'm sure I could help out with the heavy and dirty things you've got." I smirked at her.

She gave me her phone number anyway.

Someone came over and told Trixie Lynn the Father wanted to speak to her about something.

"It was nice talking to you. And, Rodrigo, we must catch up again soon. I have to go to find out what the father needs." Her voice brimmed with self-importance, and her heels clicked on the wooden floor as she left us.

"Whew," Rodrigo said.

I laughed. "Not used to cat fights in church?"

His eyes widened as he looked at me, then he laughed as well.

"Nope," he said. "Nor am I used to someone being so honest about it. My sisters used to get into it. Sometimes it descended into hair-pulling. Now that was vicious."

"I was a bit of a hell-raiser in grade school," I admitted. "Dad told me he was tired of coming to get me at school, and I needed to stop or he'd have to take a belt to me."

"Solving violence with violence," Rodrigo noted.

"Yeah. It was a different time."

"I get it. In fact, my rear got a smack more than once. So what did you do instead when someone did something you didn't like?"

"When the mean girls came calling?" I asked. "Because they aren't a myth. They are everywhere." I shrugged. "My dad told me to use my words. I got really, really good at that."

"So I see."

"Yeah. Sorry about that."

"Don't be. She was baiting you. I think you handled it just fine." He reached his hand toward me, but didn't make contact.

Something fluttered around my insides.

"Thanks," I managed to get out.

Our moment didn't last very long.

"Welcome to the congregation," a slim woman with a short haircut, who had 'former nun' written all over her, said as she reached us.

"Thank you," I said and then explained that I was only here for a short time.

She told me if I needed anything at all to feel free to contact her and gave me her number.

A number of other women followed her to introduce themselves or greet me. Some were friendlier than others. They were a mix of Latina and white, widows and divorcées, older and younger.

Trixie Lynn had a lot of competition for Rodrigo's attention.

Through it all, he remained an absolute gentleman, pleasant and courteous.

I was glad to be by his side, but couldn't wait to get out of there.

As soon as I could, I made my escape.

Chapter Eleven

A little after one on Tuesday afternoon, I stood staring at my wardrobe choices in the small closet I shared with Liz.

Was this a date?

Horseback riding had been perilously close to a date, but I'd gone only to experience riding an Arabian. He was an acquaintance before the ride, and we'd become friendlier. That was all.

I'd driven there and back all by my lonesome.

But he was coming to pick me up and take me golfing. Okay, it was miniature golf, but it still meant clubs, little balls, and hand-eye coordination that I seriously lacked.

It was a date.

What should I wear on a date? I hadn't been on one in forty years. Even "date night" with my husband consisted more of eating popcorn while we streamed a movie. I'd dress up in my most comfortable pajamas, while he'd wear sweats and a T-shirt.

Sometimes we'd even make love afterwards.

But that wasn't happening here. No way, no how. I had no interest in getting naked with a man, even my doctor. I'd keep my clothes on.

The thought forced me back to my dilemma. What clothes was I going to put on?

"Can I help?" Liz asked, poking her head in the door.

I looked at her hopelessly.

"Have you done a lot of miniature golfing?" I asked.

"Some. My grandkids love it."

"What do I wear?"

"I don't think it's the golfing that's the problem," she said. "It's the man."

"Can I call him and tell him I don't want to go?" I asked.

"A half hour before he's supposed to pick you up?" She shook her head. "I don't think so."

"A half hour! That's all I've got?"

"Diane's prepared to stall him outside. Said something about showing him how to dump."

"She wouldn't!" I protested.

"Well, then we better figure this out."

I stepped aside from the closet. "Have at it."

Liz did a quick inventory of my hanging clothes, then looked through the drawers where I stashed my T-shirts. She pulled one out, a pretty peach one that I'd bought in Georgia on our way through there. It was decorated with a discrete depiction of the fruit on one shoulder.

"Wear this with your powder-blue capris," she said. "Get dressed, then we'll do something with your hair and makeup."

"I don't want to do anything with my hair and makeup," I protested. "We're just going to play golf."

"Get dressed."

As she searched through my few bottles of makeup, I pulled on the pants and shirt.

"Your sandals will have to do," Liz said. "Cute tennis shoes would be better, but we have to work with what we've got. Now sit down."

I sat on the edge of the bed and let her fuss with my hair.

"You need a haircut," she said.

"I need a new life," I muttered. "One where I wasn't dumb enough to accept an invitation from a man."

"Oh, hush. You'll do fine." She spread a little blush on my cheeks, darkened my eyebrows, and handed me my lipstick. "Although some new cosmetics wouldn't hurt. These look like you bought them in the last century."

"Only about ten years ago," I admitted. "The cows don't care about makeup."

"He's here!" Diane shouted from the front.

"Oh, God," I said, sending up a quick prayer to Mother Mary that I wouldn't make an utter fool of myself.

As I walked to the front of the RV, familiar feelings came over me. It was the same "lamb to slaughter" emotion I'd felt when Michael had come to pick me up for a date. My parents and sisters were eager voyeurs as I'd awkwardly answer the door to let him in. That event was always followed by equally difficult small talk with my parents.

My sisters weren't having any problems now, though. They were both outside, talking with Rodrigo and admiring his car.

At least he hadn't picked me up in a ranch truck, like Michael had done on prom night. I'd almost landed on my ass trying to climb up into the cab with my long dress twisting around my legs.

As soon as I walked down the steps, Rodrigo stopped talking and looked at me, a slow smile spreading across his face. My gaze riveted on his, and that same fluttering I'd felt before occurred again.

"Are you ready?" he asked.

"As I'll ever be," I said, walking up to him.

Then that same stupid awkward moment occurred.

My sisters were staring.

Waiting.

How were we supposed to greet each other?

"Good." He looked at my sisters. "Nice seeing you again." Then he took my arm to walk me to the passenger door which he opened.

I got in as gracefully as I could.

He walked to the other side, took his seat, and soon we were off.

"Your sisters are very protective," he said as soon as we left the RV park.

"I'd hoped they would have grown out of it by now," I said.

"Hung around when dates picked you up?" he asked.

"There was only one date, but yes. The two of them and my parents."

"I understand. The parents of any girl I dated in high school were like ogres. One dad had a pair of old-fashioned silver pistols hung on the wall. He kept looking at them every time I picked up his daughter."

I chuckled. "Dating can be dangerous."

"That's for sure." He glanced over at me. "Even at our age."

"Is that what we're doing? I thought we were just friends," I said, trying to keep it light.

"We can be whatever you wish," he said.

I wasn't sure what to say to that. Would he be insulted if I didn't want to date? Which, to be fair to myself, I didn't.

"How about we concentrate on having a good time today and not worry about labels," he said.

"Sounds good to me."

"Do you mind if I turn on some music?" he asked. "I find it very relaxing when I drive."

"That's fine." It also meant I didn't have to come up with topics for conversation.

He pressed a button and a pleasant Latin singer crooned over the sound system.

"Nice," I said.

He nodded.

We settled into a comfortable silence as he drove toward San Antonio.

~ ~ ~

The miniature golf place was attractive, with lots of manmade streams and waterfalls that Rodrigo informed me were water hazards.

I nodded as if I'd understood his explanation.

He rented our clubs—putters—and a couple of balls. The scorecard he handed me made no sense, but I wasn't here to win. There wasn't a chance of that.

As we walked away from the desk, I heard something that stopped me in my tracks.

"They'll let *anyone* in here."

I turned.

The man was older, dressed in a pressed short sleeve plaid shirt, his khaki pants pulled up high on his large belly. His scowl was focused on the two of us.

Next to him, a woman half his age fidgeted with the pearls around her neck and looked in the opposite direction.

"They certainly do!" I announced loudly.

Rodrigo turned briefly, then continued down the stairs to the start of the fake golf greens.

I gave a good stink-eye to the jerk, then followed.

"You didn't have to do that," Rodrigo said.

"I most certainly did," I said. "People get away with way too much."

"It's easier to let it ride," he said. "It's better than it used to be. And most people around here treat everyone the same. It's more the tourists that seem to think the area belongs to them." Rodrigo barked out a laugh. "They never consider the things they come to see—the missions, the festivals, the food—are all contributions from the people they consider to be lesser beings. It's ridiculous."

He looked at me for a few moments, and I could almost see the wheels turning in his head.

"Thank you," he said. "You're a good person. And you're right. We need to continue to point out bad behavior. It's become too common."

The man who'd been so rude brushed past us to take over the first green space. His girlfriend—or wife, poor thing—scurried behind him.

Rodrigo and I laughed.

"While we're waiting, I'll explain the game to you," he said.

I listened and asked questions while he showed me how to putt and what the scoring meant. It was pretty simple.

Once the man left, we started our game.

Things went fairly smoothly until the fifth hole. The green was nestled between two rushing streams of water with a vigorous fountain at the top of one of them. The noise, as well as the stress I was beginning to feel from taking so many shots to get the ball in the hole, made me nervous. My hands were slippery.

I swung a little too hard.

The club escaped my grasp, flew up in the air, and landed on a rock in the water feature to our left. It ricocheted off the rock, went up, and landed right before the hole in the lower green … right after the jerk hit his ball toward it.

"Damn it! That ruined my shot! I would have made it!" he shouted. "Mark that down as one stroke. Got that?"

"Y…yes," the woman said.

"I think we should get out of here," Rodrigo whispered. He scooped up the balls, grabbed my hand, and pulled me behind the mountain supporting the fountain.

"Who threw that?" the man bellowed.

I slapped my hand over my mouth to keep from laughing.

"I'll sue you! I could have been seriously injured!"

My chest hurt from holding in my hysteria.

Rodrigo tugged on my hand.

We walked past the next two holes, and Rodrigo was lining up his shot when the man stormed through.

"Did you see anyone throw a club?" he demanded.

"No, not at all," Rodrigo said as he glanced between the bottom of his club and the ball on the green. Then with a smooth move of his body, he sent the ball rolling down its perfect path to its destination where it landed with a soft clunk.

"You have crazy people in Texas," the man said, glaring at me.

"I'm from Montana," I said with the sweetest smile I could muster. It wouldn't do for him to wonder why we only had one club between us.

"Just as bad." He glared at us one more time then stomped back to where he'd come from.

I couldn't hold it in any longer. I bent over double and started to laugh.

It only took a few moments for Rodrigo to join in. We must have laughed a full five minutes before we calmed down.

"Want to take your shot?" he asked.

"I … I … lost my club …" Hysteria threated to return.

He held out his, then placed my ball on the green.

What the hell. I was so bad at this game, a few chuckles weren't going to make any difference.

I walked over to the ball and placed the club next to it. I swung it gently back like I saw him do and prepared for the ball to develop a mind of its own and go where it pleased.

"Stop," he said.

I did.

He came up behind me.

"Can I help you? Put my hands over yours?"

He was already too close.

"Um … okay."

He reached around and placed his hands on mine. "Loosen up a little. You don't have to keep a death grip on it. It's not going …" He must have thought about what had just happened. "Never mind. Just don't hold it so tight."

I tried to loosen up, but it was difficult when I could feel his breath on the back of my neck.

"Now look at where you want the ball to go. Is the flat of the club perpendicular to it?"

I did what he asked and made a little adjustment.

"Almost." His hands guided the club a little more. "Good. Now swing back a little. Like you were."

His hands guided me through the whole stroke.

To my amazement, the little white orb followed his into the cup.

"I did it!" I threw my arms in the air, the club still in one hand.

"Easy there, Kathleen. We've only got one club left."

"Oops." I pulled my arm down and thrust the putter at him.

He had a big grin on his face. "Now isn't this fun?"

"It definitely is," I said, meaning it. Who knew that putting that stinking ball into a hole in the ground would prove so satisfactory?

"Onward?" he asked, holding out his hand.

"Absolutely." I tucked my hand in his.

Nothing had felt so natural.

Chapter Twelve

"You do show us the most interesting art," Diane told Liz as we stood in front of a painting of a large woman in the San Antonio Museum of Art.

"At least this one I can understand," I said. "Not like that stupid cow we saw in New York. I just wish she didn't need to be quite so naked."

The description attached to the wall next to the painting, told us Yemayá was a central painting of Ángel Rodríguez-Díaz's Goddess Triptych.

"Doesn't look much like an angel," I said.

"I think that's the point," Liz said. "We've worshiped the perfect for so long, that we've forgotten that the first humans honored what really mattered, the nurturing earth."

"The original earth mother," I said.

"Uh-huh," Diane muttered.

She and I could relate in a way that Liz would never understand. We'd both inherited the more stocky build of our dad's family, while Liz was blessed with the leaner frame of our mother. As time had taken its toll, we'd all seen our bodies sag, our skin become rife with blemishes, and the spots that ached multiply.

As I studied the painting, I began to enjoy the depiction of an angel closer to my body shape than the willowy angels of many churches I'd been in.

"We need to keep moving," Liz said. "There is so much to see."

"Let's take our time," Diane said. "We can always come back."

"That's right. We're here for a longer time than usual."

"It's going to go faster than you think," Liz said. "Especially now that Rodrigo is occupying your time."

"Hush your mouth," I said and moved on to the next painting.

Ever since my outing with Rodrigo, which had ended with ice cream sundaes at his favorite place, my sisters had been needling me. I ignored them, telling him—and myself—that it was just for fun while we were in the area. When we left, I would wave a happy goodbye.

However, I was beginning to suspect that wasn't going to be the case. Something about this man was very attractive. It had nothing to do with his looks or his money.

It had to do with how he treated me.

Ugh. I don't think the old-world courtesy his parents had instilled in him and how much was because he liked being with me, I hadn't figured out yet. But even the few times we'd been together made me want to be a better person, a better woman for him.

And maybe for myself.

Liz let up as we explored the paintings and sculptures of the special exhibit, which included some of the figurines from the museum's Mediterranean collection. These squat rounded female figures echoed the heavy flesh of the painting.

What would it have been like to grow up in a society that felt female bodies didn't have to be Twiggy-thin to be beautiful?

We moved on to other art collections. Liz had opened my eyes to art. I'd begun to take more than a cursory look at paintings, studying them for technique and color. I'd especially enjoyed some of the fiber art museums and historical collections we'd been to see. Creating clothing from the natural world had been going on for millennia.

"Uncle," Diane finally said. "My eyes are blurred over."

"We're going to have to come back," Liz said. "I can't believe how much there is to see here."

"What I want to see right now," I said, "is lunch."

"Sounds like a plan," Diane agreed.

We left the museum and strolled down to the Riverwalk where we chose a place that promised hearty salads, soups, and sandwiches. We managed to snag a table not too far from the river where we could watch the water flow, along with the pedestrians.

The warm Friday afternoon, one of the last days of January, had drawn a fair number of people to the city center. I was beginning to understand why. The city was a pleasant blend of cultures with a heavy Spanish influence that could soften the harsh edges of any American city. The pace seemed slower here, and the colors more vibrant. I was enjoying my time here more than I had anywhere else.

Was that because of the man? Or the city?

I pushed the thought away to concentrate on what my sisters were saying.

"I think we should do a little shopping," Diane said. "We haven't gone shopping in such a long time."

"Yes," Liz said. "I could definitely use some new things. Maybe something to put on so Walter could take it off."

"Now that's a really good idea," Diane said.

"You girls are over-sexed," I commented.

They laughed.

"You'll see," Diane said.

"Ugh. I don't think of Rodrigo that way at all." I wasn't sure I was capable of thinking of him like that. The last few years with Michael had deadened any sexual interests I might once have had. And we'd never really gone at it like rabbits.

Diane and Liz grinned at each other.

I ignored them.

We moved on to other things, discussing the art we'd liked and didn't, comparing the museum to others we'd seen, and talking about the regular stuff of life, like what to have for dinner this week. Once again, I was grateful for Liz's culinary skills. Once this was all over, I was going to have to figure out how to make something other than meat and potatoes. While I'd enjoy cereal for dinner now and again, I didn't think a steady diet of it would be healthy, or any more economical than beans and rice.

Maybe I'd fashion a greenhouse next to the southern wall of Liz's cabin. I could see myself harvesting lettuce, tomatoes, and other vegetables in the spring, summer, and fall.

We finished up our meal, then dutifully followed Liz to a nearby mall. I surprised myself by being caught up in the idea of shopping for clothes.

I'd always gone protesting and screaming when it came time for school shopping, even though it was the only time I got some new clothes. Play and work clothes had all been hand-me-downs. Even when I was grown, I'd wear something until it was threadbare before deigning to step foot in a clothing store. And even then it was usually someplace like Target for a new T-shirt. A big shopping spree took me to Murdochs for a pair of sturdy jeans.

Now I found myself staring at an abundance of blouses and shirts. It would be nice not to wear the same thing every time I saw Rodrigo. He'd asked me to go riding again, so there was one more time we'd spend together before he tired of me.

Whoa! my brain yelled. *Why should he get tired of me?*

That was the problem with marrying the boy I'd fallen in love with in high school. I didn't have any other experience to compare it to.

Michael had gotten bored, but so far, Rodrigo seemed eager to spend time with me. Since I was leaving soon, it made sense. I wasn't going to be around long enough for him to lose interest.

But was that even true? I wish I knew.

Not for the first time, I wished life came with a roadmap so I could see the future depending on the choices I made.

Now I had to make a choice about a blouse. Or maybe two. T-shirts were more practical. Maybe one of each.

Before I knew it, I had a bundle of clothes in my arms, including another pair of capris.

Once I started removing my clothes in front of the mirrors, I remembered what I hated the most about clothes shopping. All that trying on.

Staring at a body that would never be considered for any magazine cover.

Then I remembered the painting in the museum. The hell with it. I was going to look as good as I possibly could, instead of regretting I didn't look like someone else.

While I rejected most of the clothes, I came out with a couple of blouses, some fancy tees, and the capris.

Liz and Diane, far more relaxed shoppers than I would ever be, were still trying things on.

A pretty forest green dress caught my eye. It was a simple sheath, but actually had some styling to it, rather than being the straight sack designers were continually trying to push on women. The hem was full of angles, rather than being flat across the bottom.

I studied it, then found it in my size.

When I tried it on, it was as if I'd become a new person.

A new person who badly needed a hair stylist.

The dress, and the little bit of makeup I'd put on that morning, made me look and feel younger.

The hair, which I'd been wearing the same way for decades, made me look like any other older woman—nondescript and forgettable.

I didn't want to be forgettable anymore.

At some point, without my sisters, I'd see a hair stylist.

And maybe visit a makeup counter.

~ ~ ~

Exhausted, we returned to the RV by mid-afternoon, fell into our respective beds and took naps. A half hour later we roused ourselves and began to review our purchases, exclaiming over each.

We'd all bought several items of new clothes, tested new fragrances at the cosmetic counters, and explored several of the little shops. I even tried on a pair of pumps to go with my dress, but put them back as soon as I realized I'd read the price tag wrong.

After we put our clothes away, I mixed up a pitcher of G&Ts, and we prepared ourselves for cocktail hour. I was the last one outside where I found my sisters, heads together, whispering about something.

I had the strongest feeling it was about me.

"What's up?" I asked, trying to keep it light.

They looked at each other, and then Diane spoke. "We're worried about you."

"Me? For heaven's sake, why? I'm having the time of my life." I poured drinks for them, then took a generous amount for myself before settling myself in my chair.

"You weren't happy for years before Michael died," Liz said gently. "And now … well … you're almost too happy with Rodrigo."

I laughed. "You are *never* satisfied," I said. "You two kept saying I was going to fall for someone. Well, I haven't fallen for Rodrigo, but we are having a damn good time. He's fun to be around. When we pack up and leave, I'll wave goodbye, and that will be that."

"What happened with Michael?" Liz asked.

I was tempted to tell her none of her beeswax, but the concern on her and Diane's faces stopped me.

If I told them, we'd be able to share the burden. I wouldn't have to carry that awful secret anymore.

But revealing the problem would bring me so much shame, I didn't think I'd be able to bear it.

I shook my head.

"I don't want to talk about it," I said. "Not now. Probably never. So how about you let me have my fun with Rodrigo while I can. I promise you, I'll be careful. I'm not going to fall for him, cross my heart and hope to die, stick a needle in my eye." I made a cross over my heart, and they both smiled at the childhood promise we used to make to each other.

"Okay?" I asked.

"Okay," they chorused.

We held up our glasses, clinked, and took a drink.

Chapter Thirteen

Star nuzzled me as I placed the saddle blanket on her back.

"I know, sweetie," I told her, slipping her another carrot from my pocket. "You deserve a soft, bright blanket with silver decorations and long streamers attached to the corners."

The horse nodded her head as if to agree with me.

"It's a good thing you don't own that horse," Rodrigo said. "You would spoil her to death."

"She deserves it. She's a princess, aren't you, girl?" I patted her again, then walked to where the saddle was stored and picked it up.

I almost didn't recognize myself. I hadn't cooed at anyone or anything since my kids were babies. Stranger still, I was comfortable doing it around Rodrigo. He kidded me, but he did it with gentleness.

As soon as we were saddled up, he led the way out of the barn. There was a large saddle bag on his horse where he'd stowed the picnic lunch Antonia had prepared.

A housekeeper and cook was someone I could sincerely get used to having around, in spite of my desire to live alone. Maybe someone who came in once a week?

The size of Liz's house barely made it worth it.

We rode through a different section of the property. Rodrigo had told me there was a gate with access to a nature preserve. It was a good time of year for birds and even some wildlife. We'd need to be on the lookout for black bears. In recent years, they'd migrated up from Mexico and were repopulating the southern part of the state after being hunted to extinction a few centuries ago.

The morning sun was warm on the back of my new blouse, but not hot. I'd worn my least rundown hat, knowing how my face burned in too much sun. As we rode, I was lulled to contentment by the soft thud of the horse's hooves on the packed soil, the jangle of the bit, and the chirps of birds warning of our travel through their territory.

Rodrigo sat in his saddle well, the mark of an experienced horseman. Watching him ride made me feel good. I didn't know how else to explain it. Being out here in nature, with a good horse beneath me and his companionship was as perfect as it got in my world.

Michael and I had never been easy like this. There was always an agenda, something to do. In high school, he'd soaked up everything he could from the ag kids headed to Bozeman or Dillan, knowing his parents would never send him to college. On the day before graduation, he proposed to me, but didn't get around to marrying me until my dad had agreed to take him on as an assistant ranch manager. In between, he'd worked at every ranch he could, except his parents'. That ranch was being taken over by his oldest brother, and he wanted nothing to do with it.

Until I started spending time with Rodrigo, I hadn't realized how tightly wound Michael had been all his life.

Rodrigo dismounted and opened the gate to the preserve so I could ride through, before closing the gate and getting back on his own horse.

"There's a clearing by a stream about a mile that way. I thought it would be a good place for lunch."

"Sounds lovely," I said, giving him a smile.

He nodded and once again led the way.

The trees were closer and the grass taller without grazing cattle to mow it down. Here and there I could see where deer had been browsing on branches. A little bit of a breeze flowed through this stretch, fluttering the leaves. A bright yellow butterfly danced around me for a while before taking off.

All my worries, which were small at this point, drifted away.

The landscape opened up, and we were able to ride side by side.

"What do you think of chickens?" he asked.

"They lay eggs, they make a lot of noise, and they're dirty," I replied.

He chuckled.

"That's exactly my opinion. When we were children, one of us had to gather eggs in the morning. We rotated duty. Sometimes I bribed my youngest sister to take my turn. I'd rather do anything than deal with those birds."

"What were the other chores?"

"Feeding the goats, helping Mamá make school lunches, putting food and water out for the cats and dogs, scattering corn for the chickens."

"Life on a ranch," I said. "Every day … So you didn't mind feeding the chickens?"

"No. It was cleaner. You never know what you'll find under a hen. And some of them get really vicious when you're poking around their nest."

"Yep. We had them too, for a while. Michael didn't like them, so when they died off, we didn't replace them."

"That's what I did too," Rodrigo said.

"So why are you thinking about them now?"

"Juan thinks we should diversify."

I nodded. Beef could be an iffy business.

"But he's not thinking about a small operation, no. Not my son. He wants an entire field set aside for the birds. He's talking about a moving hen house."

"A what?"

"The chicken coop is mobile, so it can be moved. Juan wants to reseed an entire field with organic and native grasses, then move the coop twice a week. He says it keeps the chickens from destroying the area around their hen house, and gives them a richer diet of bugs and what have you. Well-fed chickens produce better eggs, at least according to Juan."

"Interesting. And it's true. They do scratch the area around their coop down to nothing." I thought about the whole concept. It made total sense to me, but it was still going to involve someone going out and getting eggs.

"I sent Juan to the best school I could, and he's always reading and attending conferences. He's convinced this is the way to go."

"So what are you going to do?"

"I gave him a field and told him he can do with it what he wants. The only thing he has to remember is I'm not going to go out and collect the damn eggs!" Rodrigo's laugh echoed around us.

"Sounds like a plan," I said.

"You are so easy to talk with," he said. "No one else would understand."

"I'm sure you have plenty of ranching friends," I said, but nonetheless, I was pleased with his compliment.

A few minutes later we reached a lovely meadow by the edge of a rushing stream. Rodrigo unpacked our lunch, which included a large blanket for our feast. Like the enchiladas Antonia had prepared, the sandwiches looked luscious. Rodrigo explained they were tortas, cold Mexican lunch food. They contained ham, cheese, mortadella, salt cod, sardine in tomato sauce, refried beans, lettuce, tomato, avocado, pickled jalapeños, and chipotle peppers served on a roll with three lumps on the top, that he informed me was called a talera.

"She held back the spice on yours, cara," he said as he handed me one.

"I'll be sure to thank her." Going from the bland food of Ireland to the hot spice of Mexico was taking some adjustment. I bit in.

"Amazing," I said when I'd finished chewing. "Just the right amount of spice. So flavorful." I took another bite.

Rodrigo nodded and ate some of his own sandwich.

Conversation was light as we talked. I told him a bit about the museum, which he'd been to several times, although I edited out the part about the pudgy goddess.

After we were sated and the debris cleaned up, we lay on the blanket and looked up at the big expanse of sky. Butterflies and dragonflies skittered this way and that, while a large bumblebee examined the field around us for any flowering plants.

"What was your wife like?" I asked.

Rodrigo was quiet for a few moments.

"She was a nice woman." He sighed. "This is difficult. Normally, I leave it at that, but I want to be honest with you. It's important." He turned his head to look at me. "Like I said, I've never felt this easy with a woman, and I want to honor that."

Looking back up at the sky, he continued. "When I was younger, getting to the end of high school, I fell in love with an Anglo girl. She returned my feelings. I took her to the prom and to one of my sister's quinceaneras, in spite of my parents' disapproval. My parents were old-fashioned, very against mixed marriages. They were proud Mexicans with a long heritage in this country and didn't want their blood line 'polluted.'"

Another glance. "Latinos can be just as bigoted as anyone else."

"I know how that feels," I said. "All our boyfriends were examined to see if their level of Irishness and Catholicism were up to snuff."

Rodrigo chuckled.

Then he surprised me by grasping my hand before returning his gaze to the sky.

"The girl's parents weren't thrilled either. She went off to college; I stayed home to get a crash course in running our ranch. Eventually, the pressure became too much, and we broke it off.

"My parents threw lots of what they thought were appropriate girls at me for the next few years, but I was too angry to consider them. Finally, my father told me I'd better get on with it. I was kinder to the next woman, and the one after that attracted me enough that I thought we could make it work."

"That's sad," I said. At the same time, I realized my story wasn't that much different.

"It was the old way," he said. "We had a good marriage, and I always honored my vows. I've let my children choose their spouses without interference, even though neither my siblings nor my in-laws approved. They seem happy for the most part, although one of my children and her husband have split recently."

He rolled over to face me and released my hand.

"And here I am again with another Anglo woman." He ran a finger down my cheek.

"An *old* Anglo woman," I pointed out.

"Still beautiful," he said.

The moment was getting dangerous, but I wasn't sure which direction I wanted it to go in.

"I like you, Kathleen O'Sullivan," he said. "I like you a lot."

"And I like you too, but ..."

"Yes. It's impossible. For different reasons." He stared at me. "But I'm not going to let you go without kissing you. Is that all right with you?"

I didn't know what the right answer was for either one of us.

Did I want him to kiss me?

"Yes," I said.

His lips pressed against mine. Was it his lips that were unfamiliar or being kissed at all?

My body, not as dead as I'd thought it was, responded, and I moved my lips against his, exploring, tasting. Our lips parted, but that was as far as it went.

After a few short moments, he lifted his head and nodded. "Gracias." He cleared his throat and pushed himself to sitting.

It seemed like that was all there was going to be.

Was it the kiss or me he found unsatisfactory?

"I want more," he said. "But that would be irresponsible and not respectful of you. Thank you for giving me that memory."

"Yes," I said. "Thank you."

Once again, we stared at each other. I relished the feelings that flowed between us, emotions I hadn't felt for a long time.

But he was right. This was simply a brief moment in time. We weren't going to be together long enough for love to truly bloom.

Chapter Fourteen

For the past few days, the memory of Rodrigo's kiss floated up to the top of my thoughts at least once an hour. It had been sweet, but promised more.

My problem was that I had no idea what it promised.

When I was younger and Michael kissed me, I knew what I wanted, and I was pretty sure I knew what he wanted. We wanted each other in that desperate, no-one-has-ever-felt-this-way-before sexual craving. The Lord had known what He was doing when it came to procreation. He gave us all an unbearable itch that needed scratching during our reproductive years.

But what was the possible reason for the desire I felt now?

It was probably why I'd accepted Michael's growing lack of interest over the years. It was only natural, I told myself. I certainly wasn't having any more children. I was disappointed, but I shrugged my shoulders and soldiered on like I did with everything else in my life.

My sisters and I barely talked, and never about sex. And it wasn't a topic I was going to bring up during church coffee hour!

I could imagine how that would go ...

"So Sally, are you and your husband still having relations?"

"Oh, yes. My sister and her husband stop by every Thursday night for a couple of rounds of gin rummy."

"No. I mean *relations*." I'd give a wink.

She'd look blank.

"Are you still going at it?" I'd ask.

"At what?"

"Are you having sex?" My voice would raise like I was talking to someone hard of hearing, and everyone would look at me.

"Oh, yes, my dear." Sally would lean close. "Just not with my husband. But don't worry, I go to confession every Saturday. And I swear every week the priest tells me to 'go forth and sin some more'."

That Sally always had been sex obsessed. And now I would know she was quite deaf as well.

I chuckled to myself as I let go of my imaginary conversation.

"Someone's happy this morning," Liz said. She looked at the car schedule. "What's up on Thursday?"

"I got roped into helping with the white elephant sale at church," I said. "Thursday we're going through the stuff we've got, cleaning and sorting."

"Better you than me," she said, pouring coffee and popping toast into the toaster.

"You off to your studio?"

"Yep. I think I'm close to finishing the one I've been working on since we left North Carolina."

"Taken you long enough," I said as I contemplated my own breakfast options. "Are we going to get to see this one?"

"Once I finish it, I promise I'll show it to you. It's been difficult. I tried to resurrect the style I had as a young woman, but that didn't match who I am now. So I've spent all this time trying to reconcile the two."

"What does your agent think?"

"I haven't shown her anything either. She wasn't thrilled with the change of direction when I talked with her in New York. I'm reluctant to show her anything before it's completely set."

"Makes sense," I said, nodding. Maybe I'd make myself some scrambled eggs. We had sausage in the freezer.

"I'm going to fire that accounting client." Diane emerged from the shower room where she'd finished showering and gotten dressed. She was staring at her phone. "She's left me five messages already this morning, demanding to know why I haven't answered her back."

"Isn't she in California?" Liz asked, sitting down at the table with her toast.

"Yes." Diane got her coffee.

"Why is she up so early?"

"Because she's a worry-wart. She woke up at three in the morning, concerned about how her taxes were going to work out for her this year. And if *she's* awake, she figures everyone else should be awake, too."

"I hate people like that," I said.

"Yes. As soon as we get back to Montana, she's getting fired. They're all getting fired. I'm retiring for good."

Liz and I applauded. It had been clear to us for a while that our sister no longer found joy in her accounting business. Diane had become focused on developing her photography skills. If she wasn't out taking pictures, she was working on her computer learning how to touch them up to produce the best quality image she could.

"After I finish breakfast, I'm going out to take pictures. I may be out all day," Diane said.

"What about your client?" I asked.

"I've told her I'll talk to her at our usual time. Then I'm putting my phone on airplane mode."

"That's smart," Liz said. "In spite of these handy little devices, we don't need to be at every person's beck and call."

"Freedom from technology!" Diane said, thrusting her fist in the air.

I looked at her. "Who are you and what have you done with my sister?" Diane was addicted to her computer as far as I could see.

Diane laughed. "I'm learning to be better. Really. Joe told me if I don't cut my umbilical cord with the internet, he's going to have second thoughts."

"Smart man," Liz said. With a glance toward me, she asked, "So what are you up to today?"

"Genna and I are getting together to do some weaving and spinning and having lunch," I said. I glanced at my phone. It was already nine. Maybe toast for breakfast would be a better idea.

"She's becoming quite the social butterfly," Liz said to Diane.

"I know," Diane replied. "She's got church activities, friends, and now she's dating."

"He's just a friend," I stated loudly.

"She better not get too comfortable," Liz said. "We need her to drive us home."

I ignored them. Everything was temporary. That's how it was in the RV world. There were brief friendships, parishes …

Loves.

~ ~ ~

An hour later, Genna and I were comfortably seated under her awning. She was working her odd little spinning wheel, and I was weaving. Mostly we were quiet, but every once in a while we would talk.

The time was peaceful, the gentle whir of her wheel, and the occasional thud of my ridge heddle reed providing a counterpoint to the background chirping of small birds. It was a scene as old as humans. Archeologists had found flax fibers created thirty-four thousand years ago in the Republic of Georgia; woven textiles had been discovered at a Neolithic settlement in central Turkey. People had discovered they needed clothing early on.

I could imagine gatherings like this from ancient times. People sitting together, doing what needed to be done, but enjoying each other's company while they did so. It was a pleasure that the industrial age had stripped from human work. Then the information age divided us even further, leaving us communicating through hard metal and plastic instead of talking casually within the circle of others.

"This is a wonderful way to spend time," Genna said. "It's the hardest thing about traveling for me. There are people who knit and such, but I just get to know them and they move on … or we do."

"Yes," I agreed. "It's hard to make connections."

"It must be quite an adventure for you and your sisters to go on this road trip."

"It is. We've seen so many places, and there are more on the schedule. I'm anxious to see the Grand Canyon."

"We've been. It's pretty phenomenal. Will you be going to the big Utah parks?"

"We saw a few of them on the way east. I think the latest plan is to make our way to California, see some of the coast and Yosemite and then head back to Montana." My voice dropped off as I talked.

"Don't you want to go home?" she asked quietly.

"I don't know." I debated how much I wanted to tell her. Sometimes talking to a relative stranger was easier than talking to my sisters.

Genna didn't respond but continued to spin.

I felt free to talk more or be quiet. It was a liberating feeling: someone letting me talk or not talk at my own pace.

"My husband died a year and a half ago. Cancer," I said.

"I'm sorry."

"He'd been ill for a while. I think he was relieved to go."

"Sometimes it's like that."

I let the shuttle glide from one side to the other, moved the reed, and slotted it in a new spot.

"We were having problems before that. I wasn't sure if I loved him anymore, but there wasn't much I was going to do about it. I married for life. I knew that going in."

"How old were you?" she asked.

"Twenty," I said.

"That's young."

"It seems so now, but at the time I thought I knew everything there was to know."

"I get that," Genna said with a wry smile.

"When did you get married?"

"I married my first husband when I was twenty-nine. We'd been dating for a few years, and my biological clock was kicking up a storm. I thought he was the best I was going to do."

"I'm so sorry. You're a wonderful person. I'm sure you could have had any man you wanted."

She shrugged. "You know how it was back then. We were torn between the traditions of our parents and the promise of freedom in the future. My mother had been putting pressure on me to 'find a good man' for years by that time. I thought it was my last chance." Her laugh had a tinge of bitterness. "The thing was, I wasn't even sure I wanted children, or a husband. I enjoyed work too much. It was the beginning of the computer age. I found the concepts fascinating, and it turned out I had an aptitude for it."

"But you got married anyway."

"Yep."

"Did you have kids?"

"Three. Two of them turned out okay, but one has his issues."

"I had two. Other than the usual hijinks, they've stayed on the straight and narrow. I'm grateful for that."

"You're lucky. My son's an addict. It's quite a roller coaster. I'd hoped he would straighten out someday—he's in his thirties—but that doesn't look possible. He's too much like his dad."

"I'm sorry. That's got to be tough. So are you still married?"

"No. I tried for a long time. My ex was an alcoholic. To be truthful, he tried to quit, going to rehab and such. But it would never stick. Finally, I left for my own sanity and to save my kids."

"Tough decision." If Michael had been an alcoholic, would I have been able to leave? The church was known to give dispensation in cases like that. Annulments were possible, if somewhat odd given kids had been conceived.

But Michael's addiction had been easier to hide, so I'd never considered leaving.

"The problem with addiction," Genna said, "is that it affects everyone around the addict. And for a long time afterward, even if you break it off. One of my therapists told me I had a form of PTSD. It took me a long time to get my thinking straight." She smiled. "And once I did that, I was able to find the right man, the one I *wanted* to spend the rest of my life with."

She glanced over at me. "It can happen to you too, if you let it."

I forced a shrug.

"Just remember," she said, her grin broadening. "Denial isn't a river in Egypt."

"Very funny," I said.

"But true. It's your life now, Kathleen. That means you get to make the decisions *you* want to make, not what anyone else thinks you should do."

I nodded and concentrated on the next row of weaving.

In her wisdom, Genna let the conversation go, but she'd planted some seeds that had the potential to keep me up at night.

Chapter Fifteen

Thursday morning I walked into the church's community hall at ten, the time Trixie Lynn had given me. A number of people bustled around, and it took a few moments to find her. She was walking from group to group, clipboard and pen in hand. She was as put together as ever, in cute pink Bermuda shorts, matching slip-ons, and a blouse festooned with Hello Kitty images.

With her pink headband and frosted hair, she pulled off the look, something I would never even attempt.

She spotted me and came rushing over. "You're finally here!"

"This is the time you told me to be here," I said.

"Are you sure? I believe I told you nine. Most of these people have been here since eight, eager to help."

I let her implication that I was lacking slide, but noted it. There would be time before we left to extract a suitable revenge for the put-downs she'd dished out. She'd never see it coming.

I smiled at her politely. "What would you like me to do?"

"Well, since you're so late, I've put you with the washing crew." She pointed to a far door. "There's a big outdoor sink and hose around the corner there. Things have already stacked up. There's also a few rugs that need to be beaten before they can be vacuumed. You do know how to beat a rug, don't you?"

"Do squirrels have a climbing gear?" I responded. How hard could beating a rug be?

"Huh?" Frown lines appeared on her forehead.

"Leave it to me," I said.

As I walked outside, I realized the washing crew consisted of one person: me.

Revenge was going to be so sweet.

The image of all that pinkness dumped into a manure pile made me smile.

But I was here to help the church, so I'd best get to it.

Taking the old-fashioned rug beater someone had thoughtfully provided, I took aim at one of the rugs hung over a temporarily strung clothesline and hit it solidly.

Dust immediately covered me and puffed into the air. I felt like

Pigpen in the old Peanuts comic strip.

I started coughing, and my eyes teared up.

Someone ran toward me, speaking rapid Spanish as she handed me a bottle of water. She tugged me away from the cloud of dust.

Uncapping the bottle, I took a good swig and the coughing subsided.

With a smile, she led me to the sink and gestured to my face.

I had a good idea of what she meant, so I ran the water and washed off the dirt. It was dripping, and I looked around for a towel.

She shrugged and said something in Spanish.

"Air dry, huh?" I said, waving my hands around my face.

She nodded and grinned.

She was a beautiful woman, somewhere in her late forties or fifties if I had to guess. Her hair was a glossy black, and she'd taken time with her makeup, including bright red lipstick on her still-full lips.

"Gracias," I said.

"De nada."

Then we stood for a few moments in that hopeless stance of people who'd really like to communicate but can't because of a language barrier.

I wondered what her story was.

"There you are!" An older woman, her black hair graying, and her life etched on her face came rushing from the church. She switched to Spanish and exchanged a volume of words and gestures with the woman who'd come to my rescue.

Eventually, she stopped and took a good look at me.

Then she shook her head and held her hand out to my rescuer.

The young woman shook her head and said a word even I could understand: "No!" She turned to me. "I want to help." She pointed to the rugs and the pile of things that needed cleaning.

More Spanish.

This was getting old. They'd have to sort it out themselves. There was work to do.

I picked up the rug beater and took another swing, far less vigorously this time.

A few moments later the older woman was standing in front of me, impeding my progress.

I gave her a once over. I didn't know what her problem was with me, but I figured she had one.

"You need to stay away from Rodrigo," she said.

"That's up to him," I said.

"No." A finger jabbed in my direction. "He is not meant for you."

I wanted to tell her I already knew that, but I wasn't going to give her that satisfaction.

Instead I shrugged and took a step to the side. Without giving her a chance to move, I slapped the rug again.

She coughed and gave me the evil eye, something that translated in any language.

I eyed her right back.

She glared.

I swung back the beater and took another shot.

This time she had the good sense to take a step away, although a good bit of dust still landed on her shoulders and ample bosom.

"I am his wife's sister. That is her cousin."

I glanced at the young woman who was scrubbing at a cut glass vase.

"Her husband died last year in a scaffolding accident. Someone cut corners, and he died."

"I'm so sorry," I said.

"If you are sorry, then you will clear the way for Rodrigo to do his duty and marry her so she is cared for. As you can tell, she speaks practically no English. But she is a hard worker and will make him a good wife, just like my sister did."

"None of that is up to me. It is up to your cousin and Rodrigo."

She shook her head. "I've seen the way he looks at you. Do the right thing. Leave him alone. He needs to marry within his people. There are enough gringos."

I laughed. "What are you thinking? We're going to have kids? The time is long gone for that." I held up the rug beater. "This is none of your business. If you want to help your cousin, help her learn English and get a job. And let her live her own life. Now go find someone else to bother. I've got work to do."

Turning my back on her, I gave the rug another thwack, once again delivering more dust than I'd intended.

Frustration had a way of making me forget how strong I am.

"Bravo!" a familiar voice said.

I whipped around to see Rodrigo striding toward me, and in spite of all my resolutions, my heart gave a hop of happiness. The sister-in-law was no longer in sight.

"You are just the person to beat that rug into submission," he said, then surprised me by kissing my dusty cheek. "I see you have met the dragon lady, my sister-in-law."

"Ah, yes, I did."

"And I suppose she has told you all about my duty to marry my wife's cousin."

"Um … yes."

"Not to worry. The lady doesn't want to marry me," Rodrigo said.

"She doesn't?"

Rodrigo called in Spanish to the woman who was working at the sink.

She answered him and shook her head.

"See?" he asked.

"You could have asked her anything," I pointed out. "You could have asked her if it was raining."

Rodrigo sighed and shouted over to the woman.

She turned back. With her soapy hands waving in the air, even I could see she was giving him what for.

When she got to me, she pointed at the man. "Him?" Then she laughed and shook her finger. "No marry."

Her expression turned hopeful. "You marry?"

"Oh, no," I said, shaking my head, then mimicked her shaking finger as I said, "No marry."

She laughed and went back to the sink.

"I'm deeply offended," he said. "It seems no one wants to marry me."

"I thought marrying you was a big deal. That it was important so the cousin would be kept out of poverty," I said.

"She keeps telling them she has a good job at a restaurant and a boyfriend. They don't think working in a restaurant is good enough for her, and the boyfriend is Black."

"Oh, dear. The dragon lady must be really disappointed."

"Oh, she is. But you have nothing to worry about. The cousin and her boyfriend are planning a small wedding next Christmas, so that will be the end of that."

"Sounds like you had a narrow escape." Then I spied someone else emerging from the community room.

"Is that all you're going to do?" Trixie Lynn demanded. "Stand around talking while another person does your work?" She gestured to my new friend.

"I've been rug beating." I took my stance and swung backwards.

Rodrigo had the good sense to step back.

Trixie Lynn wasn't so bright.

"You did that on purpose!" she said wiping dust from her pink shorts, getting them even dirtier in the process.

I didn't have to look over to know Rodrigo was stifling a laugh.

"Oh, I'm sorry. You did say it was dirty work." I gave her the same innocent smile I used to give my parents when I was blaming Liz for something I'd done wrong.

"Why you …" Trixie Lynn sputtered. Then she turned on Rodrigo. "Why are you out here bothering my workers?" She must have realized how harsh she sounded because she injected her next words with sweet honey. "Come back inside, and I'll show you some of the treasures people have donated. I so appreciated your gift of the Lladró figurines. That was quite a collection."

"It was my wife's," he said.

"How could you bear to part with it?" Trixie Lynn touched her hand to her heart.

She was good. Very good.

"It was time," he said.

"Well, it was very generous." She hooked her arm in the crook of his elbow and urged him toward the center. "And Antonia did a great job cleaning them, unlike some people. You have no idea how much work it is to organize …"

They drifted out of sight, and I went back to the rugs.

After some time had passed, I was done and went to help the woman at the sink. We introduced ourselves using a lot of pointing and laughing. I was polishing glassware to a shine when Rodrigo came back out.

"You escaped," I said.

"It took longer than I'd hoped. She kept going on and on about the collection. I've always hated it by the way. Collectables seemed like a long con game."

"They meant something to our parents," I said. "And even to us." I thought about the Gaelsong figurines I'd inherited from my mother. Michael added to the collection when he couldn't think of anything else to get me for Christmas or my birthday.

"I suppose," he said. "But none of this is why I came here."

"Why did you come then?" I hated the flirt in my tone, but he seemed to bring it out in me.

"I'd like to take you to a movie and dinner."

"Tonight?"

"Yes. I've missed you."

I debated. Miniature golf was one thing. A movie and dinner sounded like a much more serious date.

"Go," my new friend said with a poke in my back.

"See?" Rodrigo said with a smile. "She knows I'm good for you."

"But …" I gestured at my filthy self.

"There will be plenty of time for you to go home and get cleaned up." He moved closer. "I'd like to take you out. Please come with me."

I couldn't turn him down.

"Yes," I said, my aging heart once again going into its aerobic exercises at the thought of spending more time with him.

Chapter Sixteen

This time when Rodrigo came to pick me up, my sisters weren't home. Liz had grabbed the keys to the car as soon as she'd returned and taken Diane with her to the grocery store. There hadn't even been time to tell them I wouldn't be there when they got back.

I'd leave a note.

After a long shower, I felt wonderfully clean. There was nothing like being repulsively dirty to make soap and water seem like a gift from the gods. By the time I was done, I'd decided I was wearing the dress I'd recently bought.

Sliding it down my body made me tingle. It had been a long time since I'd worn a dress, especially a new one. I felt feminine, another sensation that was unexpected.

Was this what dating was supposed to be like?

I could get used to it.

Taking my new cosmetics into the bathroom, I applied them as the young girl at the counter had shown me. Unfortunately, I'd been unable to get a haircut, but had one scheduled before we left. After forty years as a rancher's wife and mother, it was time to explore who else I could become before life was over.

Rodrigo showed up exactly when he said he was going to.

"You look wonderful," he said, kissing me on the cheek.

"And clean too," I pointed out.

"Yes," he said with a chuckle. He walked me to the passenger door and closed it after I was settled. I had to fight the knee-jerk reaction to tell him I'd been getting in and out of cars and trucks for a very long time.

He was an old-fashioned man, comfortable with traditional courtesies. I had the feeling he treasured women, would treat them with the utmost respect, and do everything in his power to make sure they knew it.

It was a powerful aphrodisiac. I'd never experienced such regard in all my years I'd been married to Michael.

I didn't want to stop experiencing it.

"Do you like seafood or Italian?" he asked.

"What? Not Mexican?" I kidded him.

"I figured we both needed a break. I like other kinds of food, you know. And we're so rich in this country to be able to have a wonderful variety. Or do you want Thai or Chinese?"

"Seafood," I said definitively. I could get Thai and Chinese in Butte. Having seafood this close to the source was something the three of us had been enjoying since reaching New York.

"Seafood it is," he said and put the car into gear.

On the way, he asked me how the rest of the day had gone. I told him about some of the odder things his cousin and I had cleaned, and how Trixie Lynn came back several times to see how we were doing.

"One time, she pulled me aside and questioned me to find out exactly when we were leaving. She told me you were looking for something long term, so we'd never work out."

"That woman is too much in my business," Rodrigo said.

"Maybe you should give her a chance after I leave."

My statement landed with a thud on the console between us. My insides had clutched as soon as I said the words.

He was quiet for a while, maintaining the illusion that he was concentrating on driving, not on the impact of the words I'd just said.

"Trixie Lynn is not the woman I want," he said as he pulled into the restaurant parking lot.

I waited for him to continue, but that's where he left it.

As we walked into the restaurant, I tried to think of something humorous to tell him, but every bit of funny seemed to have departed. We were shown right to the table and presented with large menus covering every type of seafood a person could possibly dream up, including ceviche.

I ordered something called a redfish Pontchartrain, a rich-sounding dish that included crab, shrimp, rice, and a butter wine sauce along with the redfish. Rodrigo ordered a blackened catfish dish.

"Would you like some wine?" he asked.

"If we're going to a movie …" I said. After an active day and a rich meal, I didn't want to be snoring away while the film still rolled.

"Perhaps iced tea?" he asked.

"Sounds good."

Once our ordering was over, the minor conversational bump in the road had smoothed out. Rodrigo told me about the cows that had started to drop their calves, and the search for them in the field to tag them and make sure they were okay.

"At least you don't have to do it in snow," I said. "Every once in a while we get a mostly white calf. Man, is that a pain in the you-know-where."

He laughed. "That's why you should stay here. There is no snow."

"Montana's in my blood," I told him. "I can't ever imagine living away from there on a permanent basis."

"But what will you do in the cold of the winter next year? Didn't you say your son and his family have taken over operations?"

"Yes, but an extra pair of hands is always useful. They're talking about trying for one more child—they already have two—so that means my daughter-in-law won't be as agile as she could be."

"I understand. A woman never knows which road a pregnancy will take." He took a sip of the drink the waitress had dropped off. Then he looked up at me, his dark eyes kind, but concerned. "When will it be your turn, Kathleen?"

"What do you mean? I'm a little old to get pregnant, don't you think?"

He chuckled. "That's not what I meant. From what you've told me, you've worked hard over your life to raise your children and build your ranch for your family, including your sisters. It sounds like you and your husband did most of the work until he couldn't anymore, then you took over."

"That about covers it," I said, my smile cautious. I'd been around Rodrigo long enough to know that he thought almost like an attorney, laying the groundwork, then going in for the killer conclusion.

"I have a feeling there's more to that story," he said, his gaze direct enough that I had to look away.

My problems with Michael were going to stay buried … forever.

"Nope." I forced a smile. "Until we took off on this adventure."

He grinned, and I relaxed.

"Family," he said. "It brings me joy. Before you leave, I'll have to invite all my children and their families over to meet the women from Butte, Montana."

"That would be wonderful. Do they live close?"

"Most of them," he said, and began to tell me all about his children: Juan, Miranda, Angelica, Luis, and Miguel. We'd talked about them before, but this time I could see his pride in his children as well as his deep love for them.

"You and your wife must have worked hard to raise such successful people," I said.

"My wife was a good woman," he said. "We were good parents, I think. It was natural for us to put family first. I don't think that's true for everyone. I see so many families where people struggle even to like each other. And now, with all the division in this country, it's even easier for brothers and sisters to call themselves enemies for life. It is tragic."

I thought about a few long term feuds in my own family. My relatives were quick to anger and slow to forgive. Even my sisters and I had held grudges that we'd never talked about until this trip.

Diane's idea of the three of us taking a year to get to know each other and see the country had been so much more of a blessing than I'd anticipated. My main objective had been to get away from the house where I'd felt locked away for a long time. I didn't realize how much fun we'd have with each other, or that any of us would fall in love.

Was that what I was doing here? Was I falling in love with Rodrigo?

"But I am with a beautiful woman, so why am I talking about such painful matters?" he said with a smile. "My wife and I had a good marriage, our children are doing well, and my ranch is thriving. She's been gone for a long time, and I have the good fortune now to meet someone new, if only for a little while." He raised his iced tea, and we clinked.

The waitress brought our food not long after. My meal was divine, and I told him so.

"How is Star?" I got around to asking him.

"I think you've spoiled her," he said. "She's pining for you. You'll need to come see her again soon."

"I'd like that. It would be good to go riding with you again."

"We should trailer the horses to the Hill Country Natural Area and go riding there. I'm sure Antonia would pack us a lunch." His grin was wicked. "Unless that is something you'd like to do."

"Not on a bet," I said. "My jail sentence in a kitchen is over."

He frowned, but I could tell it was fake.

"You mean if we ever got married, you wouldn't cook for us?"

"Antonia has nothing to fear about losing her job. I know my strengths and cooking isn't one of them. Got a tractor that needs fixing, and I'm you're woman. I can sew a button if I must, but there's no guarantee the button or the thread will match the garment. Let's see, what other womanly duties do I fail at?"

"There is one I hope you do not fail at, not in the least." The wicked grin was back.

My fair skin, I was sure, blazed red. My mind raced to find a comeback.

"Nope, that's as good as it gets."

"I don't know," he said. "I think you kiss fairly well."

"And what are you implying?"

"I think you know very well what I have in mind."

"Well, you can just leave it in your mind," I said. My female parts had roused themselves and were perking with interest. Literally.

I pointed my fork at him. "We're friends. That's it. We can't be anything more."

"Why not?" His face was suddenly serious.

I looked at him in astonishment. "It's obvious."

"Is it?"

Shaking my head I took another forkful of my meal. I wasn't going to get into this conversation.

I couldn't. There were way too many minefields. My only experience with a man was with Michael, and he had failed me. That fact colored my perspective about any man, any prospective relationship in my future.

It would take an exceptional man to get past that hurdle. Rodrigo might be able to reach that bar, but there were too many other things stacked against us including culture and the fact that we lived in two different states.

All we had in common was our ranching experience and our church.

I wasn't going to think about how strong those two bonds might be.

~ ~ ~

After offering several selections, Rodrigo left the choice of movie up to me. I chose a rom-com starring some older actresses that had been stars in all the movies I'd grown up with. I needed familiarity, and I needed some good laughter.

After dinner, we skipped the soda and popcorn, and settled into the large, comfortable seats.

Rodrigo looked at the heavy arm between us with a frown. He felt under it, nodded, and then pushed it up so it nestled in between the back of our seats. The bottom was padded so it looked like it was part of the back.

"Better," he said.

I wasn't so sure about that. I was already too aware of his body so close to mine.

Why now? I'd managed to live the past decade without even

giving a moment's thought to sex. With Rodrigo next to me, I was very aware of my body's reaction to his closeness.

After all the times I'd told my sisters they were oversexed, the universe was having the last laugh.

Nothing was going to come of it though. I would be celibate unless I remarried—highly unlikely. I'd keep myself under control until we made it safely out of Texas.

Maybe I'd tolerate a few more kisses, but that was definitely going to be it.

I definitely didn't want my sisters to think I was going to turn out like them.

Rodrigo's hand clasped mine, and I turned toward him.

He smiled, and my heart went thumpity-thump, just like in the old cartoons.

This was not good.

"Do you go to see a lot of movies?" I said, in the most neutral tone I could manage.

"Rarely. I usually stream at home." He leaned closer. "It's much more comfortable to snuggle up with someone there than on these seats."

"You mean with Trixie Lynn?"

He gave a mock shiver. "Never."

"With your wife then?"

His gaze saddened. "Not really. She was always busy as we watched television: crocheting, mending one of the kid's clothes, something like that. I tried to get her to relax, but she said she didn't have time."

"I know the feeling." I'd made similar choices. It was a good way to keep distance between Michael and I, to escape the longing for something that was no longer possible.

He gently squeezed my hand. "I'd love to have you sit next to me on my couch and watch a movie," he said.

"Then why don't you take her home and do that!" some guy behind us muttered loud enough for us to hear.

We both started laughing. By the time we had our outburst fully muffled, the movie had started. Within moments, we were laughing again. This time the audience joined in with us.

~ ~ ~

"That was great," I said to Rodrigo as we left the theater.

"Yes," he replied. "That's the power of a great movie. It can take us away from reality for a while."

I nodded, but didn't feel like saying much. The movie and catharsis of laughter had left me feeling happy and content.

"I have one more stop I'd like to make before I take you home," he said.

"Where's that?"

"It's a small park. They have an observation tower there. If we climb up, we'll have a great view of the city."

It sounded like an isolated spot. Exactly the wrong place to go if I wanted to keep our relationship from going any further than it already had.

"I'm not sure," I said.

"I'll be a gentleman," he said. "You can't miss this view before you leave."

For some reason, I was disappointed with his promise.

"Okay then."

We got in the car, and he drove away from the city lights. Neither of us spoke, content to be together and quiet.

There were only a few cars in the lot of Eisenhower Park. One at the far end, almost in the shadows, had steamy windows that gave a clear idea of what the occupants were up to.

"I wonder what they'd do if we went up and rapped on the window," I said when he opened my door.

"You have an evil mind," he said. "Probably the same thing you would have done when you were a kid, and the car was the only place to explore all those luscious new feelings."

"You mean see how far the girl would go," I retorted.

"That too." His grin was devilish. "And how far did you go?"

"None of your business," I said, my face flaming with heat. I was grateful the light was dim. "But I was a virgin on my wedding night," I announced proudly, at the same time aghast that I was saying those words out loud.

"I see," he said. "I'm afraid I was not."

I was about to tell him it was okay, he was a man, when I realized what a load of crap that was. That sexist belief had wormed its way into my brain at a very young age, just like a dozen others of its ilk. Like being a virgin on the wedding night. What else was that but a man's need to make sure any progeny were his.

Ugh. What other thoughts was I carrying around that belonged back in the Middle Ages?

"Where are you going?" Rodrigo called.

I stopped. Along with my raging thoughts, my feet had carried me along the pathway a good distance. Turning around, I walked back to where he stood.

"Sorry," I said. "I got upset."

"Did I do something wrong?"

"No."

"Then?"

"It's … well …" How did I say this without sounding like more of an idiot than I already felt?

He must have understood something because he nodded. "When you're ready, we'll talk about it. But for now, let me show you how beautiful the city can be." He held out his hand.

I hesitated. Did taking his hand make me complicit in the continued inequality of the genders?

"Were you glad your wife was a virgin?" I asked.

He looked at me strangely.

"I'm not sure it occurred to me to be glad. Or even anticipate being sad if she hadn't been. I asked before … well …" He dropped his hand and looked at the ground. "I didn't want to hurt her," he said quietly.

My affection for this man grew.

"My wife and I … it was complicated." He looked up. "But I really, really don't want to talk about it now. I want to be here. With you. That's all. Is that all right with you?"

A sense of freedom flowed through me.

"Yes."

This time when he held out his hand, I took it. When we reached the top of the tower, I stared at the sea of bright lights in front of me. Rodrigo pointed out some of the landmarks, including the tall buildings surrounding the plaza where the Alamo stood.

He put his arm around me and pulled me close.

It felt natural to lean my head on his shoulder.

"It's beautiful country," he said. "The lush blankets of flowers on the hills make me feel like a very rich man every spring. God lays out his bounty in this country. It's got good feed for cattle, but other crops can be grown. There are a number of good colleges and trade schools. All of my children attended at least a two-year college," he said, pride in his voice. "My wife and I believed it was important for their development as adults. Yes, everyone needs to find an occupation, to make their way in the world, but they also need to think." He tapped his head.

"The world changes rapidly," I said. "Think of how much is different from when we were kids. A simple device like the telephone has changed our lives."

"Yes. And now we have AI. I'm not sure I understand it, but I know it's a game-changer. It will affect even ranchers. In some ways it frightens me."

"You're the one who puts little doodads on his cows' tails to find out when they're ready to drop their calves. Good thing the cows can't talk and tell you how they feel about that."

He chuckled.

"That's one of the things I like about you," he said. "You aren't afraid of speaking your mind."

"You might find you're tired of it pretty rapidly."

"I don't think so." His voice was husky. He shifted, and I found myself looking into his eyes as he lowered his mouth toward mine. His movement was slow, giving me plenty of time to object if I wanted to do so.

It was so different from either the mad scramble of youth or accepting whatever crumbs Michael gave me as his libido waned.

Rodrigo was intentional, interested, and invested in my happiness.

His lips against mine were becoming more familiar. When he pressed for the kiss to become more intimate, I went along for the ride.

I don't know how long we kissed, the lights spread out below us, our own internal glow overpowering the distant beams. As he'd asked, I was totally there, in that moment, enjoying his actions and my body's response.

When he finally pulled away, we were silent. Once again we stared into the distance, his arm wrapped companionably around me. Time passed in quiet moments. There was no need to talk. Being together was enough.

I'd rarely felt so at peace.

We strolled back to the car.

The couple in the shadows were evidently still at it, and we smiled at each other. I leaned back against the car, almost inviting him for a repeat, and he obliged.

When strong beams arced up the driveway to the lot, we pulled apart.

Thumping from the car gave us the clue that the young lovers had recognized the signs as well.

We'd gotten into the car, and Rodrigo was driving away when his beams hit the car one more time. The timing was just right to see a gray-haired man, his hair all twisted around his head and an equally aged woman stagger from the car.

"O-kay," Rodrigo said.

"They must be extremely agile," I said, thinking about the interior of what looked to be a mid-life crisis sports car now that we'd seen the occupants.

"More agile than I am," he said. "Give me a nice, comfortable, king-sized bed any day."

"Sounds good," I said without thinking.

"Then it's a date?" he said.

Even in the dim light, I could tell his smile was wicked.

"Don't get ahead of yourself, buster," I said.

"I'll light candles and spread rose petals," he said.

"Rodrigo!"

"Too soon?"

"Yes. Definitely yes!"

"Then I'll be patient," he said. He glanced over. "But I won't give up."

Instead of reminding him I was leaving, I enjoyed the glow of being wanted. At sixty-four, it was a feeling worth savoring.

~ ~ ~

Rodrigo escorted me to the door of the RV and left, but not before kissing me one more time. It wasn't as passionate as the others had been, but I had no doubt my sisters had seen it.

As soon as I walked up the few steps to the living area, I knew I was right. Both of them were sitting there, already in their pajamas, wine in hand and smirking at me.

"Isn't it past your bedtime?" I asked.

"We had to wait up for you," Diane said.

Liz checked an imaginary wristwatch. "You're very late, young lady. You'll have to be grounded for the next week," she said in a low voice that was eerily like my father's.

"Stay out of my life," I said.

"Like you stayed out of ours?" Diane said.

"We only went to dinner and the movies." I poured myself a glass of water.

"And kissing," Diane said.

"Lots of kissing," Liz agreed.

I said nothing, and the silence stretched for a bit.

"Are you okay?" Liz asked in a more serious tone.

I nodded.

"We're worried you're getting in over your head," Diane said.

Unexpected tears formed in my eyes. All kidding aside, my sisters were there for me. If Rodrigo ever hurt me, they'd go for his throat, which is why I'd never told them the truth about Michael.

"Love you guys," I said, putting my glass down.

I spread my arms out, and we indulged in a very satisfying group hug.

Chapter Seventeen

Saturday morning, I rose early, in spite of the late night before. While I quietly went about my morning routine, my sisters slumbered on.

I liked being alone in the morning, before everyone was up. I remembered my mother enjoying that time too. One time I got up earlier than I usually did and came into the kitchen to find something to eat. My mother, still in her curlers and quilted bathrobe, gave me a baleful eye from where she sat at the kitchen table. She'd been enjoying her coffee, cereal, and book, and didn't relish the interruption.

I'd gathered my own breakfast and sat there quietly until, with a sigh, she pushed back her chair and brought her bowl to the sink. Only then did my shoulders relax.

I never came out early again. I'd lie in bed and go over every moment of the day before rather than risk that look from my mother.

When I had children of my own, I understood the sigh. Time alone was rare and treasured.

By the time the coffee was brewed, Diane had stirred in her sofa bed. I poured her a cup and placed it on the table next to her.

"Thanks," she said, pushing herself up to sitting. "You're up early."

"I have my weaving class today," I said.

"Oh, that's right. I'm so glad you're doing that," she said.

"Why?"

"Because you don't do enough for yourself. Now that I have a camera, I get how important it is to have time to be creative for no other reason than to do it. I don't have to sell my pictures, they're for me to enjoy. The time I take to learn about the camera, create a shot, or just get lucky with a bird settled at the right moment on a bare limb is precious. It's almost spiritual." She picked up her cup. "I guess it's kind of the same feeling you get in church."

I was about to protest, but then I got her point. It wasn't all I got from church, but the feeling of connection to the world around me was definitely a benefit.

Did I get the same feeling from weaving?

In the past I'd used it as more of a defense. I could get people to leave me alone if it looked like what I was doing took brain power.

I suppose it was the same reason I liked fixing a tractor. People left me alone.

Other than that, weaving and tractor repair had nothing in common.

After getting ready, I waved goodbye to my sisters and left.

The drive to the fiber store was familiar since I'd been there once already.

The date with Rodrigo last night had definitely intensified the feelings I had for him. I had no idea where to go from here. Or what I was going to do with those feelings once we left.

It would take me a long time of getting to know him—or any other man—before I'd even consider a long-term relationship. After all, Michael's problems hadn't bloomed into full-fledged disasters until decades had passed. But if I looked back, I could see the genesis.

Michael had always felt one-down. It started right at the beginning when he was born the youngest. I guess it's one of the reasons we took up with each other. We both knew the feelings of being an afterthought, and the humiliation wearing hand-me-downs could bring. Teachers who knew our older siblings and held out the vain expectations that we'd be like them were also terrifying.

He had hoped his father would reconsider the family's long-standing tradition of deeding the ranch to the oldest son, but the process remained the same. Michael, who loved ranching more than anything else, was left out in the cold. That was the second reason he'd started dating me. He knew I had the best shot at running our ranch since neither of my sisters were interested in the least. As soon as I got my hands full of oil and grease and could tell one type of wrench from another, my dad told me the ranch was mine to run. He said that fixing machinery was an underrated skill; that sometimes it mattered more than knowing how to tend to the cows.

I pulled into the parking lot of the store, picked up the new loom I'd ordered as soon as I signed up for the class, and walked inside. The clerk showed me to the back room where five women and one man were already assembled. Their easy chatter made it clear they already knew each other.

The instructor, a woman who bore the same map of Ireland across her features that I did, was setting up her loom at one end of the table, and carrying on a conversation with the woman closest to her at the same time.

A pause occurred in the conversation when I came into the room, almost as brief as a comma in a sentence.

Then one of the women shifted her things on the table to provide space. She patted the seat of the chair next to her. "Come sit here between Don and me. There's plenty of room."

I put my loom on the table. "I'm Kathleen," I said as I sat down.

"Wendy," she said. "And this is Don. We're happy to meet you. New in town?"

"No, I'm only here for a short while." I explained the situation.

Someone else pushed down a spool of warping fiber. I pulled off as much as I needed and began to warp my loom as we talked. Wendy was new to the craft, while Don had been spinning and weaving for over two decades.

"I had some heart issues," he told me. "Doc said to cut down on my stress. I'm not into sports or anything like that. I had an uncle who was a weaver, so I decided to take it up. Been at it ever since." He patted his chest. "And my ticker's kept chugging along just fine."

I'd just finished warping my loom when the instructor introduced herself. She didn't have to say much at all before her accent identified her as a New England resident: South Shore below Boston, to be exact, she informed us.

She'd come from a long line of fiber artists and sheep herders, and many of her relatives still raised the animals on the green hills of Ireland. She'd been there several times, and the way she described it made me long to go there someday. The thought of sitting by an old stone cottage with my small loom as sheep grazed on a nearby green was a tempting fantasy.

Maybe I could carve out a small part of the ranch to raise the critters. Of course, that would mean learning a whole new method of raising animals that had needs very different from cattle.

How did Rodrigo feel about sheep? Traditionally, cattlemen and sheepherders were enemies, especially in states like Texas.

But somehow, I could see myself sitting in the sun in Texas and weaving far more easily than I could see it in Montana. Maybe I could teach some of the younger generation. I smiled.

I brought my attention back to the class as the instructor began to show us how to set up for lace weaving. Soon, I was engrossed in the methodical rhythm of my shuttle back and forth, smiling as the threads began to form a pattern that somewhat resembled lace.

The class lasted a few hours, but the shop owner encouraged us to come back in the afternoon to use the room to continue to work on our lace. Wendy invited me to join her and a few other friends at lunch, and I took her up on it.

"It must be fascinating," Wendy said. "Traveling the road with your sisters for a year."

"I couldn't do it," another woman said. "One or more of us would be dead before the first month was out."

Everyone chuckled.

"I'm not even sure I could do it with my husband," another said.

"Now that," I said. "I can agree on. If Michael wasn't already dead, he would be by the end of the first week."

"How would you do it?" the woman asked.

"Hmm," I picked up the hamburger I'd ordered and took a bite. "It would be much easier on the ranch," I said when I'd finished swallowing. "So many ways to die, from falling off a horse to being run over by a bunch of cows."

"Dangerous occupation," Wendy said. "Who's taking care of the ranch now?"

"My son." The answer veered us away from interesting ways to murder someone to the trials of raising children and the problems that occurred when they grew up and thought they knew what they were doing.

By the time lunch was over, I was as comfortable with the group as I'd been with my friends back home. The next few hours of companionship and weaving cemented the beginnings of friendships. It was also nice to have someone to turn to when I inevitably got stuck.

"Too bad you're leaving," Wendy said. "The local fiber guild is quite active. We're even having a sheep shearing festival at a local farm in mid-April."

"I'm sorry I'll miss it," I said, meaning it. After a lifetime of the narrow confines of my family and the church, I was happy to discover the unexpected joy of spending time with other women doing something we loved.

"Keep in touch," Wendy said. "I'd love to hear your adventures."

"I'd like that," I said. We exchanged phone numbers, I packed up my things, and left.

On the ride home, I let myself enjoy the driving, the sights I was seeing, and the total feeling of relaxation the day had provided.

"How was it?" Diane asked when I came into the RV.

"Wonderful," I admitted. I showed her and Liz the little I'd done.

"That's going to be beautiful," Liz said.

"What have you guys been up to today?" I asked.

"Figuring out the best route to get back to Butte," Diane said.

"We took the list of things we wanted to see and tried to plot out a route. Here's what we've come up with so far." Liz rattled off an itinerary that would have made me excited to get on the road a few weeks ago.

Now it made my heart ache.

"If we're going to do this," Diane said. "We're going to have to leave before we were planning."

"How much sooner?" I asked.

"About a week," Liz replied.

Both of them looked at me with sympathy.

"We can cut off some of the sights," Diane offered. "And leave a little later."

"No," I said. "That's fine. I'll be ready when you are." Leaving sooner or later wasn't going to make me feel any better or worse.

Leaving Rodrigo was simply going to be bad.

Chapter Eighteen

As soon as I got out of the car at Rodrigo's ranch, Star nickered. Instead of knocking on the front door of the house, I crossed the open space to the corral where the mare was waiting, her head over the top fence rail. She watched my progress, nodding as I got closer.

It was another glorious day with temperatures in the low sixties, a perfect riding day. It was the kind of day that begged me to plant my butt in a saddle and let the horse wander where it may.

Star nuzzled my hair with her nose as I rubbed her head. She stuck her head down as far as she could, searching for whatever I'd brought with me. Obligingly, I pulled out a carrot and gave it to her.

"You're spoiling that horse," Rodrigo said as he approached.

"She deserves it, don't you, girl," I cooed to the animal.

"She doesn't even bother with me anymore," he said. "Always on the lookout for your car. You probably didn't see, but as soon as your car was visible on the drive, she started racing back and forth in the corral."

"That's because she's a smart girl," I said. "She knows who loves her."

"I better be careful or you'll steal her right out from under me."

"And exactly where am I going to put her?" I asked. "The RV barely fits under overpasses as it is, so the roof is out. My sisters won't put up with her in the living room. And I can't tow a horse trailer along with the car." I rubbed my head against Star's cheek. "But don't worry," I mock whispered. "I'll come back and get you. Us girls have to stick together."

The horse's ears were twitching back and forth as I spoke, and she nickered her approval when I stopped speaking.

I gave Rodrigo a triumphant grin.

"Or you could just stay here," he said.

"My sisters wouldn't approve of that either."

"I think they could be persuaded. After all, they have their own men now, don't they?"

"They've fallen. It's true. But I don't need a man. Not anymore." I flexed my arm muscle. "I've got it covered."

He laughed.

"I'm sure you do," he said. "But it's more fun with two."

"Are we going to ride or are you going to stand there jabbering all day like an old woman?" I asked with a grin.

"I've got the trailer ready. Antonia packed us a lunch."

"Of course she did. I'm in love with that woman," I said.

"Are you going to steal her along with my horse?" he asked.

"It's something to consider," I said and slipped through the rails.

Grabbing one of the leads hanging over the fence, I snapped it onto a ring in Star's halter and led her into the barn.

~ ~ ~

Rodrigo knew how to handle a trailer. He was at ease on the major roads, and careful on the dirt stretch we traveled to get to a place we could pull off and park. He backed the horses out, then handed the reins to me. "Take them over there while I turn this thing around. It's a lot easier to do it now than when we return."

I led the horses to where he'd indicated, and watched him jockey the trailer around, not an easy feat in rough country. The effort required a good deal of backing up which can be a difficult skill to learn. It was one of the reasons I'd voted for a Class A motorhome and not a trailer. Even then, I'd spent a lot of time practicing solo in a near empty parking lot before I let my sisters load one item into that rig.

Now, after driving around the country for some time, I felt at ease. True there were tricky situations, especially in heavy traffic around cities, or in states that seemed to have abandoned their highways to the elements, but at least now I felt comfortable.

Rodrigo took his reins and swung into the saddle in a smooth move that indicated how good a horseman he was. My own trip to the top of Star was a little less graceful.

"There's a spot not too far up the trail where we can let the horses out to run," he said.

"Any trees?" I asked.

"Not unless you stray off the path."

"I'll try not to do that."

As soon as we reached the spot, I didn't give him a chance. I dug my heels into Star's flanks, bent over, and let her loose.

She flew like the wind, racing like I'd imagined the Black Stallion, another famous fictional Arabian, raced across the desert. Her mane flew up in the air, and I imagined her tail streamed out behind her. As I rode, I loosened the reins and let her have her head. She stretched out even farther, and it took all the strength I had in my legs to hang on.

I could hear Rodrigo shouting behind me, but didn't know what he was saying.

My limbs began to protest, and I gently pulled on the reins.

Star tossed her head, but didn't slow.

This time I put on more pressure.

With a snort, she slowed a little.

Ahead, I could see the path turn in front of the remains of a rusted barbed wire fence. If we hit that, it was going to be nasty for both of us. I didn't want to think of what that wire would do to Star's legs.

I pulled the rein to turn her and hung on with all my might.

Somehow we made the turn, but she definitely didn't want to slow down.

I hated to do it, but I yanked hard on the reins.

This time, she got the message, slowing from a gallop to a trot, and finally a walk.

"Good girl," I said, patting her damp withers. "That's what you're supposed to do."

Rodrigo came up beside me. "I forgot to tell you, sometimes she gets the bit in her teeth and is hard to stop."

"Gee, thanks for letting me know," I said.

"You stayed on," he said.

"Just barely."

"But you did."

"Yeah." I felt good about being able to do that, but I knew I was going to be ready for the RV park's hot tub later that night.

Too bad I couldn't stay in one of his guest rooms and indulge in one of those immaculately clean bathtubs.

He took the lead again as we guided our horses at a walk. As we went down the path, Star's breathing slowed, and her gait became more rhythmic. I looked around me, enjoying the scenery and letting my mind drift into a peaceful nothingness. All the petty problems of my life and the more serious ones of the world around me failed to penetrate my good mood.

We rode for about a half hour through live oaks and denser patches of mesquite. A few times as we were riding, Rodrigo pointed off to the side. With his help I was able to see a few deer in the shadows. But when I pulled up beside him, I was the one who spotted a small owl in one of the trees.

"Wow," he said. "How did you see that?"

"My dad taught me to hunt. Well, he taught all of us, but I'm the only one it stuck with. We'd do at least one trip every fall."

"Remind me never to get you mad at me," he said, his grin wreathing his face in laugh lines. His shoulders were relaxed as well, far more so than was usual when there were other people around.

"This seems like a good place to have lunch," he said, pointing to a rock cropping a little farther up the trail. "What do you say?"

"I'm ready."

"Good."

It didn't take us long to set up our lunch. Once again, Antonia had packed a delicious repast.

"You're spoiled," I told him. "No woman will ever be able to compete with her."

"She won't have to," he said. "I've promised her a lifetime job."

"Wow," I said. "A woman gets you *and* Antonia? Why are you still single?"

"You know why," he said, leaning closer, putting his hand under my chin, and dropping a kiss on my lips. "Because the woman I want has this stupid idea of going home to Montana."

"It's where I belong," I said.

"You belong wherever you want to be."

"Besides, I wouldn't last more than a few weeks."

"Why's that?" he asked.

"Either Trixie Lynn would slip a stiletto between my ribs or your sister-in-law would call in a favor and a professional hit would take me out."

He laughed. "You have a dim view of my friends and relatives."

"Oh, no. I'm being realistic. Or maybe they would band together to 'rub me out.'"

"Rub you out? Where do you get these ideas?"

"Hmm." I inspected the chicken-stuffed wrap Rodrigo handed me. "Trixie Lynn and your sister-in-law would be a formidable pair. But then they'd have to duke it out to see who got you."

"You have an over-active imagination," he said.

"Just laying out the possibilities."

"I don't care what they do to each other," he said. "I don't want either Trixie Lynn or my wife's cousin." He looked pointedly at me.

"Got it." I took a big bite of the wrap. "How does she do this?" I said when I'd finished chewing and swallowing.

"I have no idea." Rodrigo gulped some water from his bottle. "If you had to do your marriage over again, what would you do differently?"

"You mean other than not marry Michael?"

"Why wouldn't you?"

"I've got my reasons," I said.

"Which are?"

I sighed.

"It's okay," he said. "You don't need to tell me. But I've come to believe we make the best decisions we can at the time we make them. Maybe it's God's will." He shrugged. "Maybe it isn't. After all, He gave us free will so we could make our own decisions."

I nodded.

My dad hadn't liked Michael much, but hadn't done anything beyond telling me his opinion. He left it up to me to choose my path. When I married Michael, Dad welcomed him into the family with no explicit reservation.

But Dad had been right in the long term.

I glanced at Rodrigo.

Someday, it would be nice to tell him the whole story. From everything I knew about him so far, he would understand. He would be a safe place to share my story—all of it.

But that wasn't going to happen. No matter how much I was falling in love with him, I needed to go home and live my life on my own terms.

That was simply the way it was.

Chapter Nineteen

Clad in my oldest clothes, I arranged the things I was going to need on the gravel beside the front of the rig: seven quarts of oil, oil filter wrench, oil filter, five-eighths socket wrench, disposable container for the oil, and my trusty FloTool.

After watching several videos, I'd tackled our first oil change while we were in New York. It had been a bit of a disaster, and the park owners hadn't been thrilled with the oil I'd inadvertently spattered on the gravel. Diane had quieted them down with an extra payment to cover the damage.

I felt more confident, but I'd still waited until a point when my sisters weren't around. I didn't need an audience.

For a Thursday in mid-February, the weather wasn't too cold. In fact, it was quite pleasant for the chore I had to do. I hummed to myself. I'd always liked working on machinery. Grubbiness and grease didn't bother me, and there was a satisfaction in getting a recalcitrant engine up and running again. Especially when I could do it at a fraction of the cost a mechanic would charge me.

Positioning the plastic sleeve I'd created from a sewage pipe under the oil drain, I slowly opened the drain cap, keeping the cap snug against the drain until I was ready to let the oil flow. When I removed it, I also made sure my hand wasn't downstream of the oil.

I'd learned that lesson early.

The oil was almost drained when the first looky-loo stopped by.

"Whatcha doin'?" he asked.

"Oil change."

"Ya know they can do it for you at the local shop."

"Yep."

"Doesn't seem like a good idea for a gal to be doin' that."

I thought men had gotten the memo: women were just as capable as they were.

Apparently not, from what I'd experienced as I'd driven and made repairs on the rig as we traveled.

I ignored him.

When the oil had drained sufficiently, I wiped the drain threads with a rag and put the cap back on. Using the filter wrench, I loosened the filter, then got up to stretch my back.

The man was a few inches from me. He was a wizened old man with a face like an apple that'd been out in the sun too long. He was also shorter than I was.

"Did you want something?" I asked, moving forward to tower over him a bit, for once blessing the sturdy build I'd inherited.

"Um … no. I'll mosey along …"

"You do that," I said.

He scurried like a rat.

Repositioning the small tube I'd made under the filter, I removed it, letting the oil flow from it. After making sure the seal had stayed on the rig, I added the filter to a trash bag I'd brought out with me.

I'd put the new filter on and made sure everything was tight when my next visitor came by. I nodded, hoping he'd keep going.

But no. He had to watch.

What was it with RV men? They were always watching … crap flowing down the sewer pipes from their RV to the underground tanks or how someone was backing their rig into a tight spot. And god forbid someone took out a tool. They were instantly transformed into watchers with expert opinions.

Fortunately, he only stood there for a moment or two.

I'd grabbed the oil bottle and was fixing my FloTool on it when a woman asked, "What's that?"

I turned to find a petite woman who looked like she belonged on a fashion runway.

"It … um … makes it easier to get the oil into the RV." I tried to use as simple language as possible.

"Cool," she said, coming closer. "It's always a pain to get the bottle up in there. I swear, the way they design these engines. It's like they plot all night to arrange all the parts so that it's difficult to do the simplest maintenance."

My mouth almost fell open, then I blushed as I realized I'd been guilty of the exact same thing I'd blamed the men for doing.

"I think you're right," I said to her. "It's a conspiracy."

She grinned. "Can I watch? Then you can tell me where I can get one of those doohickies."

"Sure," I said. I explained what I was doing as I showed her the long tube I'd already put down the tube to the oil reservoir. "This gadget even has a stop and go button," I said. "I can keep it closed until I'm ready to let the oil flow."

We watched the oil flow down the tube. Then she made herself useful as she handed me a new bottle and took the old one and put it into the trash.

I was almost finished with replenishing the oil when a male voice asked, "What are you doing, honey?"

My new friend told him all about the oil change, then introduced him as her husband.

"Well isn't that clever," he said. "What are they called again?"

I told him.

"Shall I order you one?" he asked his wife.

"Oh yes."

"She does all the maintenance," he said somewhat proudly. "And the driving. I'm the chief chef and bottle washer."

She laughed.

"That's how I met her," he said, looking at his wife with all the love I'd never seen in Michael's eyes. "She was under the hood of my car at the local shop. Turned out she ran the whole thing, bossed all those grease monkeys around and everything. I fell in love with her the moment I saw her in those stained overalls."

They kissed and a wave of jealousy flowed over me.

"Ready for lunch?" he asked her.

She nodded. "Thanks," she told me. "That was really helpful."

"No problem. Hey, we usually have a cocktail hour in the late afternoon. Feel free to stop by. All you need is a chair and a beverage."

"Sounds like fun," she said.

With a wave, they walked away.

As I watched them go, I felt a strong pang of loneliness.

My phone, which I'd put on the picnic table before starting my work, rang. I went over to see if I wanted to answer it. After whipping the plastic gloves off my hands, I accepted the call.

"Hello," I said somewhat breathlessly.

"Hi, there," Rodrigo said, his voice warm. "How are you doing today?" .

"Not bad." I wanted to tell him the day had gotten a whole lot better with this call, but that would have been telling him a lot more than I ever wanted to say to any man.

"I have a question for you," I said.

"Sure."

"Does a woman working on a car bother you?"

He hesitated, and my heart plummeted.

"Depends on the woman," he said.

"What if you didn't know her?"

"Then I've got nothing to say, do I?" he said. "What I meant before was this. If my late wife was working on a car, I'd be worried. She wasn't mechanical at all. I fixed her sewing machine when it went wonky. But you? Watching you work on a car would be a thing of beauty."

"Oh." That made sense. I wouldn't want the chef anywhere near a motor either.

"Are you working on your car?" he asked.

"The RV. Changing the oil."

"A dirty job," he said. "I gave that one up. I admire you for still tackling it."

"Our ranch didn't make enough to have someone else do the work." It hit me again how different our lives were in terms of money. He'd never understand the hard scrabble life I'd lived.

"I remember a time like that," he said.

"What do you mean?"

"The inflation and crazy oil prices of the early 1970s hit us hard," Rodrigo said quietly. "We barely kept the ranch going. Money was tight, but it was a matter of pride to hold onto the ranch. We learned then how to make do with what we had, to fix anything and everything. You do what you have to in order to survive."

His voice had been quiet.

"You are an amazing woman," he continued. "I have a question to ask, though."

His voice lightened and I could almost see the impish grin on his face.

"Yes?" I said warily.

"Will you be my Valentine?"

I looked down at my dirty clothes, my ragged nails. I could feel the grease and grit in my hair. I laughed.

"Sure," I said. "Why the hell not?"

He laughed as well and invited me to dinner Saturday night.

A warning went off in my head. "Isn't that the day of the white elephant sale?" I asked.

"Yes. But that ends at two. And after dealing with all of those people and all of that stuff, you will have earned my dinner. I'm giving Antonia the night off. I will cook for you."

"I'm not sure that's a feature," I said.

"You cut me to the quick. I'm a very good cook."

Why not? It seemed perfect to me to have a man cook and wait on me after dealing with a bunch of women all day.

~ ~ ~

"Thank you for all you do," Liz said to me and raised her glass. Diane followed suit.

I was embarrassed but raised my glass anyway. We clinked.

"Are you ready for that elephant thingy on Saturday?" Liz asked.

"I'll be glad when it's over," I confessed. Then I thought about the dinner I was also going to have.

"Oh! What's that?" Diane pointed to my face.

"That's a secret smile," Liz said. "Our sister has a secret. Spill, girl."

I sipped my drink instead.

Liz groaned. "I told you all my secrets."

"And exactly how long did it take for that?" I asked.

"A few years," she said.

"Few????" Diane asked.

"But they weren't current secrets," she said. "They were old secrets. I'm betting Kathleen has a secret about a certain man she's been seeing. The one she keeps telling us is 'just a friend.'"

"Oh, could it be?" Diane looked at me like a puppy dog waiting for a treat.

"Cut it out."

"Wait!" Liz said. "Isn't Saturday Valentine's Day?"

"Yes!" Diane said, pumping her fist in the air.

"Would you two grow up?" I asked.

"Give," Liz said.

I couldn't wait any longer.

"Okay, yes. He's invited me for dinner on Saturday."

"Woohoo!" Diane and Liz shouted at the same time.

"Stop making such a big deal about it," I said. "We're leaving in two weeks, remember?"

"Are you remembering?" Liz asked, her tone suddenly serious.

"What do you mean?"

"It seems like you're getting awfully close with this man."

"I told you both. After burying Michael, that's all there is. I dealt with one man and his secrets enough not to want to repeat the experience."

"What secrets?" Diane asked.

Damn.

"It was just a metaphor," I said. "I didn't mean anything by it.

Really."

"Uh-huh," Diane said.

"I have a question," Liz said.

I looked at her warily.

"Remember we were talking about the Bowie knife?"

"Yes," I said.

"If you have any idea, I'd really like to know where it is. I have an idea for a painting where that would be a great centerpiece."

"I don't know where it is. Promise," I said. And I was telling the truth. Whatever Michael had done with it, it was long gone.

He'd stolen it. Just like he'd stolen dozens of other items that had once meant a great deal to me. They were family antiques; things that had been passed down for generations. Things that should have gone to Patrick and Megan.

Once I'd realized what was happening, the emotionless state I'd had toward Michael had changed. I'd begun to hate him.

Love?

That had disappeared years before.

My sisters were still staring at me.

"I need to go inside," I said, getting up to head to the RV.

"You can't keep it secret forever," Liz said.

I ignored her, but I knew she was right. If I didn't talk about them soon, my secrets were going to crush me.

Chapter Twenty

Even though I'd arrived a half hour prior to the time Trixie Lynn told me to be at the sale, things were bustling. Many of the people seemed to have taken their duties into their own hands as if they'd done this many times before.

I supposed they had. I was the outsider.

After decades in the same church where I worked as efficiently as these women, it was odd to feel disconnected. I'd only begun to figure out where the coffee cups were stored in this place. We'd be gone before I could find the sugar packets.

A woman I'd chatted with briefly several times after church service smiled at me. "Trixie Lynn had to get a last minute donation from someone's car," she said. "She'll be right back. In the meantime, let's get you a cup of coffee. You're going to need it."

I gratefully accepted the sturdy paper cup she filled with coffee.

"Thanks so much for helping us," she said. "Visitors rarely do. They attend mass and depart, like it was drive-by communion, one more thing to check off their list. Somehow I think they've forgotten the root of the church, gathering to celebrate our beliefs together."

I sipped my coffee, not in a mood to talk philosophy this morning. There were too many things already racing through my mind: working the sale without incurring the wrath of Trixie Lynn or the sister-in-law, my dinner later with Rodrigo, and how I was going to explain Michael's actions to my sisters.

Because I knew I was going to have to do that soon. The secret had begun to fester within me and was going to erupt in a very nasty way unless I did something about it.

"Oh, there you are!" Trixie Lynn came toward me with a box of what looked like salt and pepper shakers. "Just in time. Can you give these a quick clean and get them on one of the glassware tables? You're so good at cleaning."

Her smile was almost perfect. The lack of warmth in her eyes as she looked down her nose at me gave it away.

The image of an Irish washerwoman, her hair bound up by a kerchief, a full apron tied around her ample body, rose up between us.

I knew the slight for exactly what it was.

"Sure," I said, took the box, and trudged back to the outdoor sink. She didn't see my smile.

And she didn't need to know I was the one with the Valentine's Day dinner invitation.

Once I got the salt and pepper shaker collection back to its table, I refilled the coffee cup and went to find her.

She was at the front door, welcoming in the clergy as they came to inspect and bless our activities. I waited until all of the ceremonial activities were complete, then approached her for my assignment. I'd promised myself I'd be as pleasant as possible while I worked. The proceeds were going to support a homeless shelter for immigrants stuck in limbo while they waited for the government to decide what to do with them.

It was a good cause, and I owed it my best.

However, when Trixie Lynn assigned me to the table also run by Rodrigo's sister-in-law, my resolve slipped. Trixie Lynn had a nasty streak. She knew exactly how miserable my time was going to be.

Even though I knew better, the woman tried to convince me she spoke nothing more than a few words of English, limiting her conversation to orders combined with a robust vocabulary of gestures.

She let her façade slip when she was trying to convince a woman that she absolutely needed a hideous vase that belonged in a Victorian parlor two centuries ago. I watched in awe as she deftly parted the woman from her money and handed her the vase with a triumphant smile on her face.

"Well done," I said to her when she was finished. "Now cut the crap and talk to me like I'm a human being."

"Hmpf. You don't deserve it. You are taking my cousin's place."

"She doesn't want Rodrigo. If I know that, then you know that."

"My cousin is sheltered. She doesn't know the importance of a man of stature, someone who is established, who has his own ranch."

Who has money ...?

"She is a traditional woman," the sister-in-law continued. "She knows how to take care of a man. She's like my sister. She devoted herself to Rodrigo. My cousin will do the same. He'll be a happy man."

"Are you sure he wants that?" I asked, keeping my eye out for prospective customers as we talked.

"Of course he does. He's a man. Men want to be taken care of. They want to feel like they are king of all they see, and that includes their women."

"Wow," I said. "That's an incredibly old-fashioned view of a relationship."

"It works for my husband and me," she said stiffly. "That's probably why you don't have a husband. You are one of those career women."

I was saved from a reply that would have gotten me in trouble by the approach of two women who were looking for a particular brand of collectible. Having washed every bit of glass on the surrounding tables, I knew what they were seeking and that we had some of it.

"I'll be right back," I said and quickly perused the hodgepodge of things. Within a few moments, I held up the treasures.

The two women clapped their hands and took the pieces, thanking me profusely.

I gave the sister-in-law a triumphant smile as I walked back to the table.

She glared at me.

And just like that, it was on.

We were both so busy making sales we didn't have time to argue with each other. I had an edge because I knew what we had. She had one because she knew the people who were in attendance and what they were looking for.

Between us, we made a formidable team, and our table began to empty quickly.

"My, you ladies are working hard," Trixie Lynn said as she walked by our table at one point. "It looks like I'll be able to tell the Father that we have lots of money to donate." Then she strutted like a beauty queen to the next table.

"Bruja," the sister-in-law muttered under her breath.

I had no idea what it meant, but it couldn't be good.

"I agree," I said anyway.

That earned me a grudging smile, if a slight lift of corners on a straight line of a mouth could be called a smile.

The tension between us eased a little. We still fought for every customer, but the rivalry had become a little less antagonistic.

As the ancient proverb said, "The enemy of my enemy is my friend."

By the time lunchtime arrived, I was starving. Selling other people's junk was hard work.

Another group of women had prepped lunch for the workers: small sandwiches, a few salads, the inevitable chips and salsa, all washed down with iced tea, sweetened or not. I filled my plate and sat at one of the small tables that had been laid out for us. Two women were already there, one of whom I recognized from church. We chitchatted pleasantly while we ate.

Trixie Lynn buzzed from table to table, and I steeled myself for her arrival. One of the women had left by the time she reached us.

"We're having a fabulous sale," she gushed. "I think it's the best it's ever been!"

"People stared at their stuff during the pandemic," the other woman said. "And they started to wonder why they were keeping it. This is a great opportunity to get rid of things."

"But they're buying more," Trixie Lynn pointed out.

"One man's junk is another man's treasure," I said. "And that's so true at a sale. People think they're getting something special for not much at all."

"You have a point," the woman said, rising. "I'd better relieve my tablemate."

That left Trixie Lynn and I together at the table sharing an uncomfortable moment of silence.

Then she leaned forward.

"He's not what you think he is," she hissed.

I didn't respond, instead picking up my last tortilla chip and snapping off half of it with a loud crunch.

"He cheated on her, you know."

I crunched the other half. Loudly.

"She was pregnant with their fourth child. Have you had children?"

I nodded, then inspected my empty plate for more evidence to display my total lack of interest. Not that I wasn't interested. I was. It was why I simply didn't get up from the table and leave. But I had to know what she was talking about.

I just didn't want her to know it.

My tea wasn't finished. I took a sip and put the glass down, making sure the ice cubes rattled.

"Then you know," Trixie Lynn droned on. "A woman looks and feels like a beached whale. I only had one, and that was it for me. I can't imagine enduring five. Especially when your man is cheating on you." She leaned back. "It's good for you that you're leaving. He'd never be faithful to you. I'm not sure he can be true to anyone. That's why I plan on keeping him on a very short leash. Once you're out of the way, the coast will be clear."

I allowed my gaze to shift to our table where the sister-in-law was completing another sale.

Trixie Lynn waved her away. "The cousin isn't interested. She's already got a man. No, you've been my only problem."

I didn't think I'd ever been in a situation with another woman where the gloves were nowhere to be seen. In fact, I'd never been in this kind of conversation before. I had no real rivals for Michael once he'd settled on me and the ranch as the prize he was after. As far as I knew, we'd both been true to our vows.

I had had no idea it could get so nasty in the secondary market of widows, divorcées, and an imbalanced ratio of women to men.

"I'm sure he's bought me something nice for Valentine's Day," she said as she stood. "He's always done something nice in the past. He won't want to lose me since you're leaving. I'll wait you out, so enjoy yourself while you can."

With a little wave, she left me alone to unearth myself from the pounds of garbage she'd thrown my way.

I was on my way back to the table when the cousin came up to me, a good-looking man attached to her hand.

"It is him!" she said excitedly, pointing to the man next to her. "I tell her." She pointed to the sister-in-law and let loose a waterfall of beautiful sounds, none of which I understood.

The cousin dragged the man over to my table where the sister-in-law waited.

Instead of following, I lingered at other tables, pretending to be interested in some of the items.

There was an explosion of Spanish.

When I looked around, the two women were talking as much with their hands as they were with their mouths.

By the time I reached the table, the level had somewhat subsided.

"I told her," the cousin said. "She nice now."

I had no answer that was going to win me any friends, so I wisely kept my mouth shut.

The cousin left, dragging the man, who'd said nothing during the entire exchange, behind her.

"Bah," the sister-in-law said. "Stupid girl to throw away Rodrigo." She shrugged. "But it is her wish. Rodrigo is yours."

I looked around and quickly walked to the nearest person to see if they were interested in glassware.

The sooner I got out of this madhouse, the better.

Except, once I did that, I was dropping from the frying pan dead center into the fire.

Chapter Twenty-One

Somehow I survived the rest of the sale. By the time I made it back to the RV, I was bone-tired, and my mind a blur of images and sounds. Without bothering to take a shower, I waved at my sisters and fell onto my bed.

I woke an hour later.

Grabbing my robe and some clean underwear, I went into the shower. Liz was cooking something that made my stomach rumble. I could hear Diane's voice as they conversed.

Nothing compares to the first shower after giving birth, but this was up there with one of the better showers I'd taken. I needed to get off the grubbiness of the work, but I'd been dirtier. The filth I felt from Trixie Lynn's accusations was more difficult to scrub away.

Had Rodrigo cheated? He didn't seem like that kind of man to me.

But what did I know? Less than a month had passed since we'd met. As a Magic 8 Ball might say about the chances he was faithful to his wife, "Outlook not so good."

What else didn't I know? Michael had hid his addiction well. I hadn't had any idea what was going on until after both kids had left home. Then he hadn't seemed to care anymore.

I'd moved into one of the other bedrooms long before he became ill.

But this wasn't the time to dwell on that.

After slipping on my robe, I returned to my room, stared at the closet for a few moments, then smiled. I plucked the pretty dress from its hanger and slipped it on. With more skill than I'd previously had, I put on a light layer of makeup, then fixed my hair. The haircut I'd had the week before made a big difference.

I wondered if he'd notice.

Ugh. I was sounding like a teenager with a crush.

When I walked into the living area, Diane looked at me and arched her eyebrows. "Awfully dressed up for dinner, aren't you?"

"I'm not having dinner with you two, remember?"

"What?" Liz asked. "You never said anything."

I pointed to the car schedule where I'd put in the tiniest letters possible, "K: 5 to ?"

"That's not telling us," Diane complained. "Where are you going?"

"Out," I said.

"Rodrigo," my sisters said at the same time.

Liz smacked her forehead. "Valentine's Day. Of course."

"Did Walter send you anything?" Diane asked her.

"He says there's something in the mail. We had a long talk earlier," Liz said.

"Joe called too." Diane got the dreamy expression she always had when she talked about Joe.

I hoped I didn't look like that.

"See you," I said, grabbing the car keys from the hook.

"Wait!" Diane stood. "Where are you going? When are you supposed to be back? What should we do? What if he decides to ravage you?"

I burst out laughing. Liz joined me.

"I'll be fine. Since I don't believe in any of that extra-marital activity you two are so fond of, I'll be home before midnight. Wouldn't want the car to turn into a pumpkin."

"See that you are," Diane said, finger wagging at me.

"Have a good time," Liz said. "I'll save you some leftovers."

"Thanks. Good luck with her." I nodded at Diane.

"I'll do my best. Might need to get out the straitjacket though."

"Whatever it takes." I waved and left.

~ ~ ~

When I got out of the car at Rodrigo's, I walked over to Star who had her head outside the corral rails. She nickered, and I gave her the apple slices I'd brought with me.

"You were waiting for me, weren't you, girl?" I cooed at her.

"I swear you're fonder of that horse than you are of me," Rodrigo complained as he approached.

"That's the sweet thing about animals," I said. "They don't have any hidden agendas. You know exactly what they want."

"True," he said, kissing me on the cheek. "Men are also supposed to be simple creatures. We like a good meal, a wide-screen television, and football."

"There's one more thing," I noted.

"Ah, yes … that." His smile had a wicked tinge to it. "But I think most women want that as well." He slipped an arm around me. "Don't you?"

"When the time is right," I said, ducking under Star's head to escape. "Like after a wedding." I shrugged. "But since I'm never getting married again, I don't have to worry about it. It's in the 'been there, done that, got the T-shirt' bucket."

He laughed. "I'll have to see what I can do to change your mind."

I shook my head. "My sisters have been trying to convince me of the benefits, but I'm not buying it."

"I love a challenge," he said with a grin. He gestured to the house. "I've set up a table on the patio. I wanted to do something simple tonight. I'm hoping steak, salad, and baked potato will do."

"Fine with me," I said as we walked to the patio.

The small round table was covered with a dark red tablecloth. Bright dishes waited for food, and a ceramic vase filled with roses lorded over the rest.

"The roses are for you to take home," he said.

"Thank you. That's lovely."

"You deserve roses," he said. He poured two glasses of rosé wine and handed one to me. "Happy Valentine's Day to the most unusual and beautiful woman I've met in a long time."

We clinked, and I made the mistake of looking into his dark brown eyes. They were looking at me with an intensity I hadn't seen before.

The slumbering desires within me that had been stirring within me since I'd met Rodrigo jolted awake. For the first time in many years it seemed like making love to someone might be a better idea than I'd thought it to be. My breasts ached, and my lower belly softened.

I looked away.

"Thank you," I said.

He gestured for me to sit down. We chatted for a while about the white elephant sale. I told him about the flare-up when the cousin introduced her boyfriend to the sister-in-law, but didn't mention what Trixie Lynn had said. Like she'd said, I was leaving and there was no point in wondering about Rodrigo sticking to his vows.

"I'm glad the cousin finally put her foot down," he said. "It was getting a bit ridiculous."

"Me too," I said. "I was quite sure your sister-in-law was going to find a relative to do me in if I didn't disappear soon."

"You were right to be worried," he said. "I was getting a little concerned for my own safety." Tentatively, he caressed the back of my hand, the light touch letting me know the instant I objected the caress would be gone.

I didn't say anything.

He looked at me quizzically. "There's something different. Haircut?"

"How did you know?"

"Because when I think there's something different about a woman, it's almost always a haircut." He frowned. "Hairdressers are so good. They totally change how a person looks, but somehow it looks like the same style."

"The woman who cut my hair would be depressed to hear that."

He laughed, and I joined him.

This was all new to me. Teenagers don't understand subtleties, and Michael hadn't gained any skills since we'd first gone out.

"Now, if I could convince Trixie Lynn that I'm not interested, and …" He took a breath. "If I could convince you to stay, I'd be a happy man."

"That's not possible," I said without giving it much thought.

"Isn't it?"

"I made a promise to my sisters to complete this trip," I said. "I'm keeping that promise."

"Yes. You must do that," he said. He stopped caressing my hand. "It was thoughtless of me to ask." He rose. "I'll put the steak on and get the salad."

I sipped my wine while I waited, my mind a mess of emotions. If I was truthful, I wanted more time with him. Somewhere along the way, my resistance to a new relationship had faded away, just as my sisters predicted it would if I met the right man. I thought I was falling in love with him. I wasn't sure what mature love was like, so I couldn't be sure.

It couldn't be love, could it? Love would mean that I'd jump at the chance to be with someone, no matter what the apparent difficulties. And I wasn't leaving Montana.

Or was that view of romantic love outdated? These days, did the man go with the woman as often as the other way around? Somehow I didn't think so, much as women liked to say that was true.

I pushed the thoughts from my head. I'd stick to the original plan. What was happening now was simply a moment in time, although it was a very sweet interlude.

Over dinner, we continued discovering new things about each other. He told me about his children growing up, and I traded stories about my two. It was only after dishes were cleared away, and we were enjoying another glass of wine that the topic of conversation I'd been avoiding came up.

"Tell me what happened with your marriage," he said. "I have a feeling there is something that went wrong. I would like to avoid doing anything to hurt you, something that might trigger that feeling."

I debated how best to answer this. I hadn't told my sisters the problem, and I felt they should know first.

"Michael had an addiction," I said. "That's really all I want to say. I asked him to get help, but he wouldn't. Things got worse. I …" I swallowed. "I covered for him when I probably shouldn't have. Problems become worse when you keep them hidden in the dark."

He nodded and held up his glass. "Alcohol?"

I shook my head.

"I hadn't thought so, but I wanted to make sure, in case my drinking disturbed you."

"No," I said. "It isn't a problem." I held up my own glass and smiled. "I enjoy it as well. My sisters and I often have 'cocktail hours' at the end of the day.

"I will let you have your secret," he said. "As long as you promise me if I do something that makes you uncomfortable, you'll let me know."

"Yes."

"Good then. Wait here, and I will get dessert."

He returned with two plates with slivers of dark chocolate cake.

"Wow," I said. "I didn't know you were a baker."

"I'm not," he said with a grin. "I'm an excellent orderer from the best bakery in this area."

He pulled a small box from his shirt pocket. "This is for you. Happy Valentine's Day. I hope you never forget the time you spent here with me."

"Oh." I took the box, not sure what to say. A gift seemed like a lot.

I opened it.

Sparkling blue stud earrings lay in the box.

"They're blue topaz," he said. "It's the state gem of Texas."

"They're lovely." I undid the earrings I had on and replaced them. "Thank you."

"Perfect," he said. He gestured with his fork. "I hope your cake meets your expectations as well."

The cake did.

We had more wine and talked some more.

When I stood up to start taking my leave, I realized I'd had more wine than I'd planned.

He must have noticed something. "Why don't you stay the night?" he asked. "The guest room has fresh sheets."

"My sisters …" I said.

"Text them. They'll be happier knowing you're safe."

While that was true, I also knew I'd be in for some serious razzing the next day.

But he was right. It was better for me to stay.

I nodded.

"Good," he said. "I don't want anything to happen to you." He pulled me close.

I wasn't drunk enough to be unaware of what was coming next.

Or that I wanted it.

I lifted my face and welcomed his lips on mine.

Chapter Twenty-Two

The next morning I woke with a start in an unfamiliar bed. A bed with incredibly soft, white sheets. A soft breeze blew through an open window, the bright blue curtains waving gently beside them.

Wherever I was, I could linger in this dream for a while.

Outside of the hotel Liz had treated us to in New York City, this was the most luxurious bedroom I'd ever been in.

I propped myself on my elbows and looked around, then slumped back down with a smile on my face.

Nary a sock nor a pair of jockey shorts anywhere.

Heaven.

I touched my lips, and elicited memories of Rodrigo's kiss. It had lasted a long while, growing slowly more erotic. When we broke apart, we looked into each other's eyes for a long time, as if trying to solve the mystery of each other's souls.

But I also knew there was an underlying question: Which bedroom would I sleep in that night?

For me, the answer was clear.

"I think we'd better stop," I said. "We've got church in the morning."

Cold water never cooled anyone down so fast.

"You're right. And I don't wish to go to confession first," he said with a somewhat lame smile. "I'll show you to the bedroom and where the guest bathroom is."

We'd said our goodnights, and he returned to the kitchen to clean up. I'd asked if I could help, but he'd flat-out refused me.

"You're my guest," he said.

Gratefully, I'd gone about my business in the bathroom, where a fresh toothbrush and toothpaste had been supplied for guests. Antonia deserved sainthood.

I'd looked longingly at the sparkling tub, but had known I needed to get to bed.

Now morning snuck through the windows and let me know it was time to face the music. If I was lucky, Rodrigo would be sleeping in, and I'd be able to avoid him.

Before I even left my bedroom, I figured it was not going to work out for me.

"Did you sleep well?" he asked as I walked into the kitchen.

"Amazing," I said. "I could have stayed in that bed forever … at least all day."

"Then you will need to come back and spend the entire day in bed sometime," he said with a grin. "That one … I mean … not anything else. Oh, god." He wiped his hand down his face.

I laughed. "I get what you mean." I was tempted to tell him the other meaning didn't sound too bad either, but I refrained.

"Breakfast?" he asked.

"No, I really need to get home if I'm going to be there on time for service."

He nodded.

"I understand," he said. "I would like to sit with you, if that is all right."

"That would be making a statement," I said.

"I know."

My chest tightened. It wasn't a good idea, especially not for him. What if he wanted to date one of the women in the congregation after I was gone?

The image of him with someone else made it hurt to swallow.

But if this was all the time I was allotted with this man, I was going to take it.

"I'd be delighted," I said.

"I'll save you a foot of pew," he said with a smile.

"Sounds like a plan. I'd better get going."

"Yes. I suppose." He leaned in and kissed me. "Do you have your earrings?"

I nodded.

He pulled the roses from the vase and wrapped a plastic bag on the bottom. "Don't forget these."

"Thank you again," I said. "For everything. It's the best Valentine's Day I've had in … well … a long time."

"I'm glad," he said.

He walked me to the car, and Star nickered good morning.

I kissed his beard-roughened cheek and left.

~ ~ ~

The walk of shame into the RV went about the way I'd thought it would.

"Well," Liz said the moment I walked in. "Do you need to go to confession?"

"No," I said.

"Why not?" Diane asked.

"You know my position on all of that."

"I think you're carrying this too far," Liz said.

"And I think it's none of your damn business."

"Well, you certainly made what I did your business," she shot back. "Now it's your turn."

I hadn't realized how annoyed she'd been when I'd expressed my opinion about her relationship with Walter. I glanced at Diane. She'd shrugged off my opinion much more easily.

Why?

"Hey," Diane said. "Maybe give her a break, okay?"

"You feel the same way I do," Liz said.

"I feel the same way you do for *me*," Diane said. "That doesn't mean what I believe is right for everyone else." She gave me a glance with that statement.

I got the message. If I didn't want them critiquing my way of living, I'd best back off on theirs.

"Okay," I said. "I'll never say another word about how you run your relationships if you stay out of mine."

"Unless you're invited in," Diane said.

Liz nodded.

"Got it. Now, if you'll excuse me, I've got to shower and get to church."

"You want me to take care of the flowers?" Diane asked. "They're nice, by the way."

I looked at the roses in my hand.

"That would be great, thanks." I handed the flowers to her.

Liz got up. "I'm proud of you," she said, giving me an unexpected hug. "I know how much you've been resisting any kind of relationship. Rodrigo's a nice man. For you to have a Valentine's Day dinner with him is a big step."

"I'm not going to marry him," I said. "I want to make that perfectly clear. When Diane's schedule says to leave, I'm driving us out of here."

"Of course," Liz said.

I squinted at her. "I mean it."

"Yes. I know you do," Liz responded.

Again, the tone of her voice didn't fill me with confidence.

"Was it a good time?" Diane asked.

"Yes," I said, my heart filling with warmth. "Nothing fancy, but he was fun to be with."

"Let's hear it for a man who's fun to be with!" Diane said.

I looked at the clock.

"Go, go," Liz said. "We'll make cocktails later and you can tell us all about it."

"As much as you want," Diane added.

I hustled back to my room to pull out new underclothes and an outfit to wear to church. I took a quick shower and refreshed my make-up. I was beginning to understand its use to inspire confidence. With my new hairdo and Rodrigo's attention, I was feeling stronger than I had in years.

Michael had ground me down more than I'd realized.

At the last moment, I put on the earrings Rodrigo had given me.

I almost made it back outside the RV.

"Wait!" Liz said. "What are those?"

"Blue topaz earrings," I said as matter-of-factly as I could.

"Did he give those to you?" Liz asked, coming to inspect them.

Diane rushed over too. "They're beautiful. Those aren't cheap either."

I touched my hands to my ears. I hadn't thought about cost when I'd accepted them. Michael hadn't bought me much jewelry beyond my engagement ring.

Did accepting the gift mean more than I'd thought it did?

"Stop it," Liz said. "You shouldn't have said anything about cost," she told Diane. She took my hands. "Look, he gave them to you because he wanted to. He likes you … probably a bit more than that. He's letting you know how much he cares for you. That's it. Accept the gift for what it is, his appreciation of his time with you, no matter how short."

"She's right," Diane said. "I shouldn't have said anything. They look great on you. Now go knock 'em dead, especially that Trixie Lynn person."

"Amen to that," Liz said. "Now scoot!" She gave me a gentle shove toward the door.

My confidence restored, I got back into the car and went to church.

~ ~ ~

I got there in plenty of time to slip into the pew next to Rodrigo before it became too crowded. As we waited for the processional, I was aware of how close he was. There was something surreal about being in church next to someone who meant something to me, even if I didn't know what that something was.

After the first year, Michael had become a Christmas-Easter Catholic, much to my parents' dismay. No amount of talking by my father could persuade him otherwise. So I'd spent the other times sitting near my parents, waiting for the children to rejoin me after their Sunday School lessons.

Rodrigo seemed peaceful sitting in the pew and waiting.

I looked around me. I'd never sat in this pew before. It was a bit like I was sitting in a whole new church. People are creatures of habit and tend to sit in the same place in the same space. If teachers didn't have seating charts, classes sorted themselves out. Woe to the person who took someone else's place.

From my new pew, I got a different perspective on the people around me. Where I couldn't see faces before, now I could. At the same time, I was presented with a new array of hair arrangements to view from behind.

Fascinating.

The sister-in-law didn't come to this service, but I spotted the cousin, who gave me a wave and a thumbs up.

A few of the older women cut their gaze away when they saw me looking, but the men were thinking of something else, most likely their golf scores from yesterday or whatever sport they were watching this afternoon.

I tried to take Liz's tack of not caring what other people thought, but it went against my mother's indoctrination. It was *all* about what people thought of me.

Rodrigo put his hand on top of mine and squeezed gently, reassuring me that he was near, although he didn't make a big deal of it.

The organ started.

As soon as we stood, he let go.

It was okay. I was now in safe territory.

Right up until the time to exchange the peace.

I turned behind me to shake hands, and ran smack into the cold blue eyes of Trixie Lynn. She held onto my hand a little too long and a lot too firmly. By the time I extricated myself, I was ready to move onto the next part of the service.

When it came time for communion, I took it with a clear conscience. I wasn't guilty of anything beyond a nice dinner with an equally nice man.

At least that's how I viewed it.

Because of our positions in the pews, Trixie Lynn was outside before we were.

Rodrigo didn't push things by taking my hand, but every once in a while I could feel his hand on the small of my back. It kept me anchored.

I'd been aware that things would shift the moment I put my rear in the pew next to his, but I still wasn't prepared for the reality of the intensity of the feelings. My skin tingled with the observation of people around me.

The priest—God bless his soul!—acted like the two of us together was the most natural thing in the world.

Trixie Lynn planted herself in our path as soon as she was able.

"Thank you so much for your help yesterday," she gushed.

"No problem," I said. "Glad to help."

A man asked Rodrigo something, and he drifted away.

"Pretty earrings."

"Yes." I took a deep breath. "Rodrigo gave them to me last night."

"Oh?"

Rodrigo turned back in time to hear her next words.

"Just don't forget what I told you," she hissed before walking away.

"What does that mean?" Rodrigo asked.

"Nothing," I said. "Nothing at all."

Except that wasn't entirely true.

Chapter Twenty-Three

It began raining Sunday afternoon and continued for the next two days. My sisters and I watched movies on Sunday, but went our separate ways on the days that followed. Liz went to the studio she rented, Diane immersed herself in her photo program, and I spent time weaving with Genna. It felt good to simply create, watching the pattern emerge as I passed the shuttle back and forth. No decisions needed to be made about life. All I needed to do was live it.

On Wednesday, the clouds dissipated. We decided to take in some of the missions we'd been wanting to see. There was a whole array of them south of San Antonio. The Alamo may have been the most famous, but the Catholic missionaries had been busy in Texas in the early 1700s.

We set out early and headed for Mission Concepción. The grounds and the large white church gave us ample time to stretch our legs and explore. Diane snapped lots of pictures, while Liz took some with her phone, trying to get ideas that she could turn into paintings.

Not having anything to be busy with, I contemplated the purpose of the missions. To have so much faith that leaving the safety and comfort of one's homeland to come to a dangerous place to spread God's word was something I would never be able to comprehend. While I believed in my religion, I didn't feel any need to leave home and impose it on someone else.

Because that's what really happened most of the time. It wasn't only about spreading belief. The monks were often accompanied by soldiers. If the natives wouldn't accept the Christian God willingly, there were other ways to convince them to convert.

But still, between them, they left behind some beautiful architecture and places that still reverberated with spirituality, at least to me.

Even though we were together, we didn't spend much time talking, each of us lost in our own thoughts. I spent some time in the church itself, thinking about my life.

I'd always known my purpose was to take over the ranch. Once I was married, being a good wife and mother were important to me and gave me satisfaction. Was it a purpose? Probably as good as any. I'd never felt any need to make my mark on the world like Liz had done. I suspected now that she'd found photography and Joe, Diane's life might grow in the same direction.

Would I ever feel the need to display my weaving as art?

Probably not. I had the more practical bent of my father. If I ever felt I was good enough at it, I'd make gifts for people, or make clothing that could be donated to charity. Yes, that felt right to me.

"You ready for the next one?" Liz asked.

"Yep." We fetched Diane, then headed to Mission San José.

Once again, I was amazed at the architecture they'd been able to create with simple building materials. There was a rose window, full of curves displaying elements of the Baroque and Rococo styles that had been prevalent in Europe at the same time.

One of the Fathers must have been a recent immigrant.

"Imagine," Diane said. "People must have spent their entire lives working on this. They may not have ever seen it completed."

I nodded, once again marveling at the strength of some people's beliefs to impel them to envision a dream and start it down the road to completion, not even knowing that if it ever would be done before they died.

"It's been a great trip," I said to her. "I'm so glad you suggested it."

"Suggested?" she asked with her eyebrow arched. "I seem to remember I had to do a lot of arm twisting to get you two to agree."

"You know how I feel about change," I said.

"Avoid it at all costs," she answered.

I nodded.

"Is that the problem with Rodrigo?" she asked, voicing the question I'd almost been able to articulate to myself.

"I don't know," I said. "When I went riding with him, I hadn't anticipated anything serious developing. He just seemed like a nice guy. It had been so long since I'd been riding just for pleasure. And Star's a dream." I grinned. "He says I'm more in love with the horse than …"

"Than him?" she suggested.

"He didn't actually say that," I answered.

"But it was implied."

"Sorta."

"But you wouldn't be all tied in knots if you didn't feel anything for him," she said.

"I suppose so. But it's impossible."

"Why?"

"Isn't it obvious? He lives here. I live there." I pointed to the north. "Besides, that's rushing things. I don't even know what he wants. Or what I want. I swore I'd never be with another man after Michael. The risk is too great."

"If Michael wasn't already dead," she said, "I'd kill him because he obviously hurt you very badly. Are you ready to talk about it yet?"

I shook my head.

"Well, try not to let it stop you from opening up to what Rodrigo has to offer."

"Trixie Lynn said he cheated on his wife," I blurted out.

"Trixie Lynn would say anything to get you out of the picture. She's had her eye on him for ages. You're spoiling her plan."

I shook my head. "He wasn't in love with his wife. He's told me as much. The marriage was forced on him by his father."

"I didn't think people still did that in this day and age."

"From what I gathered, it didn't need to be that particular woman, just a traditional Latina woman."

"Not an Anglo."

"Exactly. He chose her because he loved her."

"Wait … I thought you said he didn't love her."

"He wasn't *in love* with her," I said. "But he cared deeply for her and loved her more over time."

"Splitting hairs if you ask me," Diane said.

"Are we talking about anything good?" Liz said as she came up to us.

"No," I said at the same time Diane said, "Rodrigo."

"Oh good. It's about time we discussed him," Liz said. "But let's do it over lunch. I'm starving."

~ ~ ~

We found a cafeteria style restaurant nearby. I felt like I was in high school again, only with a much better selection. Without shame, I carb-loaded. Since we'd gotten to the south, I'd been delighted to find macaroni and cheese as a regular side dish. Much better than coleslaw, and with potato salad it was always a risk that some fool added eggs to it.

If I'd wanted egg salad—which was gross—I'd ask for it.

When we were seated at the table, Liz wasted no time bringing up Rodrigo.

I stoically ate my food.

Diane wasted no time in blabbing what I'd told her.

Once those two had stopped clutching their own secrets like an old woman hanging onto her pearls, they'd decided everyone—which meant me—should get on board.

I was having none of it.

"Have you asked him how he feels?" Liz asked.

"No."

"How about what he wants?" Diane asked.

"Nope."

He'd already told me he wanted me to stay. I was the problem. Before I'd met him my cereal-for-dinner dreams were intact. Now he—and Antonia—had blown them to smithereens. I didn't have any idea what to do for a replacement.

"Look," I said, putting down my fork. "Let's say he wants me to stay down here, or come back when the trip is over. Where am I supposed to stay? What am I supposed to do for money? I've got a job back at the ranch."

"A job that Patrick is doing quite well," Diane said. "I've looked at the numbers since we've been on the road. They're better than they have been for several years."

"Michael was sick!" How dare she accuse me of sloughing off my duties?

She raised her hand. "That's not what I meant at all, and you know it. Liz and I are in awe that you kept it going and handled everything else as well. I'm only saying that you can relax about it. We're happy to pass the ranch along to your kids. We'll figure out the particulars when we get home.

"But that also means you can be free to live your life however you want to live it. You're no longer tied to the ranch."

I got what she was saying, and the idea terrified me.

Who was I if I wasn't in Montana?

"We'll support you with whatever you want," Liz said. "But if there's a possibility for you to get a second chance for happiness, we're all for that."

"You know," I said. "You two have become insufferable since you fell back in love."

"Of course," Liz said. "That's why we want you to try it."

"He wants me to stay," I confessed. "He told me that the other night."

"That's wonderful!" Liz clapped her hands together.

"Is it what you want?" Diane asked.

"I don't know. I feel like I don't know him well enough to make that decision. It's huge. And I can't change up my life as easily as the two of you seem to be able to do."

"He's not Michael," Liz said.

"No, he's probably got different issues."

My sisters were quiet. There really wasn't much to say in reply. We all had issues, problems that changed over time as our lives evolved. Some of us dealt with them better than others.

Diane changed the topic back to the missions we'd seen, for which I was grateful.

After lunch we continued onward to the final two missions, including a stop at the Espada Aqueduct, a small bridge constructed of stone designed to let water flow over the river below it. The water in the aqueduct was used to irrigate fields.

So much of people's lives back then, not unlike my own, had been focused on the production of food.

When we got back to the RV late that afternoon, we were all quite ready for cocktail hour. My brain was stuffed with all I'd learned and felt. Although we hadn't talked about it again, I'd ruminated on my relationship with Rodrigo as we'd wandered around the missions.

Was there a middle ground? There was nothing to say I couldn't take the RV back down to Texas when we were done with our trip. That would give me a place to stay to see if there really was anything to build on with the man.

Trixie Lynn wouldn't be happy, but that was her problem.

Thinking of her brought up the thing that she'd told me. My sisters had felt it was a lie, but I wasn't sure. If I asked him, he could refute it, just like Michael had every time I'd brought up his gambling.

That was my big secret. Michael had gambled. At first it was little things—football pools or a friendly poker game. But he began to make some money at it and placed more and more bets on a variety of things. He'd tell me he was going fishing with his friends and go to an Indian casino instead.

Things started going missing from the house, like the Bowie knife.

Then someone told me they'd seen him at one of the casinos. He'd been placing heavy bets.

Finally, that time when I confronted him, he'd told me it was none of my business. He'd hit a bad streak, but he'd recoup everything soon.

But he hadn't. He'd gotten ill instead. He'd had to pay off some nasty people, and our savings dwindled to nothing.

What if I let myself fall for Rodrigo, and he turned out the same way?

I'd be devastated.

But if I didn't take the chance, I might miss the opportunity to enjoy something better than I ever had in all my life.

Chapter Twenty-Four

What was I supposed to wear?

Rodrigo had invited the three of us to a family gathering to celebrate someone's birthday. As Liz had so kindly pointed out, being invited to a family event was an important step in a relationship. It meant moving beyond casual and into serious territory.

It had happened way too quickly. I'd barely known him a month. On the other hand, I'd known Michael all his life, and we'd dated for at least a year before I was invited to a family event. It had been another year after that before he was welcome at one of my small family birthday parties.

Besides, all of that time we'd grown up in the same place. Born and raised Irish Catholic in Butte, Montana made someone have a particular viewpoint of the world. Once we were old enough, we all drank green beer on Saint Patty's Day. A hard-knocks mining town, Butte raised its children with a rough love, toughening them up for whatever was thrown their way.

Growing up in a city that was sinking beneath your feet, home to one of the largest superfund clean-up sites in the country meant you grew up with a chip on your shoulder and your fists clenched.

I knew who I was.

Who was Rodrigo?

"You ready?" Diane called.

"Not yet."

"Okay. He's *your* boyfriend," she shouted back.

"He's not my boyfriend!" What a stupid thing to call someone who was in his sixties.

"Right," Liz shouted.

Sisters. I should leave them home.

But then I'd have to face the demon ladies of Rodrigo's family alone. He'd warned me his younger sisters clung to the traditional ways, much like his parents and his wife had done. They were not pleased he was seeing someone Anglo. Worse than that, someone who wasn't from Texas.

With a sigh, I chose a blouse and capris. He'd told me the gathering would be casual, but it hadn't sounded that way to me. A few of the family were musicians and would be playing. There would be the inevitable piñata for the grandchildren. A few of the younger generation were charged with organizing games for the children, and some were instructed to help with the three babies that would be there.

It sounded like chaos, totally different yet totally the same as a good Irish shindig.

Topaz earrings in my lobes and makeup carefully applied, I emerged from the bedroom.

"Finally," Liz said. "I thought we were going to have to go in there and dress you ourselves."

I gave her the stink eye.

It didn't work as well as it had at the beginning of the trip. She'd caught on that I was all bark and no bite.

"Stop ragging on her," Diane said. "This is a big deal. She's got to be nervous."

"That's why she has us," Liz said. "We're her wingmen … women … wingwomen."

"I'm right here," I said.

"Three musketeers!" Liz shouted.

"So do we have wings or capes?" Diane asked.

"Whatever it takes," Liz said. "No one's going to mess with our sister. And if any of the family disses her in any way …" She drew back her fist. "Pow!"

As silly as they were being, my heart just about burst in two with their support. It was going to be all right. Even if the traditional women snubbed me, my sisters would have my back.

"Okay," I said. "Let's go. I'm ready."

Liz led the way to the car, and soon we were off.

Diane was deliberately chatty, talking about a few shots she'd manipulated and her plans to go tromping around Montana when we got back.

"I've always wanted to have a photo in *Montana Outdoors*," she said. "That's my goal. It may take years, but I'm going to go for it."

"That's wonderful!" Liz said. "Those pictures are always so amazing, everything from eagles to bumblebees."

"And some of the most amazing landscape photos I've ever seen," I said. "Pictures taken by ordinary people on their way from one place to the next."

"Or someone who's planned for years to be at the right spot at the right time," Diane said.

My memory was flooded with some of the pictures I'd seen in the magazine sent out by the Montana Department of Fish, Wildlife, and Parks. The images made me homesick.

There was no way I could move to Texas permanently.

~ ~ ~

Cars were parked everywhere in the spot between Rodrigo's house and the barn. Kids and parents petted the horses, steady quarter horses Rodrigo had told me he was going to put in the corrals closest to the house. He'd banished the Arabians to a far field.

"They're good animals, but too skittish to be around kids," he'd told me. "Neither they nor the children would fare well."

Even though we'd been told to bring nothing, Liz had made up a few trays of brownies and carried them in with us. We also had a bottle of wine and a six-pack of beer.

Rodrigo must have spotted us, because he met us before we'd even made it halfway down the path. After greeting my sisters, he kissed me.

On the mouth.

In front of my sisters.

Liz merely arched an eyebrow while Diane winked at me.

"I'm so glad you could come," he told us. "And I see you have disobeyed me once again and brought food and beverages."

Liz shrugged. "Blame our mother. We never went anywhere empty-handed."

"My mother felt the same," he admitted with a smile. "Come, come. My family is anxious to meet the wild people from Montana that I've been spending time with."

Anxious to give me the once over.

I squared my shoulders. They weren't going to intimidate me. I had the pride and honor of Butte, Montana to uphold.

Even before my eyes adjusted to the dim light of the vine-covered patio, I knew they were staring. Four eyes watching every move I made. Lying in wait for my first mistake so they could tsk tsk my crassness.

Or whatever the Spanish version of tsk tsk was. And I had no doubt they had one. No matter the culture, there were always women of a certain age and disposition looking for the errors other women made.

Rodrigo made introductions, and I was quickly overwhelmed by names and relationships. There were two names I hung onto:

Esmerelda and Lucia. They were already anti-Kathleen.

But on the other end of the spectrum was the man who came up to me and immediately put his arms around me and gave me a hug.

"Don't worry about them, darling," he said. "They're horrible to everyone except the chosen few. And let me tell you, I'm not one of those."

I tried to place him in the flurry of names Rodrigo had given out.

"I'm Connor, Danny's husband. Which makes *them* my sisters-in-law, a fact that totally pisses them off." He laughed, taking my stress level down by a third.

I looked around for my sisters to introduce them, but they'd been waylaid along with Rodrigo by his son, Juan.

"Don't worry about them. I'll find them at some point. I've heard of your artist sister. Most of her work has been too kitschy even for me, but I understand she's doing something totally different these days."

"Yes. She's doing some work in a completely different style."

"Do you think she'll let me see them? I own a gallery in San Antonio. I'd love to be able to show her work."

"You'll need to talk to her about that," I said.

"I will. In the meantime, let's get you a drink. You'll need it for this group. I still have scars from my first family gathering. Oh, those women can skewer a person without saying a word!"

As I was led away to the drinks table, I looked over my shoulder at Rodrigo.

He gave me a shrug and a smile.

Connor took me under his wing and made sure I got to know his husband, Danny. He also re-introduced me to Rodrigo's brother, Felipe, the fourth child of the family, and his Anglo wife, Susan.

"Ah, yes," she said. "The sisters are *not* pleased. But I am. I've never seen my brother-in-law this happy. You're good for him. I hope you stick around."

"Well," I said, "I actually live in Montana. My sisters and I are on an extended road trip in an RV."

"How fascinating!" she said. "You must tell me all about it."

By the time I finished telling Susan about our adventures, my sisters and Rodrigo managed to catch up to me.

"How are you doing?" he asked me.

"I've had a delightful time with Connor, Danny, Felipe, and Susan."

"Good. They are the safe ones." Rodrigo introduced my sisters to the four family members. The discussion of RV life picked up from where we'd left off.

"I can't imagine going anywhere for that long with my family," Felipe said with a shake of his head. He was a good looking man with thick gray hair and a mustache to rival Rodrigo's. His smile was slow and his love for his wife evident. "Even my wife and I would have to have some space, I think."

"It would have to be a very large RV," she agreed with a grin.

"We've had our moments," Diane agreed. "Fortunately, we all have different interests so we can get away from each other. Whenever we're somewhere for any length of time, Liz rents a studio. She's a very popular artist."

"Yes," Connor said to Liz. "I can't wait to talk to you. See if I can show your new works in my small gallery."

"He's modest," Danny said. "His gallery is one of the top ten in San Antonio."

"I'd love to discuss a show with you," Liz said graciously.

"And what do you do?" Susan asked Diane.

"I've recently taken up photography," she said. "I'm spending a lot of time getting to know my camera and some of the online programs I can use to edit the pictures I take." She pointed to me. "And Kathleen's a weaver."

"What a talented family," Susan said.

"You're a weaver?" Rodrigo asked, almost at the same time. "You never told me this."

"It didn't seem important," I said. "I do it for myself. And I'm still learning."

"She's making the most incredible-looking lace," Liz said, startling me. I hadn't thought she'd noticed.

"You can weave lace?" Connor asked.

"Not me. I'm just learning. But yes, people can weave lace."

"I agree with Susan," Connor said. "A very talented family." He looked at Rodrigo. "You've chosen well."

"Um," I said. "We're just friends. No one's chosen anyone." I needed to put the record straight.

Pain flashed in Rodrigo's eyes. It disappeared quickly.

"That's true," he said with a smile I knew was false. "After all, they're off on their adventure in a few weeks."

"And you can't convince them to stay?" Danny asked.

"Not so far," Rodrigo said.

"Well, we'll have to help you out," Connor said.

"Thank you," Rodrigo said to his brother-in-law. "But I think I'll handle this on my own."

"You have to forgive Connor," Susan said. "He's so helplessly in love with Danny that he thinks everyone else should be in the same state."

"I've got the same problem," I said, nodding at my sisters.

The laughter that followed eased the tension somewhat, but I still felt badly for the hurt I'd given Rodrigo.

I hadn't realized how invested he was in our relationship. Like my sisters said, family introductions were a big deal. I wish I'd believed them and begged off from the party.

But it was too late now, and I was going to need to deal with the fallout.

"I'll be right back," I said. "I need to visit the powder room."

I turned away, and Diane followed. "It's a one-seater," I whispered.

"Just checking to see if you're okay."

"I will be when I'm done in the bathroom. Which I'm doing. Alone. By myself. Okay?" For some reason I was seriously aggravated.

"Sure," she said, and veered off toward the drinks table.

I went to the guest bathroom and frowned at my face in the mirror. This whole situation was getting way too complicated. What had started as a friendly horseback ride was turning into a family drama worthy of a telenovela.

It was a far cry from the world I'd envisioned for myself after we returned to Montana, and I settled into Liz's old house. There, I'd imagined blissful mornings of sleeping in while someone else milked the cows. Showers with lots of hot water. A toilet where the seat was always down.

A girl can dream, can't she?

I took care of my business, thoroughly washed my hands, and left. Instead of returning to the chaos on the patio, I went to the kitchen to see if Antonia was there, masterminding the whole event.

"Ah, Kathleen," she said when I walked in. She bustled over and gave me a solid hug. "It's so good to see you again."

"You too. Looks like you've been busy."

"It's mainly organizing. The family brings everything. At least they think they do. There is always the person who brings filling for tacos, but forgets the shells, or sour cream, or guacamole."

"It's hard to remember everything."

"Si. I spent yesterday making stacks of tortillas."

"You make your own?"

"Yes. It's not that much work, and they taste so much better than store bought. I can show you sometime."

My immediate reaction to spending more time in the kitchen was revulsion, but I hesitated with my refusal. What would it be like to spend time with this kind, talented woman who had no problems teaching an Anglo how to make tortillas? It would be something I could learn for myself, not because it needed to be on the table at any particular time.

"I would have liked that," I said. "But since we're leaving in a few weeks, that won't be possible."

"I'm so sorry to hear that," she said. "And you won't be back after your trip ends?"

"I don't think so."

"That's too bad. You're good for him. He's had a lot more energy since you arrived. Before that, I think he was at a loss. Juan's been taking over more and more of the ranch duties, and I don't think Rodrigo knows what to do for the next stage of his life."

"I know the feeling." As much as I was looking forward to all my alone time, I wasn't sure what I'd do with myself. I'd been busy for almost four decades.

But a man wasn't the answer. No, I'd have to figure out the next stage of my life on my own. Rodrigo would need to do the same.

"Well," she said. "If you do come back, the offer stands."

"The offer to do what?"

I turned. One of the two sisters who'd been watching my every move, stood in the doorway. Esmerelda?

"Teach her to make tortillas."

"Pah!" Esmerelda spat out, almost literally. "She'll never learn. She was raised on corned beef not chili con carne."

"Anyone can learn anything," Antonia said, a slight chastising in her voice.

"Not when they're that old."

I'd had enough.

"I'm no older than you," I said. "I learn things almost every day. Maybe not big things like tortillas, but it could be a word or two in Spanish. Like la anciana. I think it fits you perfectly. To be an old woman, you need to think like la anciana. I do not."

I turned to Antonia. "Thanks for the offer. I'll think about it." Then I turned back to Esmerelda. "And, if you ever want to learn to drive a Class A RV motorhome, I'm your woman. But you're probably used to driving a Ford sedan, not a truck, being a woman and all."

"I ... I ..."

I left Esmerelda sputtering and Antonia with a grin on her face.

As I left, I realized I shouldn't have done that. Where the older sister might have been an enemy, she was definitely one now.

Oh well, only two more weeks. Maybe one more ride to say good-bye to Star. Then we were off to the Grand Canyon.

I slipped onto the patio and watched the festivities for a while. There was lots of laughter, a few serious discussions, and a group of teenagers who had migrated to the darkest corner of the space. As I watched, a girl and boy slipped from the group and off the patio.

Moments later, one of the older men walked in the same direction. As I watched, the teens snuck back onto the patio, eyes focused on the ground.

One of the benefits of a large family was that someone was always on the lookout for bad behavior.

Esmerelda stalked back onto the patio.

But who kept the adults in line?

"Hello again," Juan said, coming up to me. "Do you need anything? A drink perhaps?"

"Thank you," I said. "I'm fine."

"That's good. My father wouldn't be happy if you weren't attended to."

I chuckled. "Did he really say that?"

"Not in so many words, but it was how he was about Mamá. As the oldest son, I was charged with attending to her, along with my sister, Miranda." He pointed to a woman about his age who was talking with a few other women.

"I'm sorry your mother passed," I said. "You must miss her."

He nodded. "It was difficult for my father."

"He must have loved her very much." Even though Rodrigo had denied the feeling, a person couldn't be married for decades without developing *some* feelings.

The rumor Trixie Lynn had passed on snaked through my memory.

"He loved her and cared for her," Juan said. "And I'm sure he misses her, but ..." He gave a gentle shrug.

I waited for him to continue.

"It's not important," Juan finally said. He smiled. "Are you sure you don't need anything?"

"Quite sure."

"Okay." He started to move away, then turned back. "Don't let my aunts get to you. They're hopelessly old-fashioned, and everyone ignores them. Makes them mad." This time the shrug was genuine. "Serves them right."

I grinned at him.

"Thanks," I said.

"No problem."

After he left, I looked around for my sisters. Liz was engaged in conversation with several women, while Diane was seated by a young girl, listening intently to whatever the girl was telling her.

My sisters were good people, able to rise to the occasion and beyond.

The clink of coins caught my ear, and I turned toward the sound. A small group of people surrounded a felt-topped poker table. Some were emptying bags of coins in front of them while one person was shuffling cards. They were chatting and smiling as they set up the game.

My breath stopped.

I stared at them for a few more moments before realizing Rodrigo wasn't there. Then my lungs began to inhale and exhale again, and I turned away. Spotting a chair in a quiet corner, I went there to sit down. I hadn't been sitting for more than a few moments, when I noticed a wide-eyed boy making his way toward me. I figured him to be about six, with the thick black hair and wide mouth that many of Rodrigo's family had, including him. Rodrigo's grandson, Marcos.

When the boy saw I'd spotted him, he looked away.

Deliberately, I turned my head in another direction, but was still able to keep an eye on him from my peripheral vision.

Once he realized I wasn't watching him, he resumed his steady walk toward me.

I stayed quiet, and soon was rewarded with the feel of a small body leaning close to me. A hand reached out and touched my hair.

Unsure whether or not to move, I waited a few seconds while he explored the texture.

Then, I slowly turned and looked at him. "Hello," I said with a smile.

"Hello," he said, not removing his hand from my hair.

"My name is Kathleen," I said.

"Hi Kathleen," he said, maneuvering his mouth around the syllables.

"And who are you?"

"Marcos," he said.

"Marcos is a nice name."

He shrugged and stopped stroking my hair. "You have different hair," he informed me.

"Yes. It used to be kind of red. Now it's gray."

"My tia's hair is gray, but it doesn't look like yours," he said, pointing to one of Rodrigo's sisters, who was technically his great-aunt.

"I bet her hair was black like yours once."

He slapped his hand on his head, and his eyes widened. "Will my hair become gray?"

"Not for a long time. And then you'll look very distinguished."

"What's 'stingished?"

"Handsome," I said. "Like him." I pointed to Rodrigo, who turned around at that moment, spotted me, and started walking my way.

"That's Abuelo," the boy said.

"Oh? Is that your Papá?" I pointed to Juan.

"Yes. You know my papá?"

"I've met him."

"I love my papá," Marcos said.

"Of course you do," I said.

"I see Marcos is entertaining you," Rodrigo said.

"Yes, we're having a good conversation."

"This lady says you're handsome," Marcos helpfully said.

"Oh, did she now?" Rodrigo asked.

"Yes. She said I'd look like you when I got old." The frown came back. "That won't happen for a long time."

"No, Marcos," Rodrigo said. "Not for a long time."

"Okay. Bye!" With a wave, Marcos ran off to join some other kids, probably all related to him in one way or another.

"He's cute," I said to Rodrigo as I stood.

"Handsome, huh?"

"The word I used was actually distinguished, but he had a little problem with that."

"I can imagine," Rodrigo said. "But I'll take that too. Are you having fun?"

"Yes. It is interesting to see so many people related to you."

"And you haven't yet met my own papá," he said. "He's in an assisted living facility not far from here. He finds it hard to walk."

"Wouldn't your sisters take care of him?"

Rodrigo laughed. "They tried. He spent a few weeks with each and then decided assisted living was a better choice."

"Smart man," I said with a chuckle.

The clink of coins broke through my consciousness again.

"Is that a regular thing?" I gestured toward the poker table.

"At gatherings? Yes. There's usually a game going. Friendly. Small change. No one is going to go broke at that table. Have you ever played?"

"No."

"It can be a fun game—you need skills in strategy and observing other people. But a lot of us like games of pure chance. In fact, the parish is running its monthly bingo game next week. You should come with me."

"You play bingo?"

"Only at church. It's for a good cause. I didn't used to go, but Antonia told me if I didn't leave the house more often she was going to quit. Losing her was not an option."

"Definitely not."

"So you'll come with me?"

"Um … I don't know." My chest squeezed a bit.

"Please. Just for fun. I'll buy you a couple of cards, and we can have a good time. All the money goes to the church's outreach programs."

Surely I could make it through a bingo game.

"Okay, I'll go."

"That's great! We'll have fun."

"We have to plan a time to go riding again, soon," I said, wanting to move on from the whole subject of gambling in all its forms.

"Yes. That's true. Does Tuesday work for you?"

"I think so. I'll text you."

"Good. I want to spend every moment I can with you before you leave."

"Oh?"

"Yes. It will take every minute to execute my campaign to get you to come back."

"Well, now I'm warned. My guard will be up."

"Then I'll have to leave you defenseless."

"Just how are you going to that?"

"Like this." He pulled me close and kissed me.

Right there.

In front of God and everybody … including his sisters.

Chapter Twenty-Five

As soon as I swung into the saddle on Star's back, a sense of peace and rightness descended on me. The Arabian was the horse I'd needed all my life. Although I'd read the horse classics as a kid, books like *Black Beauty*, *Misty of Chincoteague*, and *The Black Stallion*, I'd considered them fantasies. Dad had treated horses like every other working animal on the farm. They weren't pets, they had to earn their keep.

The idea of keeping a horse to ride, an animal that served no other function, would be crazy to him.

Because I'd adored my father and took every bit of his teaching to heart, I'd treated animals the same way.

Until Star.

There was a connection with the horse that I'd never felt with any animal before. I'd never adopted a kitten or claimed one of the many dogs as mine like Liz and Diane had done. Part of it was the reality of ranch life. I didn't want to come home one night and find out we were having Jenny-burgers for dinner.

Part of it was a strange reluctance to give myself totally over to anyone or anything.

I'd picked the worst time to change that attitude.

"You're a good girl, Star," I whispered, leaning over her withers and patting her neck. "I'm going to miss you."

"Ready?" Rodrigo asked as he, too, swung into the saddle.

"Yep."

Once again Antonia had packed a lunch. We were taking the path through the ranchlands that led to the preserve. The gentle clop of our horse's hooves on the ground was soothing. My body swaying to the rhythm of the horse lulled me. I could almost sense that God was in his heaven and all was right with the world.

If I was being honest, it wasn't only Star I was going to miss. Though I'd only known Rodrigo a short while, I'd become comfortable with him. There was an ease between us I'd never had with Michael. When we'd gotten the horses ready to ride this morning, there was no need for a lot of chatter. Our attention was on our horses, but the connection between us had still been there. Little things, like stepping to the shelf where the hoof pick was normally stored and having him hand it to me.

While we rode, we knew when to let our senses enjoy the sights, smells, and feel of being on a horse in beautiful country, and when to talk.

It was easy.

I wasn't sure I'd experienced easy companionship ever before in my life. My relationships with my sisters were sometimes heavy with baggage from the past. As time had worn on between Michael and me, we'd gone in our own directions. There was a rhythm to our daily lives, but it was always underlined with tension.

It wasn't this.

I smiled without effort. All around me, I could see the buds of the trees beginning to form, months earlier than they'd even think about it in Montana. Songbirds flitted around, on their way from wherever they spent the deepest part of winter to their nesting regions farther north. Even the smell of spring was in the air, that seductive combination of new grass and warm earth.

What if I did come back down in the summer? Or better yet, what if he came to Montana?

Where would I put him? I wasn't ready to share my bed, even if I did put aside my lifelong belief about sex belonging within the confines of a marriage.

The sexual revolution had passed me by long before I was born.

"Heavy thoughts?" Rodrigo asked.

"Not really," I said, unsure if that were true or not. "Just appreciating the day."

"It is a glorious one," he said. "This is the time of year I appreciate Texas the most."

"Spring in any place is glorious," I said. "All that new birth and life."

"I wonder what it would be like to have a year of spring."

"What do you mean?" I asked.

"Travel to places that are experiencing spring. Move slowly north as the season travels to the northern reaches of Canada, then pick up again in the Southern Hemisphere as the season begins down there."

"That sounds fun when you talk about it, but having been on the road for over half a year, I'm not ready to do anything except stay home."

"You're right," he said. "It does sound like fun, but the reality would defeat me. I like the steadiness of living here, seeing what my family has built, and watching the new generation take over." He shook his head. "Although that isn't as easy as I'd hoped it would be."

"What do you mean?"

"Every time Juan wants to change something, I'm resistant. Of course, my father was the same with me. I'd get a lecture about how the family had been running this ranch for centuries, and he knew what worked. It was tough to convince him the world was evolving and sometimes change was good."

"These days it seems like the world is changing at a dizzying speed," I said.

"Technology is taking over everything," he said. "Even things that are better left alone. Next thing you know they're going to put chips in us to fix what someone thinks is wrong with us. Our differences, which I believe are our greatest strengths as people, will be lost."

"I agree with you," I said. "Seems to me we lose more every day in our rush to be faster and more in control of everything. There's nothing like sitting on a back porch and watching the sun set."

"No," he said. "Especially if you are sitting there with someone you love."

There was nothing I could say. I didn't think I loved him. But I wasn't sure. Sometimes I thought I had no firmer grasp of what love was than I did when I was sixteen.

He seemed to grasp that I was done talking and moved his horse back ahead of mine. Soon we were riding through an open field at a slow canter, a gait that blew the wind through my hair and pumped up my heart rate as I used my muscles to maintain the horse's rhythm.

We settled down for lunch in the meadow we'd used before, not too far from a stream that was fuller than it had been. There were no mountains nearby. How far had that water had to travel before it reached the part where it flowed in front of us?

Not unlike the lives Rodrigo and I had had to live before we reached this exact moment in time together.

I watched him as he unloaded our picnic. There was economy in his movements, a man used to physical labor and how his body worked. As I waited, I realized my body was sending messages of awareness to my atrophied brain. My breasts tightened and warmth rushed to my abdomen. There was a flush to my skin.

Was I aroused?

It was such an alien feeling I almost laughed aloud.

But like a loose tooth that my tongue could never leave alone, I kept staring at the man. I tormented myself by remembering his kiss and wondering what his work-roughened hands would feel like on my most intimate places. I tried to remember my flesh as it once was, not the soft sagging that aging had brought to my shape.

At some point he looked up and caught me.

My cheeks flamed, and I quickly looked away.

"Hungry?" he asked in a way that clearly played on the double entendre.

"I'm always ready to eat whatever *Antonia* dishes up."

His grin was mischievous. "Nothing else?" he asked.

"Not at all."

"Liar," he said and leaned over to kiss me. He took his time with it, his lips exploring in a way that hinted at more pleasures that could be had.

It took all my strength not to wrap my arms around him and pull him down on top of me. Never had I felt so wanton, so ready to ignore everything I'd been taught in order to be satisfied in a way I never had been.

Finally, he released me.

"Well," he said. "That was interesting."

I lost the battle to ignore the statement.

"Why?"

"Because there was a lot more heat in that kiss than there's ever been before," he said. "You've always been in control, and I think it just slipped a little there."

"Everything's still the same," I declared.

"If you say so." He handed me a plate.

I picked through the offerings Antonia had sent, knowing everything would be delicious. It was only after we both had our plates full that I decided to respond to his comment truthfully.

"Okay. Yes. Something changed," I said. "But I'm not ready to put a name to it."

"Fair enough," he said.

"I don't do flings. I've been with one man my entire life. All of this is alien territory to me."

"While I did have relationships before and after my marriage," he said. "I was faithful to my wife, so I understand."

Were you? I wanted to ask. Trixie Lynn's rumor was still digging at me. But there were other things to discuss. Things that didn't descend so rapidly into perilous emotional waters.

He propped himself up on one arm and plopped a grape into his mouth. Once he'd swallowed, he said, "I've just bought another horse."

"Really? Arabian?"

"Yes. A yearling. Barely trained, but he has a good bloodline. I'm thinking of breeding him to Star."

"Poor Star. Being pregnant is so hard."

"Yes, but then we'll have a beautiful little foal. I'll even let you name it." His expression became serious. "Let me tell you what I dream about when I'm drifting off to sleep."

"Sure."

"As hard as it is for me, Juan's going to take over the ranch. He'll move into the big house with his family. It's only fair. I'll spend some money renovating the house he and his family have been using, and then move in there." He smiled at me. "There's plenty of room for two. Even two full bathrooms so you can have one all to yourself."

"I—"

"Antonia mentioned how much you liked her nice, clean bathrooms."

"Traitor."

"I just reminded her of who pays her."

I laughed.

"Anyway, I want to concentrate on raising and breeding Arabians. It will give me something to learn. Life is always enhanced by something new, don't you think?"

"Yes," I said, wondering what new things I could learn during Butte's winters.

"Not running the ranch would give me more time." He looked at me. "More time to see if I could convince the woman I care for to stick around. I could also live in Montana part of the year if that would sweeten the deal for her.

"We could make it work, Kathleen. If you're willing to try, that is."

My heart stirred again.

All my common-sense arguments railed against the idea of doing anything with this man.

But in affairs of the heart, common sense rarely wins over love.

"Let me think about it," I said.

"That's all I can ask," he said.

I asked him to tell me more about the new horse while we cleaned up.

Before we got back on our horses, we took a walk to the stream and indulged in more physical exploration.

I was really getting to enjoy this kissing stuff.

Chapter Twenty-Six

"A night of bingo sounds like fun," Diane said.

"It does!" Liz agreed. "It's been so long since I've played."

"I don't think I've done bingo since we were kids," Diane said. "Remember we got a set one Christmas? Mom would call out numbers while she did the ironing."

"I think she made them up," Liz said.

As I listened, I was mystified. I didn't remember bingo at all.

"We had to use pennies then," Diane said.

"Didn't Kathleen swallow one?" Liz asked.

No wonder I didn't remember.

"Um … I think so."

The pair of them turned to glare at me.

"What?" I asked. "I don't remember any of it. If I swallowed a penny, I seem to have survived."

"Yes, but Mom didn't let us play as much after that," Liz complained.

"It was hard enough for her to iron and call out numbers. But you were into everything when you were little."

"Yeah, we had locks on every cabinet you could reach," Diane added.

"I had to do that for Megan," I remembered.

"Serves you right," Liz said.

"I was a kid. You can't be seriously holding a grudge this long."

Diane and Liz looked at each other.

"We'll let it go if you let us come with you tonight," Liz said.

"As long as you promise not to swallow anything," Diane added.

"I think they use dabbers now," Liz said. "You know, those magic marker thingies."

"Oh, yeah."

"Rodrigo invited me," I said. "I don't remember him asking you two as well."

"He'll be delighted," Liz said. "He likes us."

"Yes. I promise we won't horn in on your date," Diane added.

"It's not a date."

"And the Pope's not Catholic," Liz said.

"It's a free country," I said with a shrug. "If you want to go to bingo, go to bingo."

"Is he picking you up?" Diane asked.

"No. Like I said, it's not a date."

"R-i-i-ght," my sisters chorused.

Truthfully, I was a little relieved they were coming. I was nervous about going. For the last few nights I'd been having nightmares, reliving the arguments I'd had with Michael, my stomach dropping with despair at the memories of our ever-dwindling bank account.

If my sisters were there, I could pretend it was all in fun. Rodrigo had promised he didn't take gambling seriously, but bingo is where Michael had gotten the bug.

My late husband had gotten a real high out of winning. It was losing he couldn't take. He'd get angry, blaming the casinos for cheating him, then yell at me for not being more supportive. Once he'd come close to hitting me, but something in my face must have stopped him.

If he'd followed through, I would have left.

At least that's what I told myself. I'd never had to make the decision.

With a flurry of activity, we got ready and were out the door in time to get to the church at six.

Rodrigo was waiting for me.

"I'm so happy you all decided to come!" he said with enthusiasm.

"Oh, we're not here to horn in," Liz told him. "We'll sit somewhere else."

"Nonsense," he said. "You're family and family sticks together."

Diane gave me a knowing glance.

After checking to see if anyone else was looking, I stuck my tongue out at her.

She shook her head with a smile.

We paid our money and got our cards. Rodrigo handed out dabbers, and we managed to find four seats together.

"I feel a winning streak tonight," he said.

I nodded, biting back the fear that statement brought up.

He chatted with Liz and Diane, not appearing to notice how quiet I was.

I could get through this. Rodrigo wasn't Michael. He couldn't have built a successful ranch if he had a gambling problem.

Or maybe he was just good at it, like Rhett Butler.

The caller got our attention and the games began. I tried to get into the spirit of the thing, and a few times I almost faked myself out enough to enjoy the game. But then a new wave of angst would wash over me, and I'd be pulled back into memories of the past.

Liz won the first game.

During the second game, I noticed Trixie Lynn. She spotted me about the same time and gave me an expression of disapproval.

I looked back down at my card.

"You missed one," Rodrigo said, pointing.

"Oh, yeah." I dabbed absently.

A moment later, he shouted, "Bingo!"

I dropped my dabber, and it clattered to the floor.

As we waited for the card to be checked, I attempted to retrieve it, bending myself into a pretzel shape to get between the chairs and under the table, giving my neighbors an unasked for view of my large bum.

How did I get myself into these situations? Or was it the O'Sullivan curse? Diane kept falling into water when she was going out with Joe. Even Liz had fallen into a pond.

Since I'd yet to take a water-logged tumble, maybe it wasn't true love with Rodrigo.

"Ow!" I banged my head on the table.

"What are you doing under there?" Rodrigo asked.

"Dabber." I held it up triumphantly as I emerged, red-faced, from under the table.

"I had extras," he said.

"No need."

"Okay," he said. "Everything okay?"

"Just dandy."

The next game began. As the numbers were called with no winner, tension ramped up in the room.

Finally, Rodrigo yelled, "Bingo!"

Again?

This time I held onto my dabber.

"I like winning," he said, after his card had been checked. "I could get used to it."

My chest tightened. All I could do was nod.

A few more games went by. Diane won once, as did Trixie Lynn.

Then Rodrigo won again.

With that game, we were out of cards, which was a relief.

"Guess that's it," I said.

"It doesn't have to be," Rodrigo said. "We're having so much fun. And I'm on a winning streak. Let me get us a few more cards."

"Um …"

"C'mon, Kathleen," Liz said. "Don't be a spoilsport."

It was my fault for never telling my sisters what had happened with Michael and me. Like them, I'd kept my damned secret to myself, and now I was paying for it.

"Sure," I said, caving. "But only a few."

"Bueno!" Rodrigo said and went to get the cards.

Diane inspected me. "You okay?"

"Sure. Just tired. I didn't sleep well last night."

Liz examined me. "You do look tired. Don't get sick now. We've got traveling to do, and we need our driver."

Rodrigo returned with the cards and his luck continued to hold as he won two out of the next three games.

My stomach became more and more nauseous.

Finally, we were out of cards.

"We have to go," I said, standing up with relief.

"If you must," Rodrigo said, standing as well.

Was that the gleam of winning in his eyes? Or was I imagining things?

He walked us out. Diane and Liz went on ahead to the car.

"Can I make you dinner on Friday night?" he said. "Our time together is short, and I must work harder at convincing you to come back when summer is done." He smiled. "Or maybe I can come to Montana to see you?"

"I don't know," I said. "There's a lot of work to do to get ready."

"But you have to eat," he said.

"I … yes … but …" The fear I'd felt in the church hall lingered.

"What's wrong?" he asked gently. "All evening I've felt like there's been something bothering you. Is it something I've done? Tell me. We can only fix it if you tell me what it is."

This was my chance to come clean. He was right. I knew it. Maybe I was only imagining things.

But if I told him, I'd have to admit my failure as a wife. My husband had strayed, not with another woman, unless you believed luck was a lady. But he'd been unfulfilled in some way, so he'd gone looking for the answers in a casino hall, no different from someone who searches for wisdom in the bottom of a bottle.

And as soon as Rodrigo realized what I'd lived with, how our hardscrabble ranch had remained that way because of Michael's gambling, and I'd done nothing about it, Rodrigo wouldn't want anything else to do with me.

I shook my head.

"There's nothing to talk about," I said. "I'll get back to you about dinner." I took a step away, then remembered my manners. "Thank you for suggesting this. It was fun."

Even I could tell I was lying.

"Goodnight," he said, taking my hand and kissing me lightly on the cheek. "We'll talk soon, okay?"

"Sure," I said. "Good night." With an incomplete smile, I extracted my hand and went to join my sisters.

~ ~ ~

Liz and Diane had kept up a constant chatter as we drove home, for which I was grateful.

It was only when we got home that they turned on me.

"What is up with you?" Diane asked.

"Yes, you've been downright weird all night," Liz concurred.

"I told you. I'm tired. That's all."

"That is so not all," Liz said. "Remember me? I've lived in your general vicinity for most of our lives."

"I don't want to talk about it," I said.

"Something tells me you need to do just that," Diane said.

"You're not my therapist."

"Maybe you need one."

"Take care of your own business!" I tossed my purse on the couch, not caring that Diane would have to move it before she made up her bed for the night.

"Whoa," Liz said. "Wait a minute. I don't know what's up, but we're only trying to help. Obviously, something was bothering you tonight, something major." She cocked her head. "Does this go back to whatever you aren't telling us about Michael?"

I was too frightened to tell them. The same litany of reasons I'd gone through with Rodrigo ran through my head. True, they wouldn't leave me in the lurch. They were my sisters.

And Liz's secrets had been far bigger than my own.

I should tell them.

They stood there, expectant.

I opened my mouth, but nothing came out.

A lifetime of keeping quiet was a habit that was too hard to break.

"Goodnight," I finally squawked out. "Thanks for coming with me. It was fun."

I walked to the back bedroom and closed the door firmly behind me.

Then I lay down on the bed without bothering to get undressed. What a mess.

I'd really begun to think there might be something with Rodrigo. I'd let myself hope that I'd get a second chance at this love stuff. I could see us together, growing old, watching sunsets on a porch in Montana or a patio in Texas, or maybe even on a beach in Hawaii.

God, how I wanted to experience that deep connection before I died.

But was it even possible for me? Diane and Liz provided good examples, but I didn't have faith enough I could turn away from the pain of the past to reach for a better future.

A tear rolled down my cheek.

I was paralyzed. As I lay there, I sent out a prayer to Mother Mary to guide me.

Then I got back up and got ready for bed, wiping away my tears as I did so.

Chapter Twenty-Seven

As soon as it opened the next morning, I was at the fiber store. I didn't need anything … except serenity.

I still had two projects I was working on: the table runner and the lace project. Both of those had languished over the last few weeks. I should start weaving again. The lace pattern took a lot of concentration. It would keep me from thinking about things that might have been.

If my mind was too distracted, though, I could make mistakes. That would be unfortunate. It was coming along nicely. The table runner took concentration, but my fingers were familiar with the pattern, and I was almost doing it by rote.

After receiving three texts from Rodrigo this morning, I put my phone on airplane mode. There was nothing I could say to him right now. I'd let myself mourn a little more, then send him a final text telling him it wasn't going to work for me and to have a nice life.

A phone call would more polite. But I couldn't bear to listen to his voice right now.

As for seeing him, that was out of the question.

So here I was with my first love: yarn. My mom had taught me to knit, just like she had with Liz and Diane, only with me it had stuck. I loved the repetitive motion that produced an actual thing that someone could use. Once she took me to the store—a discount place—to see the varieties and colors of yarn, I was hooked. There was yarn that was so delicate it could be used to crochet the doilies that my great-aunt loved, and other so bulky, fuzzy, and colorful, I could create wild scarves as gifts for my few friends.

Later I began to learn about the multitude of varieties of sheep, as well as other fiber producers like alpacas and camels. Spinning yarn and using it to create garments was a craft that went back almost to the beginning of human history.

It had always been mind candy to me, as well as a distraction.

Surely, it could be enough to stop the movie reel of my time with Rodrigo from running over and over again in my mind.

"Can I help you?" one of the sales clerks asked.

She looked familiar.

"I recognize you," she said, her smile broadening. "You came to the lace class. How is that going for you?"

"Slow, but steady," I said.

We chatted for a few moments about the challenges of the craft, then she said, "You have a good time browsing and let me know if you need anything."

It was one of the best traits of fiber stores and bookstores. Sales clerks were there to help, not hover. I'd visited quite a few fiber places on our trip, and they'd all been filled with friendly folk ready to chat about anything non-controversial.

People talked about personal problems and yarn problems, but politics and religion were left at the door. Just the click and swish of ancient tools and the continual murmur of women's conversations.

Serenity.

Maybe I should knit something in the evenings while we were watching television. It wasn't too early to get started on Christmas gifts. I could find a nice tweedy sweater pattern for Liz, who was moving to the Hudson Valley after we finished our trip.

I was going to miss her. We'd lived on the same property for a long time, and I was used to seeing her there. We hadn't always been the closest confidantes, but no one had known me longer than my sisters. Diane would be moving to Butte to take up her relationship with Joe, but she'd be living in an apartment close to his house.

Remnants of church teachings, and his children, kept her from moving in before any official ceremony.

Since Diane had been living in the San Francisco Bay Area for decades, she'd need a nice, thick sweater ... or maybe a hat, scarf, and mittens set. My son and his family could always use new warm clothes, as they'd been Texas residents for a long time.

Did they even use knitted garments in Texas? What was I going to make up for Rodrigo?

My breath caught in my throat.

There was no need to give anything to him. I was tossing him out like yesterday's trash.

Fool.

No, no, I tried to convince myself. This was the right thing to do. He should find someone else, someone he'd known for a long time.

The image of Trixie Lynn rose in my mind. I shuddered. As soon as I left, she'd try to get her hooks into him. He'd resist, but eventually, she'd wear him down. The sisters would tsk, but she would put them in their place.

I tested the texture of a delicious deep blue sport weight yarn. It would look beautiful knitted up in a vest that would keep him warm for early morning golf games or late night porch sitting.

My heart started to ache all over again.

I'd so clearly imagined us sitting together watching the sun set on one of our ranches. He'd said he was willing to come to Montana. Not move there permanently, but spend time there.

Did I really want to spend any more winters in the state?

I'd enjoyed this time without snow or the freezing temperatures that chilled the marrow of my bones so much that it took days to leave.

Was I being resistant because I was being realistic, or had Trixie Lynn's suggestion wormed its way into my brain and grown into a full-sized monster?

I'd never given Rodrigo a chance to defend himself. He'd told me he didn't cheat on his wife, but there was still suspicion in my heart, suspicion put there by that woman, just as she'd intended.

And the gambling? Was I overlaying the pain I'd experienced with Michael on a fun night of bingo years later?

Or was fear of change still driving my life?

I'd resisted this trip, and it had been one of the most wonderful experiences I'd ever had.

"That's lovely yarn, isn't it?" the sales clerk said.

"Yes."

"It's the perfect weight for Texas. We don't need the heavy sweaters of the north, but an extra layer can make a difference sometimes. Do you have something in mind?"

If only she knew.

Some bubble of hope hadn't died.

"Not yet, but let me take enough to make a sweater," I said. Better to have more than I needed from the same dye lot than risk not having enough, even if I wasn't sure what I was going to do with it.

"Sure thing." Her smile brightened. Sweater sales were always going to be more satisfying than the single skein required for a hat.

With my purchases all neatly placed in a basic shopping bag with the shop's logo, I left the store. While I hadn't achieved serenity, I felt more at peace.

Yarn had a way of doing that.

~ ~ ~

"Kathleen!" Genna called as soon as I got out of the car at the RV park.

"Hi," I said, unsure if I was happy to see her.

"It feels like ages since we've had time to weave and spin together," she said. "Things must be heating up with that guy you told me about."

"That's a long story," I said.

"Then tomorrow will be perfect."

"Why?"

"My husband's got a big fishing trip scheduled with a group. It's one of the reasons he's down here. He helps wounded veterans—amputees and that sort of thing—learn to fish again."

"How wonderful," I said.

"It is. He gets great satisfaction. From surveys they can tell that it's a real boon to the veterans as well. Apparently fishing is as relaxing as spinning or weaving."

"My dad loved to go fly fishing," I said. "Always alone, though. He'd never take any of us. He needed his alone time."

"We all do," Genna said. "So I'll see you tomorrow? I picked up some cheeses and other things from some of the local markets. I'd love to share."

"Thank you. I think we have some berries I could add." Genna was one of the kindest and most generous people I knew. We'd have to keep in touch.

~ ~ ~

The next day I brought over the table runner to work on. I didn't think my brain could handle the intricacies of the lace pattern.

We settled into our crafts in the shade outside her trailer. The soft new age type music she had going in the background was soothing, as was the air temperature. Weaving outside at the end of February was something that wouldn't have ever crossed my mind.

After a period of catching up, we were quiet for a long time.

"How are things going with you and the man you met?" Genna asked when we took a break to nibble at some of the delicious cheeses and crackers she'd bought. "Are you staying after your sisters leave? Or coming back when your trip is over?"

"Neither," I said.

"Oh?"

"It's not going to work out," I said. "There are too many unknowns."

"Well, you won't figure them out if you don't spend time with him," she said.

"The logistics to do that are crazy," I said.

"You do most of the driving on the rig already, don't you?"

I nodded.

"So what's the big deal? You just drive it back down here, give it a few months, then see where you're at."

"You make it sound easy," I complained.

"I know. Sorry about that," Genna said. "It wasn't easy for me."

"What do you mean?"

"Let's go back outside, and I'll tell you about it," she said.

When we were settled back into our chairs, she began.

"I was married for twenty years, pretty much straight out of high school," she said. "It sounds a lot like what you've described. We were teenage sweethearts. He was captain of the football team, I was a reluctant cheerleader. I did it more to be with him at the games than because I wanted to be a cheerleader." She smiled. "Of course, cheerleading was very different back then. We were just there to root our team to victory. It wasn't a competitive sport."

"Sometimes it feels like every feel-good thing we ever did has been taken over by people trying to make money from pitting us against each other," I said.

Genna laughed. "That sounds right to me." Her fingers gently pulled fiber from a clump she had in her hand while the wheel magically made yarn.

"We did all right for the first ten years," she continued. "We had our kids. Our relatives were close by, and our jobs went okay. He worked in manufacturing, and I was a nurse. Then the factory moved somewhere else—not overseas, I think they were just going south back then. He lost his job along with half the town. It was tough finding anything with a high school diploma and no experience other than a factory job."

The wheel slowed and came to a stop. She looked over at me. "I'm telling you this because I want you to know everyone has secrets. Everyone has moments in their lives when they wished they'd done things differently. Keeping this to ourselves only makes the shame fester. We need to share and support each other so we can break free of the past and find a more joyful future."

"What happened?" I asked quietly.

The wheel started up.

"Seeing how much he could drink became his next job. It took a long time before it really began to affect us, and I put up with a lot, more than I should have. He got odd jobs while I kept working. The kids made it to high school."

For a few moments she didn't say anything, and I respected the silence.

"I thought I could ride it out until they left home, but one night he came home and told the kids we were only in this situation because I refused to move. If I really supported him, he said, I'd move south where he could find work. It was only because I refused to go that we were poor." She glanced at me. "Problem was that was the first I'd ever heard of it.

"I tried to tell him that, but I saw something in his eyes I'd never seen before. I told the kids to go to their rooms. They were reluctant to go, but I insisted. Once they were gone, I told him he needed to stop drinking, get counseling, and then we'd discuss moving." The wheel slowed, but didn't stop.

"He backhanded me."

I felt the statement like a punch in the gut.

The wheel seemed to go at a faster and faster pace. A tear trickled down Genna's check.

"I'm so sorry," I said, feeling like what I'd dealt with was nothing compared to her trauma. "Did you leave him?"

She shook her head.

I moved my shuttle back and forth. The air around us practically vibrated with her anguish.

No matter how long ago this had happened, the hurt remained. I knew that. Nothing ever made it go away. You just learned to deal with it.

Some of us did it better than others.

"He never hit me again," she said. "He got counseling, said we needed to stay together for the kids' sake, and I agreed. I did move into the guest bedroom. Being intimate just seemed wrong."

I nodded. I'd done the same when I could no longer deal with Michael's lies and excuses.

"He joined a church," she said. "When he did that, I thought we had a chance. Maybe we could pull it together. Maybe I could forgive him so that we could learn to love each other again."

Somehow, I believed, it got even worse before they split.

"The church he joined was very conservative. They believed in traditional roles, family run by a male head of household." She gave me a wry smile. "It was too late. I was used to doing things my own way."

She stopped the wheel to draft some more fiber. "Unfortunately, my husband traded in one addiction for another. He soon became a leader in the church, and my failure to become a compliant, submissive wife chafed. The boys pretty much ignored him."

Starting up the wheel, she chuckled. "Oh, the lectures he began to give me. Once he tried to get me to agree to domestic discipline."

"What's that?" I asked. The term seemed vaguely familiar, but I had no idea what it actually meant.

"Spanking your wife when she gets out of line."

"What? You can't be serious!"

"For real."

"Insane." I tried to imagine placing myself over any man's lap for discipline.

I started laughing, and she joined in.

"What did you do?" I asked when we finally calmed down.

"Exactly what we just did. I laughed at him. His face turned so red I thought he was going to have a heart attack. That's when I realized the total absurdity of the situation. He wasn't going to change. Neither was I. I filed for divorce the next day. He protested a bit when I told him he had to move out, but our boys had gotten as tall as he was, and both were doing sports. He left."

"That's quite a story," I said. "You must be incredibly strong."

"We all are," Genna said as she started up the wheel again. "No one realizes how strong women are because we use our strength quietly. We endure things we shouldn't have to. Sometimes we forget how strong we are, and we let others do things around us and to us they shouldn't be allowed to do. That's why we need to support each other, give each other the strength to take a clear-eyed look at what's actually happening and take action if necessary."

I nodded and concentrated on my weaving.

What was supposed to happen now? Was I supposed to share? Were we bonding?

It was the reason I'd never joined a self-help group. I was fine with listening and supporting. It was talking about myself that was difficult.

There was too much shame.

"Whew," she said. "I need a break. How about you? Let's go inside for a bit and have something to eat. I've got a nice bottle of Riesling if you want to crack that open. Or iced tea—unsweetened. I've never gotten used to the sweet stuff."

"Me either," I confessed.

She laid a sheet over the spinning and weaving to protect from any birds with overactive digestive systems, and we went inside.

"How did you meet your new husband?" I asked.

"At work. He was a pediatric doctor. His wife had died of complications in childbirth, and he'd never remarried. I did a rotation under him. First, I fell in love with how he handled the kids. He knew when to be gentle and when to josh or get stern. Then I fell in love with him." She held up the wine in one hand and a pitcher of iced tea in the other.

I pointed to the tea.

"Fortunately," she said. "He fell in love right back."

"It's great when it works out that way."

"You should give him a chance," she said.

"Who?"

"The guy you've been seeing."

"We've got nothing in common."

"I find that hard to believe. You wouldn't have seen him multiple times if you had nothing in common. Tell me what you've been up to. I love romance."

"There's no romance."

"Has he kissed you?"

"Um ..."

"That's a yes. There's romance. So spill."

Maybe I should have had the wine after all.

But suddenly I felt a need to talk about Rodrigo, if for no other reason than to explore my feelings for him.

This was a safe place to explore. I loved my sisters, but they were far too used to telling me what to do since they were older. Having just rediscovered love for themselves, they were also very opinionated on the subject.

So I relived all of my experiences with Rodrigo, from the hilarious miniature golf fiasco to viewing the city at night to our horseback rides. As I talked, I became more aware of the intensity of my feelings in such a short time. He'd been considerate at every turn.

"My problem, I think," I admitted to Genna. "Is that I don't know what's real and what's not. Is it all an act? Or is that who he really is? I was so wrong about Michael."

"Why don't you tell me about Michael," she said softly.

I took a deep breath. "I think I'll take a glass of that Riesling now," I said.

She nodded and poured us each a glass.

I settled into one of the chairs in the RV and started to talk. I told it from beginning to end, even though I may have said some of the information before. The logical explanation was as much for me as it was for her.

"Like you," I began. "We were high school sweethearts. Not standouts in the school, just some of the ranch kids that hung together for the most part. Some of the guys joined athletics, and a few of them took their shot at college, particularly in schools with ag degrees. Most of us were middle-of-the-road kids, looking for a high school diploma. We might go on to a trade school or community college, but that was about it. Unlike my sisters, I felt no need to leave Butte."

"You were happy there."

"Yes. Especially after Michael and I got together. I felt complete … you know, satisfied. I knew who I was going to be, and it was exactly what I wanted. I'd be a rancher's wife, his partner, and a mother." The feelings of contentment I'd felt so long ago drifted around me like a ghost's mist.

"My dad didn't like him, but eventually accepted him because Michael was the one I'd chosen. Maybe Dad saw a weakness I didn't know was there." I shrugged. "Whatever it was, Michael and I were happy for the most part. Every couple has its ups and downs, and we weren't any different."

I sipped the wine.

"Liz used to babysit when we wanted to go out. We started going to bingo games at the church. It was fun at the beginning, but then Michael really got into it. He bought as many cards as he could and wanted to stay to the end. I'd be ready to go long before he was. For me it was a fun night out. Looking back, I can see it was more than that for him."

"An addiction," Genna said softly.

"Yes. Then he started going to the casinos. He told me he was fishing with some friends, but he lied. He'd spend all weekend gambling. It was fine when he was up or at least breaking even. But then he began to lose." I put my glass down and clenched my fingers together. "I didn't catch on for years. But then we needed money to get Patrick equipment for soccer camp. That kid had worked all year to save up enough to go for a week. When I went to buy the stuff, Michael told me we didn't have the money. I couldn't believe it. He'd always insisted on doing the finances, and I let him."

"Money is always tricky. If one person handles it, the other person doesn't really know what's going on. And it's so hard to talk about it."

"True. I'd always had access, but I hated things like balancing a checkbook. Give me a machine, and I can figure out what to do," I said. "But numbers? Ugh."

"So what did you do?"

"I should have called Diane. She was a bookkeeper. But I was too embarrassed. So I slogged through it alone. I'd always had access to our accounts—I'd insisted on that—I just hadn't paid much attention to them. I began to notice several large withdrawals, always on the Friday before Michael said he went 'fishing.' Sometimes they were repaid, but most of the time they weren't. I confronted him with what I'd found."

"That was brave."

"I was angry. My kid needed something. You know how that feels."

"I do. Did he tell you the truth?"

"Not right away. He started with it was none of my business, but when I pointed out it was a joint account, he got defensive. You see, I have a trust fund from my grandparents—we all do. That's how I paid for the kids' college educations. He told me I'd never shared that with him." I could feel the anger and tension rising within me all over again. "I was so mad. I reminded him that he'd spent his life on our ranch, that we got a good salary, and that it would probably be *our* children who inherited." I took a deep breath. "When he finally admitted to the gambling, I told him he needed to quit. He refused. He swore he'd make up the money somehow."

"Did he?"

"No. Instead I set up a second account that was mine only. It was complicated, but I squirreled away enough money to take care of the kids. Patrick went to camp. And, like you, I moved into the spare bedroom."

"I'm sorry to hear all that. I bet it was difficult."

"Yes. But I did it."

"Did he ever quit?"

"No," I said. "Well, he did once he started getting ill. He was forced to. But if he'd been able to do so, he would have been out that door. Gambling came first. Our kids took second. And that's what burned me the most. They should have come first, damn it. They should have come first." To my horror, I burst into tears.

Genna put her arm around me, and bless her soul, she just let me cry.

Chapter Twenty-Eight

When I woke the next morning, I knew what I had to do.

Not having the courage to talk to him directly, I texted after breakfast.

I'm sorry I've been distant, I began after the greeting. *I've got a lot of things to think about.*

No response. No little dots.

I waited.

Finally, he responded.

I hope when you're done thinking, we get to talk.

Yes, I typed.

Good.

I took a deep breath and then asked, *Could I come ride Star? By myself?*

Again, the moments of no response.

When do you want to come?

This morning.

I have a golf game this morning, but Juan will be here. He can help you.

Then it's okay?

Yes.

Thank you, I typed.

It's good to hear from you, he wrote.

I wasn't quite sure how to respond to that. I wasn't ready to talk to him yet.

Thank you again. I'll be in touch soon, I wrote.

Good. I'll tell Juan to expect you.

I put my phone down, an ache in my chest. He was a good man, but I wasn't ready to give him the answer he wanted.

"Would you mind if I took the car this morning?" I asked Liz. "I know you said you wanted to paint last night, but I'll be back around lunchtime."

"No problem," she said, stretching. "I'm feeling lazy this morning. I think I'll just sit around, drink coffee, and read a book."

"I've got a report I've got to finish for my client," Diane said. "I don't need it either."

"Where are you going?" Liz asked.

"Horseback riding. Alone," I said, forestalling any questions about Rodrigo.

A half hour later I was at the ranch. Juan was waiting for me.

"Dad said you were coming by to take Star out for a ride."

"Yes. I wanted to ride up to that meadow he's taken me to a couple of times."

"I know the one. It's a lovely spot. Let me get you saddled up."

"It's okay," I said with a smile. "I know my way around."

"Sure?"

"Positive."

"Let me know if you need anything," he said. With a wave, he walked back toward the main house.

I walked to the corral through the barn. Star was waiting for me, greeting me with lots of head bobbing and nickers.

"Hello, you beautiful girl. Shall we go for a ride? Just the two of us?" I snapped on her lead, and she followed me into the barn.

Less than a half hour later we were out on the trail. She was prancing as much as walking, as if she was as anxious as I was to get out of the house.

When we reached the flat spot, I let her have her head, keeping low on her neck so I didn't get knocked off by a branch again. She ran faster than I'd ever let her go. The wind streamed her mane and my hair behind us, the fresh air feeling like it was cleansing my mind of cobwebs and painful events of the past. Soon all I was aware of was the bunching of muscles beneath my legs and the thunder of Star's galloping hooves.

I let her run as long as the trail allowed it. When I finally pulled her in, I was amazed to find I had tears running down my face. I thought I'd shed them all the day before.

Once I'd finished sobbing, Genna had draped a knit blanket over me and told me to sleep. Quietly, she began to clean up around me. By the time I awoke, she'd brought in my loom and her wheel.

"How about an old movie?" she asked. "I've got some herbal tea brewing."

I nodded, unable to speak.

She'd found an old romance on one of the streaming stations, and we'd settled in. When the movie was over, I'd felt sufficiently recovered. We'd bid our goodbyes, and I'd headed home, grateful to have met someone as kind, generous, and understanding as she was.

There were lots of good people throughout the country, I'd

discovered. We needed to stop looking for what makes us different and concentrate on how we are the same.

As Star slowed, I wiped my eyes.

Then I gave her lots of pats. "Good girl," I said. "That was a nice run, wasn't it?"

She nodded her head, the bridle jangling with her still pent-up energy.

It was obvious she needed more exercise than she was getting. If I were here, I'd ride her almost every day. Never had I been so in tune with a horse, or any animal for that matter.

I let Genna's revelations from the day before play out in my mind. She'd told me she'd had to thoroughly let go of the past in order to be able to love again. "Not everyone is Michael," she'd said.

She was right. I was painting Rodrigo's actions with the brush I'd learned to use from my late husband. It wasn't fair to him. I did need to clear the air.

And then what? I felt like I was falling in love with him—probably what had made me so ready to run—but was I sure? Didn't I need a lot more time to be sure?

Romantic movies and books had plenty of "instalove" plots, but I wasn't sure I was built that way.

But what was I going to learn about Rodrigo that I didn't know already? Yes, there were a few things that were bothering me, but simply asking the questions would resolve those issues one way or the other.

His family loved him, people at church had nothing but good things to say about him, and he'd always treated me with kindness and respect.

My sisters had had the advantage of knowing the people they fell in love with again. Both had second chances with someone they'd cared for once.

Not only was Rodrigo a stranger two months ago, but his culture, and that of the state of Texas, were very different from the one I'd spent my life knowing. People in Montana were close knit. Call someone in the government, and a real person answered the phone. It might likely be someone I knew.

Things were changing as newcomers brought "efficiencies," but the old ways were pretty entrenched. Montanans liked to do business with people they'd seen in the flesh and shaken hands with.

Somehow, I didn't think the Texas government worked that way.

If I made the decision to come back, I was taking a chance on more than the man.

What if I hated Texas? Would I make our lives miserable?

No, I had to decide on the whole thing.

We reached the meadow, and I slid off the horse to lead her to the stream to drink.

Rodrigo said he'd be willing to spend time in Montana. With our children taking over our respective ranches, we'd both have more time.

Maybe I'd take up golf.

I laughed out loud at the image of me teeing off and my club going sailing like it had at the miniature golf place.

Maybe we could go to Hawaii. I'd always wanted to see the islands. Or even farther, to Australia where they had all those bizarre animals.

There was a lot I needed to discuss with Rodrigo.

But first I needed to decide if I was really in love with him.

Or did I?

Didn't I really know that already?

"What do you think?" I asked the horse.

Star kept drinking, but shifted her feet.

Her rear pushed against me.

While I'd been thinking, I'd moved closer to the edge of the stream. What I hadn't realized, was that I was standing on an unstable edge.

The shifting of the horse made me change my own balance. The bank crumbled beneath me, and I pitched forward into the stream.

"No!" I yelled as I twisted my body to avoid doing too much damage. As it was, I landed hard on one hip, but I had plenty of padding there.

That wasn't the worst of my problems.

"Yikes!" I screamed. "That's cold!"

Star took her head out of the water and stared at me.

I pulled myself to standing, an effort that made me even wetter.

"This is all your fault," I scolded Star.

She gave me a horse's version of the stink-eye and went back to drinking.

Great. What was it with O'Sullivan women and water? Diane had fallen in several times when she'd gone out with Joe. Liz had landed in a pond.

And here I was, dripping wet from a stream.

At least Rodrigo wasn't here to see me.

I pulled off my boots and emptied them before putting them back on.

Careful of where I put my feet, I led Star away from the stream and got back into the saddle, my soaking wet pants landing with a wet plop on the leather.

Hopefully, I'd dry out a bit before we got back to the stable.

My hope was ill-founded. The air around San Antonio wasn't nearly as dry as that of my home state. And Star wanted to play a bit when I hosed her down, causing me to drench my shirt all over again. Somehow I managed to get the tack off the horse, and the animal cleaned up and back in her corral without Juan showing up.

Once I was done, I hustled to the Jeep and made my escape.

~ ~ ~

"What happened to you?" Liz asked when I walked into the RV.

"Don't ask," I said.

"I just did," she said.

Diane looked up from where she was working on the computer. She looked me up and down, then grinned.

"You fell into the water!" she exclaimed.

Liz took a closer look.

"You did!"

"Damn horse pushed me in," I said. "It was nothing."

"Oh, it was everything," Liz said.

"True love," Diane said.

"With my horse?" I asked.

"With the man," Diane said.

"He was nowhere around me," I said. "I went riding by myself, remember?"

"Doesn't change a thing," Liz said. "It's the O'Sullivan curse. Fall in love?" She extended one arm, palm up. "Fall in water." The other arm took the same position.

"You two," I said.

"Admit it," Diane said, her tone serious. "You love him. Or you're falling in love with him. So what are you going to do about it?"

I wanted to deny her assertion, but suddenly I was tired of trying to fight what was evident to everyone, including me.

"I'm not sure," I said. "There are still issues, things that need to be discussed. And the logistics are crazy."

"Got that," Liz said. "But if he's the right man, then you'll find a way to make it work. It's as simple as that."

I hoped she was right because, to my surprise, I was ready to take a leap for love.

Chapter Twenty-Nine

The next day was Sunday, and I went to early mass. I wasn't ready to confront Rodrigo or deal with Trixie Lynn. I spent the rest of the day reading, weaving, and watching a movie with my sisters. They sensed my mood and didn't tread on any sensitive subjects.

Sunday night, I slept well, but when I woke I knew there were still things I needed to think through. So I planned a few days doing what I did best: fixing things.

After breakfast, I started with the inside of the RV, since both my sisters had taken off for the day. I streamed country music loudly through the RVs speaker systems and went to work.

Beginning with the back, I checked every shelf for looseness, tightening some screws here and there. Unlike a mobile home that stays put, the jostling of the RV on the road tends to make things fall apart. Screws and pipe fittings loosen. People complain about the constant repair motorhomes need, without realizing the dual function of home and vehicle puts a lot of stress on things.

Especially considering the state of some of the roads. They didn't just have potholes—some of the nation's highways had genuine craters. More than once I'd thrown things across the RV while swerving to avoid a spot where the road seemed to disappear.

Thankfully, more road crews seemed to be out. It was a pain to go through the one-lane construction zones, but having safe roads was worth the inconvenience.

Once I'd taken my screwdriver to every shelf in the place, it was time to check the pipe fittings. Under the kitchen sink, the p-trap was loose. When I inspected it more closely, I realized it had cracked around a fitting.

It was going to need to be replaced.

I got a piece of paper and noted the fix that needed to be made. Then I continued to check the fittings in every other pipe. When I was done inside, I'd start on all the fittings under the RV. That should keep me going most of the day.

The routine was soothing. My mind began to wander to the problem at hand: Rodrigo.

He'd talked about wanting to be together, but how would that work? I was in my sixties. If I wanted a second chance at happiness, there wasn't much time to waste. Did he want to get married? Was it important enough for me to insist upon?

Yes. My beliefs were part of who I was at my core. They were old-fashioned, and I felt no need to insist that everyone believe what I did, but if Rodrigo and I were to make it work, he'd need to accept my beliefs. We would need to get married.

What about intimacy before marriage? The church was basically against it, but there were plenty of priests who turned a blind eye to the practice, especially if the couple was in a committed relationship.

I'd deal with that if and when it happened.

When I was hungry, I made a sandwich and poured a glass of iced tea, sitting outside to enjoy it. While I sat, I nodded at people going by, listened to the birds in the nearby brush, and enjoyed every bite of my meal. No matter what happened between Rodrigo and me, I'd finally let go of some of the bitterness I'd clutched for so long.

Anger and bitterness were often only harmful to the people who held onto them.

Genna texted me to see how I was doing. I told her I was fine and invited her and her husband over for cocktail hour.

It took most of the afternoon to go through all the pipe fittings under the motor home. Fortunately, most of them appeared solid. I didn't look forward to any problems dealing with gray or black water.

Just thinking about it made me shudder.

By the time I'd cleaned up and taken a shower, my sisters were home.

"Cocktails?" I asked.

"Absolutely," Diane replied.

"Sounds good," Liz said. "I've got something to show you." She pulled out a canvas she'd tucked behind one of the chairs.

It was an amazing portrait of an older woman half asleep in a chair. The lines on her face echoed her age, but there was also a hint of the young woman she'd once been. That expression had been mirrored in a painting the woman was holding of a teenage girl, presumably one of the old woman herself.

It took my breath away.

"That's amazing," I said.

"Isn't it?" Diane asked.

"Thanks," Liz said. "I took a photo of it for my agent, and she says she believes she has a place for it in a gallery in San Francisco. My old gallery is happy with the old work I have." Liz was famous for her pen and watercolor art which she'd sold under a pseudonym. She smiled. "She suggested I present this under my own name. If this is the direction I want to go, I need to claim it."

I nodded. Maybe that was what this trip was really about: reclaiming the pieces of ourselves we'd given up for one reason or another.

"So that's what I'm going to do," Liz said.

"Great idea!" Diane exclaimed. "Now how about those cocktails?"

I laughed and went to mix up a batch of gin and tonics, our drink of choice.

"By the way," I said. "I've invited Genna and her husband, Don, to stop by."

"That's nice," Diane said. "It's fun to have other people over."

We'd just started on our first round when Genna and Don showed up. She'd brought wine and he, a few beers. I got her a glass, and we settled in for a nice chat.

For a long while we talked about the places we'd been, which is something people motoring around the country like to do. They hadn't spent much time on the East Coast, so they were fascinated by our descriptions of the Hudson River Valley.

"Your sister says you're an artist," Genna said to Liz.

"Yes," Liz said. "I've been working in a studio in San Antonio while we've been here."

"She just finished a painting," Diane said. "Show it to her."

With a little bit of prodding, Liz showed the picture. She'd changed so much since the beginning of the trip. So had Diane. They'd released their secrets and moved on.

Tonight was the night to tell them about Michael. It was time for me, too, to come clean.

Despite my protests, Diane told Genna and Don about my tumble into the creek.

"It's a tradition," she said. "When I met my old boyfriend in Yellowstone—totally unexpectedly—he tried to teach me how to fish. Every time we went near water, I managed to fall in."

"Hard to avoid water when you're fishing," Don said with a wry tone.

We laughed.

"But Liz fell in the water after going through a maze," Diane pointed out. "She was dating her ex-boyfriend. And, plop! Into the water she goes!"

"It sounds like you sisters are destined to be with men you've known before," Genna said.

"Except for Kathleen," Diane said. "She's found someone totally new."

"Well …" I said, glancing over at Genna.

My new friend's face didn't reveal her in-depth knowledge of what was going on between Rodrigo and me.

"But she *still* fell in the water," Diane said with a chuckle.

"It's got to be true love then," Liz said.

"I think you're getting ahead of yourselves a bit," I said.

"I'm sure it will all turn out the way it's supposed to," Genna said.

"I agree," Don said, taking her hand. "It took us a while, but we found each other."

"Had you known each other before?" Liz asked.

"No," he said. "But I knew I was in love with her not long after we met. She took a little convincing."

They smiled at each other. There was no doubt in my mind that the love they shared was deep and long-lasting.

After another half hour or so of talking, they left. We took our drinks inside, and Liz started making dinner. Diane turned on the news, but I ignored it. It didn't seem to change or get better.

Like many people I'd talked to, I missed the feel-good, human interest stories that used to accompany our local news so long ago. When people doing good things was celebrated, instead of the news being about the worst behaviors humans could inflict upon each other.

I shook off the melancholy and concentrated on the book I was reading until dinner was ready.

After dinner, Diane and I cleaned up while Liz browsed on her tablet.

"Can we talk?" I asked after the last dish had been dried and put away.

"Sure." Liz put her tablet aside, and Diane settled into a chair.

"I don't know why we all felt a need to keep secrets," I said. "You two have opened up about yours, and now it's my turn." I took a large sip of the water I'd poured, wishing it was something a little stronger.

I looked at my sisters, unable to speak anymore.

They nodded their encouragement.

I took a deep breath and began the story of Michael's addiction and my complicity in it.

They were quiet all the way through as I told it. To me, it was almost like another person was sitting next to me reciting it like it was a puppet.

When I was done, I was dry-eyed, but drained.

"Oh, sweetie," Liz said. "I'm so sorry. That had to have been horrible. No wonder you were always so short on cash."

"It's so hard when the man you love betrays you," Diane said, her voice sad with her own memory of her ex-husband's lies.

"I should have been stronger," I said. "I should have given him an ultimatum."

"That would have been very difficult for you," Liz said. "Mom and Dad set such a strong example of what a marriage was. They argued, but there was never any doubt they would stick together. They made a vow and had every intention of keeping it. Like you, their Catholic faith was so strong, they couldn't even imagine a divorce."

I nodded, and then the tears began to flow.

"I never thought you'd understand," I said.

"Why not?"

"You're so different. You seemed to flaunt everything Mom and Dad stood for, and you were so strong in your conviction that they were wrong."

"Yeah, well, see how well that turned out for me," she said.

"I get it," Diane said. "It took me a long time to accept the idea that I needed to get a divorce. It went against everything I believed in. But I'm glad I did." She shook her head. "And I did put things in motion to get an annulment."

"Really?" Liz asked.

"Really. I want to have a clean conscience with Joe."

"It's not stopping you from doing the horizontal mambo," Liz said.

Diane reddened. "That's different."

Liz laughed, and I had to join in.

Diane stood up and walked to me. She reached down and urged me up.

"You've held the ranch together," she said.

Liz joined us.

"You raised two amazing kids," Liz said.

"We're proud of you," Diane said.

"Very." Liz put her arms around Diane and me.

Diane and I did the same.

A group hug never felt so good.

"Now," Liz said. "Get out there and get your man."

Chapter Thirty

"Hello, Rodrigo," I said when he picked up the phone.

"Hello," he said, his voice warm. "I'm glad you called."

"Thank you for being patient. I had things to sort through in my mind."

"And are they in order now?" he asked.

"Well, not perfect order," I said. "But some things are clearer. We need to talk."

"That would be good. Do you want me to come there?"

"Um, no." While living in an RV was nice, it didn't lend itself to entertaining, except outdoors. And this wasn't a conversation I wanted to have when we'd be interrupted by well-meaning travelers.

"We could meet at a park," I suggested.

"Or you can come here. Antonia is off tonight."

"How about I bring pizza?"

"I haven't had pizza in a long time," he said. "That would be wonderful."

"Cheese, pepperoni, onion, olive?"

"Perfect."

We settled on a time, chatted briefly about our days, then hung up.

After letting my sisters know I was taking the car, I set off to get the parts I needed to make repairs. We were leaving the following Monday, and it was time to get things completed.

If I focused on that, I didn't need to think too much about the sadness that was occupying my body.

~ ~ ~

The pizza store I chose was one of the more popular ones in the area, so it was a wait before my pie was ready.

Rodrigo didn't come out to meet me, but Star put her head over the top rail of the corral and nickered. I blew her a kiss and told her I'd get to her later.

When he answered the door, I was struck again by the kindness in his eyes. Whatever else, he was a nice man, an attribute I didn't think women valued nearly enough.

"Let me take that," he said, plucking the box from my hands. "Come in."

I walked into the cool adobe home and shut the door behind me before following him to the kitchen. Even though the sun was close to setting, the kitchen maintained its warm atmosphere. Bright Mexican ceramics lit up terra cotta tiles, while a gas fire burned in one corner. The kitchen table had thick legs and caned chairs. Very different from the patio table or the formal dining room no one seemed to use.

"I'm hungry," Rodrigo said. "I hope you don't mind if we eat first. I've been training the new horse all day. I don't think I've worked that hard in a long time."

"Sounds good," I said. Putting off a difficult conversation always seemed like the easy path to take.

Rodrigo nodded and pulled out plates, flatware, and orange- and yellow-patterned napkins. Two heavy glasses also made it to the table. "Beer?" he asked.

"Yes."

We sat at the table, and each grabbed a piece of pizza. For a few moments, we did nothing but eat and purr our approval of the greasy mess.

"I can't believe it's been so long since I had a slice," he said.

"Our doctors would be horrified," I said.

"Let's keep it a secret then," he said with a grin.

Then we both reached for a second piece.

~ ~ ~

We had cleaned up and were settled into chairs on the patio, letting the night sounds whisper around us. In the distance, lights were on in the house that Juan and his family occupied.

"Have you decided when you're moving?" I asked.

"We're talking about May to give his wife a new house for Mother's Day."

"I'm sure she'll appreciate that," I said.

"She's a little worried about it, to be truthful," he said. "She sees the size and worries about the upkeep." He chuckled. "I think she's also worried he's going to want children to fill all the bedrooms."

"Will he?"

"I know he wants one or two more, but when it comes to the important decisions, she has the final say. He once told me he makes the unimportant decisions, like which newspaper to subscribe to, while she is in charge of vital matters like how they should run their lives."

"Seems like a good division of labor."

"Then that is how we will do it if you decide to give us a chance." He turned toward me. "And have you?"

The time I'd been avoiding all evening was here.

Even so, I took a moment to indulge in the quiet of the space around me. The ranch was far enough away from roads that we barely heard the traffic. While there was a pole light by the barn, it was sensor operated. The horses had settled in for the night, so it was dark. Overhead, the stars shone brightly. It was a sight I'd appreciated more since we'd begun our travels. There were so few spaces in the east where one could get a good look at the heavens at night.

"I need to tell you about my life with Michael," I said. "It will help you understand."

"Okay," he said. Then he reached over, gave my hand a slight squeeze, and let go.

Falling in love with this man had been easy. If only deciding what to do about it came with the same effortlessness.

Slowly, I began the same tale I'd told to Genna and my sisters. Rodrigo listened quietly, but at some point he placed his hand on mine.

"No wonder you had such difficulty at bingo," he said. "If I'd known, I never would have suggested it."

"I thought I could handle it," I said. "Until I was talking with a friend, I didn't realize how deep the wound had gone."

He nodded. "It's amazing how deep emotional hurts can live. I find myself still sorting through things that happened to me as a kid. I had a good childhood, but no one's parents are perfect. As for the army..." He shook his head. "I don't think I'll ever sort that trauma out in my lifetime."

"Was it bad?" I asked, then realized how stupid the question was.

"All war is bad," he said.

Then we were quiet for a while. I was exhausted from telling the story again, and he seemed to sense I needed the time to recover.

Letting the night work its magic, I sipped my beer.

"I think..." he said. "I think it will be important that we talk about our finances. I know you and your sisters have your ranch tied up in trusts of some sort, and I've done the same with this ranch. We should be clear with each other about how all of that works. And if we move forward, we need to discuss how we're going to do it financially. It's something couples don't do enough of, I think."

"Yes. It's not a very romantic subject," I said.

"But it's one of the things that can foul up a marriage," he said. "One of many."

"I've always believed many problems come down to one basic thing: communication. If couples make an effort to communicate, to say what's real for them, to be heard when they speak, then the marriage has the best chance of surviving."

"It's difficult to do all of that."

"I know. It's something I've realized was absent in my own marriage. Gabriella was brought up in a home where the man ruled. Her mother was submissive to her father's will, and the girls were brought up that way too."

"I don't think her sister learned that lesson very well," I said.

He barked out a laugh. "She's got a tongue, that one. Yes, she got beyond her mother's message. Her husband is the definition of henpecked."

I laughed too.

Then the other problem prodded me.

Rodrigo was right. Communication, no matter how difficult, was essential.

"Trixie Lynn told me something that's been bothering me," I said.

"She might have told you anything to get you out of the picture. She is quite clear in her desires to snare me as her next husband."

"I know. Since you've told me you and your wife weren't totally in love with each other, I'm worried what she said might be true."

He took a deep breath and stared into the night. Then he returned his gaze to me. "Let me guess. She told you I had an affair when my wife was pregnant."

"Yes."

"Remember I told you I had been in love with an Anglo woman before I married my wife?"

I nodded, remembering the story.

"My father told me I'd fall in love with Gabriella the same way, but I never did. My wife was too passive. She didn't have the spunk I'd admired in the other woman, the same energy I value in you." He smiled at me.

Warmth filled me. Michael had never appreciated hearing my opinion or my drive to get things done.

"I loved her as much as I could. She bore me fine children, more than I really wanted, but I love them all. Our house was always beautifully kept, our meals plentiful, and our families always welcome." He took a swig of beer. "She was pregnant with Luis when the woman I'd once loved came back into town. Gabriella was having a difficult time of it, and her sister had moved in to help. There is only so much of my sister-in-law I can take, so I spent too much time with my friends, often at cantinas. And, yes, I drank a little too much."

His fingers tapped the arm of the chair.

"One night she came into where I was visiting with other ranchers. We embraced like old friends, and went to a separate table to talk. She'd just been divorced from her husband and was curious to know what I was up to. When I told her our fourth child was due in a few months, she was disappointed. Like me, she'd always had a fantasy about our relationship." He paused, then took another deep breath and continued. "The rumor went around. All we did was meet a few nights and talk. It was always in public. I never cheated on my wife. I swear on the life of Santisima Madre Maria, I was faithful."

I nodded.

This time I reached for his hand. We entwined our fingers.

"I believe you," I said.

"Gracias."

We were quiet for a long time after that.

~ ~ ~

It was only later, when we were settled on the couch having a cup of coffee before I headed home, that we delved back into serious matters. I'd begun to realize that I wasn't going to have all the answers I needed to make a decision before we left.

I could come back when everything at the ranch was settled, but I might take a long drive only to discover I'd made a colossal mistake. Or I could decide to let it go and feel the ache of something that might have been for the rest of my life.

"If I came back, I would bring the RV," I said.

"Yes. Of course. I would expect nothing less," he said. "I know you value your faith as much as I do, so leaping into bed together is not something you would do." He traced a finger down my arm. "But I do want to do that someday soon. I am very attracted to you."

My body turned up the heat, and soon I was very aware of my sexuality, an awakening I'd only felt since I'd met him.

"Yes," I said.

"We could give ourselves time, and then decide," he said. "Whatever happens, we would walk away friends, okay?"

"That would be good."

"So you'll come back?"

I wanted to say yes …

"I don't know," I said. "I really don't."

"You need more time." I could sense his withdrawal.

"Yes."

"Is there anything else you need from me to make that decision?" he asked.

I shook my head.

"It's me," I said. "I'm … well … I promise I'll make a decision by the end of March. Will that be okay?"

"It will be agony," he said, the ache in his voice apparent. "But I will wait."

I rose from the couch.

Wordlessly, he walked me to the car, giving me a soft kiss before I sat down in the driver's seat.

He closed the door.

As I drove down the driveway, he waved.

Would this be the last time I ever saw him?

Chapter Thirty-One

I was an utter fool. And there is no fool like an old one.

This was a man who aroused feelings in me I hadn't felt in a long time, not since I was much younger. And the desire I felt now was so much more complex than that raw emotion that had driven me as a teenager. It wasn't just a need for sexual release. I desired true intimacy with Rodrigo.

Neither of us had the bodies of young people. But intimacy wasn't only about the body. There had been an episode of an old television show—something with teachers and Burt Reynolds—that had stayed in my mind. In it, one of the other characters, a skinny balding guy with glasses, had to take over teaching sex education.

He was awkward and embarrassed. But the thing he came up with stuck with me. He told those young teens that the greatest sexual organ was the mind. He was trying to get them to understand the respect that was required when engaging in sex, even if it was the fumbling around of teenagers who had no idea what they were doing.

But now I knew he was right in ways far beyond what the television screenwriters had tried to indicate.

What I desired with Rodrigo was far more than physical contact, although I wanted that too. No, I wanted a relationship where our minds and hearts were totally engaged along with the physical aspects.

And in my heart, I knew it was possible with him.

Then why couldn't I just tell him I was coming back? Was I waiting for a sign from God or something?

"Crap! Ouch!" I stuck the finger that I'd pinched into my mouth. Then I got up too rapidly, smacking my head on the bottom of the RV. Damn these small spaces.

"You okay?" Diane asked, bringing out some of the trash she and Liz had found. They were in charge of going through all the inside storage units, cleaning them out, and restacking things.

"I will be," I told her.

My sisters had been very good about refraining from talking about Rodrigo or asking me what I was going to do. I was grateful.

With my head and finger down to a dull throbbing, I went back to work. Although I was being a bit overzealous with the maintenance I was doing, we were headed off into large stretches of nothing, and breaking down was an experience I could live without.

~ ~ ~

By mid-afternoon, Liz called it quits.

"We're not leaving until Monday," she said. "That gives us three more days to get everything done."

"But what if something needs fixing, and I need to search for parts?" I asked.

"Kathleen, you're beginning to sound like an old lady. What if … what if …" Liz said.

"It's because she is an old lady," Diane said.

"I'm younger than you are," I shot back.

"Maybe chronologically, but not in spirit."

"Oh," I said. "Here we go again. Just because I'm not leaping into bed with Rodrigo doesn't mean I'm an old lady. I've got principles. That's all."

Liz shook her head. "That's not it at all."

"Definitely not," Diane agreed.

"I'm not sure even you know what's stopping you," Liz said.

I didn't have a comeback for that.

"I'm taking a nap. Then a shower. Then we're having cocktails," I said and walked away.

Fortunately, I'd done enough physical exertion that I fell asleep quickly. But my dreams were vivid. I was racing across the plains on Star's back, trying to chase a distant figure on a black horse. I knew I needed to catch up.

And I knew I never would unless I changed something. What I needed to change remained elusive. The road forked a few times, and I always urged Star to the right-hand fork, even though she wanted to go left. I was determined that I was right.

By the time I woke I hadn't caught up to the person on the black horse.

With a sigh, I banished the dream. It didn't really mean anything.

After showering, I mixed up a batch of gin and tonics. My sisters were already outside, under the awning. The day had turned warm with a hint of the stronger summer heat to come. The humidity made the air feel heavy.

As I settled in, Liz looked over and opened her mouth to say something.

"Don't," I said.

"I just want you to be happy."

"Then let me be."

"You are one stubborn woman."

"I'm Irish," I said. "Comes with the territory. Besides, you're one to talk. How many years—no, decades—did you hide your paintings from me?"

"That was …"

I glared at her.

She shrugged.

I opened my book and drank some G&T. Soon I was caught back up in the gritty world of drug runners and the people who tried to bring them to justice.

A faint noise that seemed out of place penetrated my consciousness. My sisters must have heard it too, because they looked up from their books. Wasn't that horse's hooves clopping on the pavement?

I put down my drink and book and waited.

A horse, flowers attached to the mane and a floral ring around his neck, nosed around the corner. Rodrigo, sitting proud in a polished saddle with gleaming silver, was himself decked out in a black suit with silver trim. His boots shone from a vigorous polish, spurs jangling from the heels. A large felt sombrero sat upon his head.

Behind him, just as flamboyant with flowers and trim, Star followed.

My heart was in my throat.

He dismounted, and I stood up and walked to him. Vaguely, I was aware of my sisters following.

"Mi dulce, Kathleen," he said. "My sweet, sweet lady. I know I said I would wait until the end of March for my answer, but I miss you every moment. I know you care for me as much as I do you. You've told me that. I want to spend time with you, the rest of my life if you'll let me."

He handed me a soft leather folder. Then he handed me the reins to Star's bridle.

"I'm making you a commitment," he said. "I want you to come back and give me … give us … a chance. Star is my promise that if we can make it work and when the time is right, I'll ask you to marry me. Please accept my gift and my love."

Diane pulled the folder from my hand and scanned it.

"The horse," she said. "He's giving you the damn horse."

"Let me see," Liz said. After a moment, she added, "Oh my god, he is."

All I could do was concentrate on his dark eyes while he waited for an answer.

I could do this, couldn't I? All the man wanted was for me to spend more time with him. That was it.

Except it wasn't. Because if I came back, I'd have no choice. I was already half in love with him. More time would complete the job.

Star plodded over and nudged my arm.

There was laughter, and all of a sudden I became aware that a crowd was gathering nearby.

"Yes," I finally said. "Yes, I'll come back."

His moustache quivered as he smiled.

"Thank you," he said, then leaned forward to kiss me.

I was quick to respond.

The laughter turned to hoots and clapping.

I could feel my stubborn old Irish face redden.

"Care for a ride?" he asked.

"I'd love it," I replied.

Making my way to Star's side, I maneuvered myself into the saddle, then followed Rodrigo from the park. I had no idea where we were going, but out of there was good enough for me.

He led me a short way down the road to an entrance to a nature preserve. I hadn't realized this was here, but Diane had mentioned something about going to a green space to take pictures. This must have been what she meant.

The path was wide enough for us to ride side by side. We rode quietly, a blanket of contentment wrapped around us. It was a glorious Texas day. The birds were having lots of conversations, and I could see all kinds of critter tracks.

At one point a creek arched close to the trail. Rodrigo stopped, suggesting we water the horses.

For the first time since I'd promised to come back, we had a moment to ourselves. We stood face to face. He ran his fingers down my cheek.

"I'm already in love with you," he said. "I didn't think it was possible to fall in love that quickly, but it happened. Maybe it's because I know how short life can be at this point. We need to grab our happiness while we can."

I nodded.

"I'm so glad you've agreed to come back. I wish you didn't have to leave," he said.

"I know," I said. "It would be easier. But I think it's for the best. I never thought I would meet someone at this point in life. After Michael, being alone was all I could dream about. Marriage didn't bring me the happiness I'd thought it would."

"We have the chance to reinvent it. Neither of us had the best, but now we can create the relationship we want to have."

"Does that mean I can have cereal for dinner?" I asked.

"Absolutely. As long as we can have our meal in front of the television if we want."

"Sure." I grinned.

"I'm also going to put a hot tub by Juan's house once I move in. I don't know about you, but the idea of a long soak after working sounds good to me."

A wicked thought appeared in my head.

"Is that a clothing optional hot tub?" I asked.

"Well ..." He kissed me.

It was a kiss that went on for some time.

When it was over, we remounted the horses.

"You don't have to give Star to me," I said. "I'll come back anyway."

He shook his head vehemently. "The horse is yours. She's always been yours, really. She claimed you. But ..." He raised a finger. "I'm hoping you'll allow me to breed her."

"I'm sure we can come to a suitable arrangement," I said.

He laughed, and we started back the way we came.

When we reached the RV park, I slid off Star. "Now I'm going to be gone for a while," I told her. "But Rodrigo will take good care of you. And I'll spoil you rotten when I get back."

Star nickered. Whether or not she understood me was up for grabs.

"Stay for dinner?" I asked. "Liz is cooking, so you'll be safe."

"I'm sorry. I can't stay. I have to get the horses back. The RV park let me bring them in here for a little while, but they didn't want it to be too long."

"Okay," I said, disappointed. "I understand."

"It won't be long," he said. "We'll talk. I'll tell you how my move to Juan's house is going, and you'll let me know about your trip, okay?"

Tears welled in my eyes. It felt like I was leaving part of my heart behind.

"It will be okay," he said and pulled me close. He held me tight for a few moments, then stepped back. "I love you," he said. After a soft kiss to my lips, he got on his horse and rode out of the park.

Chapter Thirty-Two

Rodrigo and I talked daily from then on until the day I pulled the RV away from San Antonio. I had to work hard to keep the tears away. Driving with blurry eyes was not a good plan for a safe trip.

My sisters and I took a few days to reach the Grand Canyon. While the Alamo had been smaller than my imagination had made it, the canyon's expanse and beauty were beyond anything I'd conjured in my mind.

We got up early one morning to watch the sun rise. Wrapped in our down coats and mittens, we could see our breath. At the high elevation, winter lingered, unlike the sultry weather of southern Texas. We'd been spoiled.

Watching the light spill over the jagged towers and cliffs that made up the canyon infused all of us with the knowledge there was something grander than we were, whether we wanted to call it Mother Nature, science, or God. There was a presence that couldn't be denied.

Younger people whooped when the sun reached them on the precarious ledges where they'd perched to watch the event. They were so free with their lives, not realizing how very short they were.

But it was the nature of humans, and all I could do was remember the feelings of freedom, hope, and optimism that being young had given us. Probably just as well we had that time to remember when the realities of our aging bodies hit us later in life.

Now I had a second chance, a serendipitous morsel of sweetness.

Once I returned, I would do everything in my power to make it work with Rodrigo.

From Arizona, we headed west through Nevada to California's Death Valley, another surrealistic landscape, then across the barren area of the Mojave Desert. It seemed like everywhere we went, solar panels and windmills announced the switch to renewable energy.

Once we reached the Pacific Coast Highway, we headed north. The western ocean shores were dramatically different from the wave-washed beaches of the eastern seaboard. The water was a lot colder too!

Once again we were thrust into the density of a lot of people. While there were stretches of magnificent redwoods on the ride, there was also the packed area of Silicon Valley, San Francisco, and the cities north of it to navigate around.

All of this was new to me, although Diane excitedly announced familiar spots.

Every night, the three of us would pull out our phones and describe our events to the men in our lives.

North of California, we traveled two-lane roads across Oregon to pick up Interstate 15 and head for home.

It had been an amazing trip.

~ ~ ~

March the following year ...

"You're beautiful," Liz said. "Just like a bride should be."

"Isn't it a little ridiculous to be a bride in my sixties?" I asked, staring at myself in the full-length mirror. It had taken weeks and dozens of three-way video calls with my sisters, but I'd settled on a cream dress with an asymmetrically-flared skirt. The waistline and high boat neckline had roses embroidered on them.

I wore a small clip of pink roses in my hair.

"It's not ridiculous at all," Diane said.

As my bridesmaids, she and Liz were dressed in pink dresses with similar lines. Emma, Patrick's daughter, was being dressed for her role as flower girl by her mother. Juan's son, Marcos, was ring bearer.

All of this had been discussed down to the last detail over the past few months. Rodrigo's sisters, still unhappy with my presence, nonetheless felt it was their duty to supply much needed and unasked for advice.

Somehow I'd managed to make it through without turning into bridezilla.

A good measure of that was due to the man I was marrying. He'd made sure I had plenty of time to ride Star, either with him or alone. We took quiet dinners either in the RV, or at his new place. One night he'd surprised me with cereal for dinner!

He'd installed a hot tub as he'd said he would, and we spent lovely evenings there.

As a wedding gift—as if a horse wasn't enough!—he'd had contractors create a second master bath with a deep tub and separate shower that was for my use only. I'd laughed when I'd seen it, but I'd been filled with love.

He was a man who listened carefully to my needs and desires, no matter how strange they may be.

And now here we were.

Diane's Joe and Liz's Walter were in attendance, as were my children and their families, but that was almost it for our side of the aisle. The last two additions were Genna and Don. She'd given us a beautiful hand-spun and knitted throw for our couch.

The number of people on Rodrigo's side would have seriously unbalanced the church, so we decided to avoid that particular tradition.

"Ready?" Liz asked.

"As I'll ever be."

We left the small room and walked to the sanctuary, waiting outside the door for the processional music to begin. Emma was bouncing up and down, and Marcos was giving the ties on the ring bearer's pillow a serious inspection.

I hoped they made it to the altar.

The music began, and Megan urged Emma forward. With a beatific smile that would have suited the Virgin Mother, she walked down the aisle, tossing flower petals here and there.

Wide-eyed, Marcos followed, taking his role seriously, his tiny shoulders held high with inborn pride.

Diane smiled and stepped out, followed by Liz.

I walked down the aisle alone. None of this giving away stuff, thank you very much. I was my own human being, more than ready to declare my love for my future husband.

When I got to the front, I passed the small bouquet of roses to Diane and turned to Rodrigo. We'd written our vows ourselves, and they were full of the promises we'd made to each other: loyalty, honesty, friendship, and respect.

He'd already proved he knew how to romance me.

Taking our first mass together at the railing was more powerful than I'd realized it could be. I was truly blessed.

Soon he was slipping a plain gold band next to the simple band with a yogo sapphire he'd given me for an engagement ring.

As we walked back down the aisle, my heart burst with joy I'd never known was possible.

We joined the priest in the reception line, greeting the people who'd come, including Trixie Lynn.

She pressed a small box into my hand. "I'm sorry I gave you such a hard time. I can see how happy you make him. He deserves it."

"Come back to the house," I said, touched by her gesture. "You're welcome at the reception. It's very informal."

"Antonia cooking?"

"Of course. As soon as she gets back from church." I nodded at the housekeeper and cook who was a few people behind Trixie Lynn.

"Then I'd be glad to come," she said.

"Good," I said.

"Well done," Rodrigo whispered in my ear after she left. "You're a good woman."

"I'm a smart woman," I said. "I'd rather have her on my side than against me."

He chuckled.

We rode back to the house in his sedan, slipping by the main house to park at what was to be my new home. He pushed open the door, then scared me half to death by picking me up.

"Put me down! I'm too heavy!" I yelled. "You can't do this at our age. You'll be laid up for weeks!"

By the time I finished objecting, my feet were already on the living room floor.

He laughed, then pulled me close.

"I love you," he said, then kissed me.

Thoroughly.

~ ~ ~

By the time we got to the reception on the patio, it was in full swing. Rodrigo's sisters were in their usual corner, surveying the crowd with disapproving stares. Daniel and Connor were swaying together in a corner, out of tempo to the DJ's upbeat music.

An elaborate piñata hovered from the center of the overhead beams. Marcos and some of his cousins stood under it, slowly explaining the purpose to three of my grandchildren.

Enticing aromas wafted from the open kitchen window, and chips, salsa, and guacamole were already out. Clusters of people chatted, some softly, some loudly. A few of Rodrigo's relatives vied over entertaining the Anglo guests with stories that no doubt had more than a hint of embellishment.

"Do you think they'd notice if we went back to the house and finished what we started?" Rodrigo asked, wrapping his arm around my waist.

"Not right away, but eventually," I said.

"Too bad."

"Yes." I leaned in for a kiss. Although it had been a while, I was looking forward to our time alone later.

People clinked flatware against glasses.

I guess we weren't as unobserved as we'd thought we were.

~ ~ ~

The rest of the reception was a bit of a blur. I spent time with my children and my sisters, as well as with Rodrigo's family, including my new grandchildren. They were a delight, absolutely willing to play with their new Anglo grandmother without giving it a second thought.

Marcos instructed my aim when I took my turn at smashing the piñata. After I'd made a few wild swings, he fell to the floor laughing.

Rodrigo, long a master at these things, broke it on the second swipe, to the delight of all the children who scrambled for the candy that descended. Patrick's and Megan's children were ecstatic over this new game.

"Thanks, Mom," Megan said. "They'll be on a sugar high for the rest of the day."

I shrugged. "We'll just have to wear them out. We'll take them to see the horses later."

"Did he really give you a horse to convince you to come back?"

"He did. Although it didn't take much convincing."

"I can see that. He seems like a good man. And he makes you happy, happier than you've been in a long time. I'm glad for you, Mom." She leaned in and kissed my cheek.

Both my children had accepted Rodrigo's presence in my life easily. It made me realize that I hadn't been hiding much from anybody.

With a wicked grin, Liz had a chat with the DJ.

Soon, Irish music blasted from the sound system.

Liz grabbed my hand and Diane's and soon we were kicking up our heels in a horrendous version of an Irish dance. We'd all been taught as kids, but there hadn't been much chance to dance since then.

After watching for a few moments, Patrick, Megan, and their spouses joined in.

Walter and Joe followed.

Rodrigo shrugged and danced his way toward me, his natural sense of rhythm assisting him.

Juan grabbed his wife. Their kids followed. Soon most of the guests were laughing and dancing as the cultures merged in a riotous celebration of life and love.

It was a wonderful reception.

And, later, after the guests had left, Rodrigo and I went back to his … our … house.

Butterflies darted in my stomach, and desire raced through my body as we walked into our bedroom.

With tenderness and awareness, we made love for the first time, then fell asleep wrapped in each other's arms.

Chapter Thirty-Three

The following July in Montana ...

Diane

Liz and I double-checked her old house to make sure everything was ready for Rodrigo and Kathleen. They were arriving today.

Liz and Walter had come in a few days ago. They'd stayed in the house for a few days, but had found a nearby Airbnb to rent for the two weeks they were going to spend near the ranch before they visited some other parts of the state.

"It's going to be good to see them again," I said, as we put clean sheets on the bed.

"Yes," Liz agreed. "After that year together, I was ready for us all to go out on our own, but I didn't realize how much I'd miss you two."

"Me either."

We smiled at each other, companionable in a way we hadn't been only a few years ago.

Once we finished, I lay the quilt I'd brought over the foot of the bed.

"That's lovely," Liz said, stroking the top and examining the pattern.

"Joe's mom made it. He called her 'the mad quilter.' He's got way too many of them, and figured it would be a good idea to spread them around."

"Didn't his kids object?"

I laughed. "Bug forbade him to show up with any more quilts a few years ago, and Tess is more focused on her work on sanitation projects in underserved communities to nest."

"Sounds like something we should get Kathleen involved in," Liz said with a grin. "She's an expert on poop!"

I laughed. "We'll put them together when Tess gets here."

"She's coming? I thought it was only Bug and his family."

"Last minute decision. She had a little time off." I had to look away. Joe and I were keeping the real reason secret until after Kathleen arrived. "What about Stephan and his family?" I asked. "They're still

209

coming, right?"

"It was touch and go there for a while. Willow picked up a bad cold, and they were worried it was going to turn into the flu or something worse. But she kicked it off. They arrive on Friday. Ivy is so excited she's having trouble sleeping. For some reason, she has a very distinct memory of Kathleen."

"They did bond while we were there."

"Kathleen has a way with kids. Amazing, considering how sharp her tongue can be with the rest of us."

"That's true."

We moved on to the bathroom, checking there were ample toiletries and towels.

"Kathleen's going to enjoy this," I said.

"I don't think as much as she would have before. Apparently, Rodrigo is indulging her every whim when it comes to bathrooms. She has her own, you know. It even has a heated floor."

"She deserves it after putting up with so much from Michael. I'm amazed she didn't divorce him."

"That never would have happened. You know that."

"Yes." Much as I admired Kathleen for her deep faith and absolute convictions, it would never be a way I could live my life. Joe was much more a church-goer than I was, and we'd finally reached a point where I'd come with him on occasion, but not consistently. As for confession … that wasn't going to happen. If it cost me communion, so be it.

But when he'd asked me for one important change on that stance, I'd capitulated for the sake of the man I love.

After making sure the house was ready, we drove back to the ranch house. Patrick had put on a new extension for his growing family, including a second bathroom and an upgraded kitchen. Kathleen may have put up without a dishwasher, but Patrick's wife, Sydney, was having none of it.

"Any word from Kathleen?" Sydney asked as she greeted us at the door, her hand on her round belly in that way all pregnant women seem to adopt.

"She texted that they were about an hour out," I replied. "Of course, that was about a half hour ago."

"That will work. Patrick and Walter just came back from checking on the flock of sheep," she said. "They're cleaning up, so they'll be ready."

"How are the sheep working out?" Liz asked.

"They're a lot less work than those damn milk cows were," Sydney replied.

We laughed.

Patrick had finally convinced his mother the milk cows were too much work and not worth the investment in new, automated equipment. He'd sold them and bought sheep, believing ranchers would need to diversify to succeed.

Emma raced down the hallway and threw herself at Liz. "Miss you, Auntie Liz."

"I miss you too, sweetheart."

"Can't you come back?"

"Aunt Liz has a family too," Sydney said. "Her granddaughters would be lonely if she moved back here."

"Where are they? Will they play with me?"

"I'm sure they will when they get here," Liz said. "You're all about the same age."

"Oh, good," Sydney said with mock horror. "More kids to get into everything."

"It's the way of life," I said, trying to feel positive about my own lack of children. I now had Bug's kids to spoil, but the ache of loss would never really disappear.

"Hey, love," Joe said, giving me a firm kiss and wrapping his arm around my shoulder. "Why so gloomy?"

"It's nothing," I said, brightening with his attention. "I have everything I need now." I pulled him close and kissed him with a promise of things to come.

"Get a room," Liz said.

"There are minors here," Sydney added. "Keep it PG."

"How else are they supposed to learn?" Joe said with an evil grin.

"They have plenty of time, Uncle Joe," Sydney said with a wag of her finger. Even if she wasn't a blood relative, she had a lot of Kathleen's mannerisms. "Now you all come into the kitchen, get the fixings for iced tea, or gin and tonic, or whatever you want and go out on the front porch to do your waiting. I've got to get these kids fed."

"I'll help you," Patrick said, coming into the living room where we'd been chatting. "You need to get off your feet for a while."

"Thanks," Sydney said, giving her husband a beaming smile of appreciation.

We did as we were told. Soon I was relaxing in one of the Adirondack chairs with a gin and tonic, Joe beside me with his beer. On the other side, Liz had her drink in her hand. Walter, also with a beer, finished up the row.

The pitcher of drinks stood ready for Kathleen on a nearby table.

Ten minutes after we sat down, the RV came rumbling into view.

Liz

My heart leapt a little when I saw the RV come down the driveway. The wedding had been beautiful, but hectic, and I was ready for some downtime with my sisters.

Now, *that* was a phrase I never thought I'd say.

While we were in Texas at the wedding, we'd committed to an annual family reunion with the three of us and anyone else we could manage to drag to Montana. July seemed like the right time, a great pause between the euphoria of "It's summer!" and the reality of shortening days.

Although it had taken some convincing, Stephan had agreed to come, especially after his wife and children had weighed in. His work was starting to sell, thanks to the support of the agent we'd found, but it still wasn't enough for him to quit his job.

That would come in time. My son was a talented artist.

Mom would have approved of his fanciful work, but not of the strong nudes and vulnerable faces I had begun to sell. The new paintings were being met with acclaim from serious art critics in a way my earlier work hadn't.

It pleased me.

Even Walter's work was beginning to move locally. He was content to do local landscapes for the tourists. He'd told me one high powered artist in the family was more than enough.

His daughters still hadn't come around to my presence in their dad's life, but I wasn't giving up. I was hanging around for the rest of our lives so they'd need to get used to it.

As the RV came to a stop, I rose with the others to go out and greet the weary travelers. Joe opened the screen door to the house and shouted to Patrick that his mother was here.

Kathleen had been behind the wheel, so Rodrigo was the first one out.

He looked tired. It had been his first long road-trip with Kathleen, and I knew how exhausting it could be moving from one place to another. Plus he had to take up the slack for all the duties Diane and I used to do.

I wondered who was cooking. It would be safer not to ask.

Kathleen climbed down from the RV, looking happier than I'd ever seen her.

The three of us wrapped our arms around each other for a big hug. Soon, like the others, I had tears streaming down my face. It was so good to be back together.

Finally, we were a family again.

"Hiya, Mom," Patrick said. Emma was already tugging at Kathleen's shirt, while her younger brother was clasped in Patrick's arms.

"Oh, Patrick," Kathleen said, breaking up our hug. "It's so good to see you!" She turned to the little boy in his arms. "Look how big you've grown!"

Patrick's son buried his head in his father's shoulder.

"He'll come around," Patrick said.

"I know," Kathleen said with a smile. "Now who's this big girl?"

"Emma! You know who I am!"

"Of course, I do! You've gotten bigger too." Kathleen wrapped the little girl in her arms.

"Gin and tonics are ready," I said.

"Thank goodness!" Kathleen said. Then she turned to Patrick. "Where do you want me to put the rig?" she asked.

Patrick started to speak, but Rodrigo stopped him. "I'll take care of it," he said to Kathleen. "You go talk to your sisters."

"Thanks," Kathleen said with a large smile.

We went back to the porch.

Sydney came out on the porch and gave Kathleen a big hug. "It's good to see you."

"My, you've gotten big there," Kathleen said. "How are things going with the pregnancy?"

"As well as they can be. She was a bit of a surprise, and doc says my body wasn't quite ready for her. He wants me to rest more than I did last time."

"She?"

"Well, we don't officially know, but in my heart I believe she's a girl. A girl that's going to be healthy and strong, aren't you?" Sydney patted her bump. "But right now, I'm going to head to the bedroom and take a quick nap. You ladies enjoy yourselves."

"We will," Diane said as she poured a glass for Kathleen.

"How is wedded life?" I asked Kathleen.

"Bliss. I never thought it could be this good," she said. "So when are you and Walter tying the knot?"

I took a sip of my own drink before answering. Social norms were important to Kathleen, but I could care less.

"We're not," I said. "We decided it wasn't important for us."

"And Stephan's okay with that?" she asked.

"He wasn't at first, but he's so happy we're together, he's accepted our decision." I looked her straight in the eye. "So you will have to do so too."

She shrugged. "It's your life. You have to decide how you want to live it."

"Who are you, and what have you done with Kathleen?" I asked.

"I'm not sure," she answered slowly. "Maybe it's finally that I understand what unconditional love really feels like. When you have that, it's tough to be as judgmental about how others run their lives."

"Hear, hear," I said. "I know what you mean, and I'm so happy for you!"

"Me too," Diane said, raising her glass.

We toasted, and went back to catching up until it was time to gather on the newly constructed back porch for dinner.

We said grace over a meal of steak, potatoes, salad, and corn, then dug in. Halfway through the meal, Joe clinked his fork on his beer bottle.

"Now that you're all here, we hope you don't have any plans for Saturday afternoon," he said with a grin.

"Why is that?" I asked, surmising the answer.

"Because you're invited to a wedding!" Diane yelled.

"I was supposed to tell them," Joe said.

"You were taking too long! I've been bursting all day!"

Everyone laughed.

"We'll be there!" Kathleen said. "Maybe it will be an inspiration for Liz and Walter!"

The old Kathleen was still kicking around there somewhere.

Good thing. Too many changes at once were hard to take.

I leaned toward Walter.

"Not happening," I said.

"I know. And I love you more for it," he said.

Then he kissed me.

Kathleen

Rodrigo and I stood at the edge of the patio watching everyone gather.

"Your family is a lot larger than I thought it was," he observed.

"I don't think I've ever seen them all gathered in one place," I said.

Both of Joe's children and his son, Bug's, family were there for the ceremony and later celebration. Stephan's family had made it as well. It was good to see Liz in her rightful place as grandmother. Walter made her laugh. Now that her secrets were released, she was glowing and her art had reached new levels.

While I'd continue to tweak them about their marital state—or lack thereof—I wasn't really concerned. I'd meant what I'd said earlier. Receiving unconditional love makes it easier to hand out.

My daughter, Megan, and her family had also made it in time for the celebration of love between my sister and Joe. It was a long time coming. After her first painful marriage, Diane deserved all the happiness she could get. I was glad that Joe's son, who hadn't been a fan to begin with, had thawed toward my sister.

Bug's kids hadn't had any problem accepting a new grandmother, especially one who doted on them as much as Diane did.

I slipped an arm around my husband's waist.

"Thank you," I said. "Thank you for loving me."

"You're wrong," he said. "I am the lucky one. I never knew what I'd been missing."

"Do you think it's time for the surprise?" I asked.

"Definitely."

We made our way to the RV and came back with a bright piñata.

Emma spotted it first and started jumping up and down. Megan caught sight of it and groaned.

"What's up?" Stephan asked her.

"Kid sugar high," Megan replied, pointing.

"We can't have a celebration without a piñata!" Rodrigo declared.

"Candy! Candy!" Emma shouted.

"Thanks, Mom," Patrick muttered. "I'm on bedtime duty tonight. It's going to be impossible."

"We're making memories, kid," I said. "A difficult night is worth it once in a while."

"Oh, sure, now you say that. But I remember …"

I held up my finger, then pointed where Rodrigo was attempting to get on a bench to tie the toy to the rafter.

"I'd like to stay out of the hospital," I said.

Patrick dashed over, meeting Bug at the bench. Together they convinced my husband to relinquish the job.

"I could have done it," Rodrigo said.

"I'm sure you could have," I said.

"You put them up to this." He glared.

"Only because I love you …"

His gaze softened, and he leaned in to kiss me.

Patrick suddenly loomed over me.

"Now what?" he asked.

Rodrigo reached for the stick he'd propped against a rail and took a blindfold from his pocket. "The bride goes first," he said, holding out the blindfold to Joe. "Would you tie it around her eyes?"

"Oh, brother," Diane said. "Can't we skip this part?"

"Where's your spirit of adventure?" Joe asked.

"I'm afraid I'm going to knock a kid's head off instead of what I'm aiming at."

Following Rodrigo's instruction, Joe led Diane to the piñata and turned her around three times.

"Okay, honey, swing!"

As Diane took aim, Rodrigo grabbed Joe and pulled him back, waving everyone else back as well.

Diane took a wild swing and almost connected with a hanging plant.

"Not my plants!" Sydney yelled. "Someone point her in the right direction!"

Orders were yelled to my sister, but after two more tries, Joe took over.

He wasn't any better than Diane.

Liz and Walter went next.

Then it was my turn.

Unknown to Rodrigo, I'd been practicing. Being married into a Mexican family, it seemed like a useful skill to have.

Once I'd been turned around, I listened.

Wind fluffed the paper on the colorful donkey.

I took a deep breath and swung.

Candy started to rain down on my head, and I was almost bowled over by a bunch of little kids.

With a laugh, I pulled off my blindfold and grinned at Rodrigo.

He gave me a thumbs up, grabbed my hand, and took me to the bar where the G&Ts were kept cold.

~ ~ ~

Later that night, we sat side by side on our temporary porch and watched the sun set, just like we'd promised each other we'd do as often as we could.

I held his hand, and we were silent. The day had been exhilarating, but had taken a lot of energy.

In some ways, the journey we'd begun on the RV was finally over. Diane and I were married, and Liz was as married as she'd ever be. We were closer than we'd ever been in our lives, and our extended families had taken the first steps toward knitting together.

The next generation was taking over. Life goes on and changes happen. Most of our recent ones had been good.

I leaned my head against my husband's shoulder.

"I love you," I said softly.

"Yes," he said. "I love you too. And I will for the rest of my life."

We didn't know how long that would be, but then and there I vowed I'd live every day with purpose and joy, making sure Rodrigo knew how much he was loved every single day of his life.

Because that was what he showed me every day.

Love.

~ ~ ~

What made the three sisters decide to go on a road trip? Find out in the short story, *Starting Out*, one of three short stories in **Sweet Romance Novellas**. Go to https://www.CaseyDawes.com to get your free ebook!

Author's Note

I love my readers!

When I began talking about my serialized novel set on a Carolina beach, one of my readers reached out and connected me to a man who lives on Oak Island on the North Carolina shore. I had a delightful conversation with Jeff who gave me the low-down on the island, his business rescuing furniture and painting it the correct colors, and other colorful ideas. You'll recognize him in the series as Sam.

Thank you Bobbie!

This serialized format for me. Some of you will love it, some of you won't. If you're on my mailing list, by mid-September 2024, you'll get a complimentary copy of the first book. Go to https://www.CaseyDawes.com to sign up!

Casey

About the Author

Casey Dawes writes non-steamy contemporary romance and inspirational women's fiction with romantic elements.

Her women's fiction series, Rocky Mountain Front, explores the five siblings from a ranching family living in Montana, the people who love them, and the characters in the small town in which they live. Previous to that she wrote a 5-book contemporary romance series about friends and family on the Central Coast. Her latest series features love between "seasoned" heroes and heroines in a small Montana town.

Currently, she and her husband are traveling the US in a small trailer with the cat who owns them. When not writing or editing, she is exploring national parks, haunting independent bookstores, and lurking in spinning and yarn stores trying not to get caught fondling the fiber!

Other Books by Casey Dawes

Coharie Beach Café

This is a clean, sweet romance set on a North Carolina beach. It is a serialized novel told over six separate books, currently only available as an ebook.

Coharie Beach Café (Carolina Sunrise Book 1)
Coharie Beach Café (Carolina Sunrise Book 2)
Coharie Beach Café (Carolina Sunrise Book 3)
Coharie Beach Café (Carolina Sunrise Book 4)
Coharie Beach Café (Carolina Sunrise Book 5)
Coharie Beach Café (Carolina Sunrise Book 6)

Promise Cove

Return to Promise Cove
Spring in Promise Cove
Hope in Promise Cove
Winter in Promise Cove
Promise Cove Wedding
Summer in Promise Cove
Away from Promise Cove

Beck Family Saga

This series revolves around a Montana ranching family—women's fiction with a touch of romance!

Home Is Where the Heart Is
Finding Home
Leaving Home
Coming Home
Starting for Home
Finally Home

RV Park Romance Series

Brand new romantic comedy series!

Grown-Up Second Chance
Her Son's Secret Father
Her Texas Cowboy

California Romance Series

Two mothers, two daughters, and one friend explore contemporary romance on the California coast.

California Sunset
California Wine
California Homecoming
California Thyme
California Sunrise

Montana Christmas Series

A new adult contemporary romance series set in Missoula Montana— just right for the holidays!

Sweet Montana Christmas
Montana Christmas Magic
Second Chance Christmas